BOMBS AWAY!

Behind the Nye's Annihilators' 449th and 450th Squadron, Lt. Col. Charles Olmstead stared from the cabin of *Pretty Baby,* the lead plane of the 332nd's other two squadrons. Olmstead would break off from the other Annihilator units when they crossed the French coast, because he would fly slightly north-northeast to attack the important railroad bridge at Letripad. This span was on the line that came from the low countries and into France. Without this bridge across the Seine River in northwest France, the Germans could not carry rail traffic to the Atlantic wall defenses on the Normandy coast.

Olmstead's *Pretty Baby* carried a quartet of thousand-pound delayed-fuse bombs in the bays and the Lieutenant colonel looked forward to attacking the Letripad Bridge, certain that he and his fellow B-26 pilots would knock out the spans. He squinted again at the dreariness ahead of him . . . .

OTHER BOOKS ON THE WORLD AT WAR
by Lawrence Cortesi

D-DAY MINUS 1	(1318, $3.25)
THE DEADLY SKIES	(1132, $3.25)
PACIFIC HELLFIRE	(1179, $3.25)
PACIFIC STRIKE	(1041, $2.95)
TARGET: TOKYO	(1256, $3.25)
VALOR AT LEYTE	(1213, $3.25)
VALOR AT SAMAR	(1226, $2.75)
THE BATTLE FOR MANILA	(1334, $3.25)

Available wherever paperbacks are sold, or order direct from the Publisher. Send cover price plus 50¢ per copy for mailing and handling to Zebra Books, 475 Park Avenue South, New York, N.Y. 10016. DO NOT SEND CASH.

D-DAY MINUS ONE

LAWRENCE CORTESI

ZEBRA BOOKS
KENSINGTON PUBLISHING CORP.

ZEBRA BOOKS

are published by

KENSINGTON PUBLISHING CORP.
475 Park Avenue South
New York, N.Y. 10016

Copyright © 1984 by Lawrence Cortesi

All rights reserved. No part of this book may be reproduced in any form or by any means without the prior written consent of the Publisher, excepting brief quotes used in reviews.

First printing: January, 1984

Printed in the United States of America

D-DAY
MINUS ONE

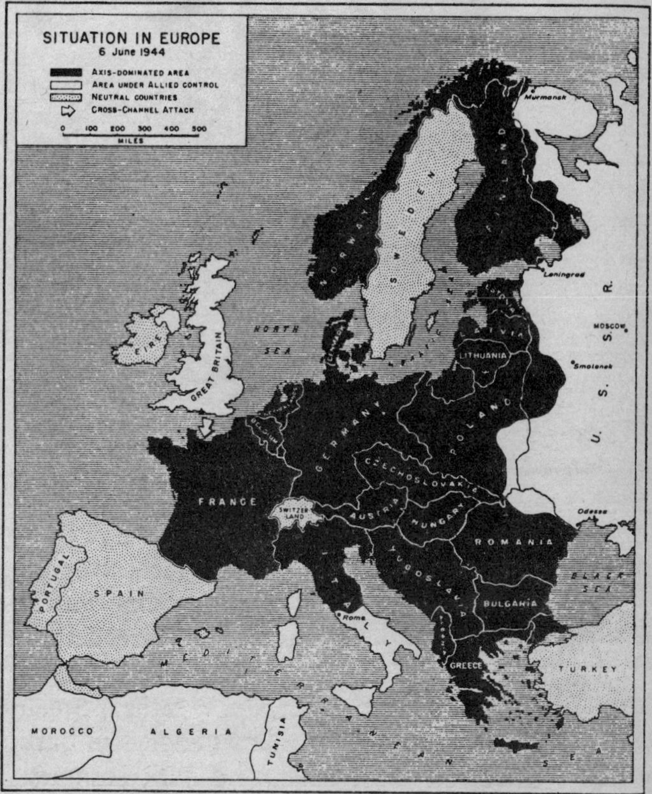
SITUATION IN EUROPE
6 June 1944
Axis-dominated area
Area under Allied control
Neutral countries
Cross-Channel Attack
0 100 200 300 400 500
MILES
Murmansk
FINLAND
NORWAY
SWEDEN
Leningrad
U. S. S. R.
MOSCOW
Smolensk
NORTH SEA
EIRE
GREAT BRITAIN
LATVIA
LITHUANIA
POLAND
GERMANY
BELGIUM
FRANCE
SWITZERLAND
CZECHOSLOVAKIA
AUSTRIA
HUNGARY
ROMANIA
Odessa
BLACK SEA
YUGOSLAVIA
BULGARIA
ITALY
Rome
GREECE
TURKEY
SPAIN
PORTUGAL
MOROCCO
ALGERIA
TUNISIA
MEDITERRANEAN SEA

CHAPTER ONE

By late May of 1944, Paris, France was enjoying warm, spring weather. Residents moved about the city in shirt sleeves, traffic became heavier, the countless gardens had sprouted an array of colorful flowers, and trees were in full green foliage. But there was an ominous atmosphere hanging over Gay Paree. The vitality of its citizens, in evidence despite German occupation, had not heightened as was usual with the onset of warm weather. Small and large groups of Parisians huddled in dark cellars, closed apartments, and dark crannies, where they discussed the same subject: the coming Allied invasion of the continent.

German soldiers, from full generals down to *Wehrmacht* privates and *Luftwaffe* lance corporals, had also become strangely inconspicuous. Few of them indulged in their usual strolls through the streets of Paris, and few maintained either their relationships with pretty French women or their friendships with the men, associations that had prevailed in Paris for nearly four years. A wall of mutual coolness had emerged between the German occupiers and the French civilians, for both sides knew that one day soon Paris would be occupied by British and American troops.

Yet Hitler raved on about defeating the Allies with his determined *Wehrmacht,* his panzer divisions and his new types of arms.

"Our secret weapons will bring the Anglo-Saxon enemy to his knees," the Fuhrer ranted during a speech on 20 May 1944.

Hermann Goering also ranted, promising that the growing strength of the *Luftwaffe* would destroy the Allied air forces over the skies of Europe. "The *Luftwaffe* has never been stronger," he told a jittery German public. "Our enemies will never penetrate *Festung Europa* (Fortress Europe)."

But no one in Europe really believed the two Nazi leaders. The past year had brought two realities to the continent. The Allies had wrested the skies over Europe and they had built a military force in England that sprawled over half of the British Isles. By May of 1944, everybody on the continent suspected that an Allied invasion was imminent.

Both civilians and soldiers had seen the

masses of Allied planes drone across the skies of *Festung Europa* almost daily with near impunity as they bombed German industry, production facilities, assembly plants and communication systems in both the occupied countries and Germany itself. True, *Luftwaffe* interceptors and AA gunners had invariably shot down large numbers of these bombers, but the Allied air fleets continued to come across the English Channel in large formations.

How could anyone on the continent believe that the day of reckoning was not fast approaching for Nazi Germany?

Few questions remained as to the expected invasion. Where would Dwight Eisenhower land his American and British troops? Calais? Boulogne? Le Havre? Cherbourg? Where along the 200-mile stretch of French coast that fronted the English Channel? And when the Allies did establish a beachhead, how long would they need to sweep the 150 miles inland to capture Paris?

Not only had the Parisians become more obscure and reserved, but the French underground had become more active. More Frenchmen joined the partisans; more arms had been smuggled into Paris, perhaps more than the Germans themselves had in the French capital. And the secret radios: partisans now operated them by the thousands to keep London informed continually on the movement and strength of German forces, or to report on German defenses along the French coast. The barrage of secret messages had become so widespread and so frequent that German monitors could not begin to locate more than a fraction of them. Allied intelligence knew every move the Germans made. They even knew what Field Marshall Gerd von Rundstedt, CinC of the German Armies of the West (AOW), ate for breakfast.

The Armies of the West encompassed three army groups. Army Group B under Field Marshal Erwin Rommel included the Seventh and Fifteenth Armies that were responsible for defenses along the Channel coast. Army Group G, under Gen. Johannes Blaskowitz, included the First and Nineteenth Armies that were scattered throughout northern France, Belgium, Holland and northwest Germany. Army Group H, under Field Marshal Gunther Blumentritt, included the Sixth and Thirteenth Armies, and these forces were scattered from central and southern France into Luxemburg and across the border into Germany.

AOW included fifty-six divisions, of which fourteen were armored divisions. Of Rommel's sixteen divisions in western France, he maintained six of them, one an armored division, in the Normandy area. The other ten divisions were stationed in other areas of the Channel coast between Cherbourg and Calais. Of the other forty divisions in AOW, the twenty from army Group G in the north sector had five armored divisions and the twenty Army Group

H had in the south sector had four armored divisions.

Field Marshal Rommel had been building defenses for several months. The hero of the old Afrika Korps had won command of Army Group B in 1944 and the OKW (Oberkommando der Wehrmacht) had ordered him to develop shoreline defenses of the French Channel coast in order to repel any invasion. Rommel had worked hard to strengthen the Atlantic wall, using his own soldiers and forced laborers from occupied countries.

Rommel had constructed dozens of concrete coastal pillboxes and installed 547 naval coastal guns along the French and Belgian coasts between Orne and Loire to defend the Brittany, Normandy and Cotentin peninsulas. The field marshal had also saturated the waters offshore with every type of obstacle—teller mines, hedgehogs, and tetrara gates, the Element C states.

At Normandy itself, besides the mines offshore and the C states on the beaches, Rommel's five divisions from his Seventh Army manned trench defenses, bunkers, and pillbox gun positions. Still, he continually grumbled about the lack of enough armor, and he worried about getting *Luftwaffe* air support.

On 30 May, Rommel received a summons to AOW headquarters in Paris to complete final plans for a defense against an Allied invasion. The energetic Army Group B commander welcomed this conference, hoping he could persuade Field Marshal von Rundstedt to release more armored units for his Normandy defenses, and hoping he would get more *geschwaders* of aircraft on the air fields in northwest France. Soldiers of the general staff watched curiously as the VIPs entered the AOW headquarters. They knew that something important would come from this meeting.

Gerd von Rundstedt, a dour, thin faced, aging field marshal, had become rigid in his actions and thinking. He rarely listened to advice from his general staff or his field commanders, and he often ignored orders from the Fuhrer. No smooth relationship existed between him and Rommel, whom he often disparaged. Rommel often called von Rundstedt an old crank who turned a deaf ear to any constructive suggestions from experienced field officers. In turn, von Rundstedt referred to the Army Group B commander as a "pseudo hero." Rommel enjoyed the confidence and patronage of Hitler, while von Rundstedt enjoyed great influence with the OKW high command. Both could do as they pleased. The two field marshals had learned to live with each other.

Those arriving at the AOW conference expected another confrontation between von Rundstedt and Rommel, and they would not be disappointed.

Besides the two field marshals, the others at the conference included General Blumentritt, CinC of Army Group H; Gen. Johannes

Blaskowitz, CinC of Army Group G; Gen. Kurt Warlington, the AOW chief-of-staff; Gen. Hans Spiedel, Rommel's chief-of-staff; Field Marshal Hugo Sperrle, *kommondo* of Luftflotte 3; Gen. Dietrich Peltz, commander of the Jagdkorps IX bomber command; and Gen. Werner Junck, commander of the Jagdkorps II fighter command.

"Gentlemen," von Rundstedt began, "surely, there cannot be a single soldier in the German armed forces who does not know that the enemy will soon attempt an invasion of the continent, perhaps within the next few weeks. Our latest intelligence indicates that the Allies have amassed over fifty divisions of troops, including a dozen armored divisions and several paratrooper divisions. We have at present sixteen divisions of Army Group B defending the Channel coast from Calais to Cherbourg. In the event of an invasion, Army Group B would need support. We must therefore consider the role of reserve divisions from Army Group G, Army Group H, the three independent panzer divisions, and Luftflotte 3 *geschwader* units."

"I must tell you, Field Marshal," Rommel spoke quickly, "that we lack enough armored divisions for the Channel defense. You must release to me at once the three panzer divisions that are in reserve."

"I have toured your defenses," von Rundstedt answered icily, "and I can tell you that you have done a poor job. You have not constructed enough bunkers, not enough beach wire obstacles, and not enough trenches. You received thousands of laborers to work alongside the soldiers of your command, but the defenses are not up to the standards we expect."

"I have done all that was possible, considering the failure of the AOW to furnish the promised equipment and supplies," Rommel retorted. "The fifty million mines—where are they? And where are the twelve hundred coastal guns? I have less than six hundred. I was promised enough concrete to build a minimum of five hundred emplacements, but I have received material for less than two hundred. And where are the twenty thousand tons of steel beams that were ordered to build the girder stakes? I have not received five thousand tons of beams for such construction."

Von Rundstedt did not answer.

"I am sure the enemy will attempt their invasion on the Normandy beaches," Rommel continued, "and if we are not prepared, the fault must lie with those who failed to send the promised material and not with me and my troops."

"I must remind you, Herr Field Marshal," von Rundstedt quipped, "that only you among the AOW commanders believe the enemy will land on the beaches beyond Bayeux. What could the Allies possibly accomplish by landing there? Roads inland are at a minimum and there are no good rail lines. There are no port facilities whatever, not even for a dinghy. High ground lies beyond the beaches and the terrain is poor. Logic would tell us the Allies will attempt an invasion at one of the good Channel ports: Calais, which is only twenty-two miles from Dover, or at Cherbourg with its fine port on the Cotentin peninsula, and where the enemy could make excellent use of the harbor. Even the Le Havre area would be a better place to land troops than on the Normandy beaches."

Now it was Rommel who did not answer.

"We know the Allies have assembled thousands of troops at Dover, across the Channel from Calais, and at Plymouth and Weymouth, directly across the water from Cherbourg," von Rundstedt said, gesturing.

"They have also massed troops and equipment at Portsmouth, opposite the Normandy beaches," Rommel answered sharply.

"Field Marshal," the AOW CinC said, "if the enemy sends an invasion flotilla to the Normandy beaches, such a movement would be a mere diversion to deceive us while they sent their main forces to either Cherbourg or Calais. I would suggest that you stop working so hard at the Bayeux beaches and concentrate your defenses at Calais and Cherbourg. If the enemy lands troops at these two ports areas and you are ill-prepared, you must accept the responsibility of any failures."

Von Rundstedt sighed and then continued. "I will tell you, Herr Rommel, that you will get the three reserve panzer divisions. However, I cannot release them to you until we are certain we know when and where the invasion will come."

"Are you suggesting that you do not trust my judgment?" Rommel asked.

"I am only telling you that no one knows for certain where the Allies will attempt their amphibious landings, and it would be foolish to send any kind of reserves anywhere until we know where such reinforcements should go. If the Allies do indeed land at Normandy, a quite remote possibility in my opinion, I will surely send reinforcements there."

"You mean the panzer divisions," Rommel said.

"Yes," von Rundstedt nodded, "the Twenty-first Panzer, the Twelfth SS Hitler Jugend, and the Panzer Lehr Division. They are the best. They are well-equipped and now resting in encampments east of Hasselt. They can be quickly moved out of Belgium to Calais or wherever they are needed."

Rommel nodded.

Now the AOW CinC turned to the other army group commanders. "General," he looked at Blaskowitz, "your forces are disposed in northern France, Belgium, Holland, and northwest Germany. When the invasion comes, you will be expected to send as many reinforcements as possible from your First Army through Hasselt, Limden, Louvain and Verdun. Men and equipment must be mustered at the Lille marshalling yards. Your Nineteenth Army units will move southward and muster in the Verdun and Lesnil marshalling yards east of Paris. They will then move swiftly westward to the Calais and Le Havre areas to aid Army Group B."

"I understand, Herr Field Marshal," Blaskowitz said.

Von Rundstedt now looked at Blumentritt. "General, your Army Group H forces are extended from Poitou beyond the Bay of Biscay and to the east through Lyons, Strasbourg, and into Freiburg, Germany. Your forces from the Sixth Army will move directly across central France over the Le Fitte and Vernon Rivers and then into northwest France. They can then aid Army Group B units in defending the Cherbourg area. Your Thirteenth Army units, particularly the panzer divisions, will muster in the Dijon and Limidan yards and then move swiftly up from the south of France over the Le Fitte and Vernon bridges. They will then be in a position to aid Army Group B units in the defense of the Cotentin peninsula."

"We will not fail," Blumentritt said.

"You will receive full orders with detailed instructions," von Rundstedt continued. "If we move reinforcements to both the north and south extremes of the English Channel, these forces can move swiftly into any position along the two hundred-mile coastal front. While we do not know exactly where the Allies will try to land, we must be in a position to act."

"Yes, Herr Field Marshal," Blumentritt said.

The AOW CinC looked at Field Marshal Hugo Sperrle, the CinC of Luftflotte 3 that was responsible for the aerial defense of France and the low countries. "Herr Sperrle, if we are to stop any invasion, we must have air support. No matter how many infantry, artillery, and panzer units we have at our disposal, and no matter how strong our Channel defenses, without the *Luftwaffe* we could not possibly hope to stem an invasion. The enemy will no doubt send air units over the English Channel in large numbers and we must meet them with fighter interceptors that can shoot them down. We must also have bombers to attack and disrupt the emeny's amphibious forces."

"We are aware that the enemy intends to invade Europe in the near future," Sperrle said, "and we have taken measures to prepare Luftflotte 3 for a response to such an invasion."

"Good," von Rundstedt said.

Field Marshal Sperrle shuffled through some papers in front of him before he continued. "We have improved and strengthened twelve to fifteen of our bases in the west. I regret to say, however, that our forces are limited because we are still awaiting the promised new aircraft and new crews. At the moment, we have about eight hundred aircraft available to meet any invaders."

"I see," von Rundstedt said.

Sperrle turned to General Peltz of the

Jagdkorps IX bomber command. "Deitrich, please explain the disposition of your bomber *geschwaders.*"

"Yes, Herr Sperrle," Peltz answered. He scanned some papers on the table and then continued. "We have at our disposal 325 bombers to attack the enemy's beachheads, as well as 75 ground support and 95 tactical reconnaissance aircraft. Most of these bombers are based at our main French airfields in Edex, Beaumont, Lamar, Lesnil, Orival and Ambria-Epinoy, with other bombers and tactical reconnaissance units at Beauvais, Juvisey, and Maisons-Laffitte. All of these bases are quite close to the English Channel, and, thus, the aircraft are within easy range of any amphibious force. But I have yet to receive the additional 500 bombers and crews as well as more supplies of fuel, bombs and ammunition. Perhaps, Herr Field Marshal I," he gestured to von Rundstedt—"you can press the OKW in Berlin to speed up deliveries of these reinforcements."

"I will do what I can," the AOW CinC said.

"I believe that air reinforcements are imperative if we are to conduct a satisfactory bomber campaign," Peltz said.

Von Rundstedt nodded and turned to Sperrle again. "And what of the fighter defenses?"

Sperrle looked at Gen. Werner Junck. "Werner?"

The Jagdkorps II fighter command leader nodded and also thumbed through some papers on the table before he spoke. "I must tell you that we do not have enough fighters to stop any huge formation of Allied bombers that would accompany an amphibious landing. We have but 270 single-engine fighters and 45 twin-engine fighters. Full *gruppens* of these aircraft are at five main bases: Lille-Nord, Chartres, Abbeville in western France and at Cormeilles and Conflants outside of Paris. We have other fighters at Rouen, Athis, and a few other airfields. I too am awaiting air reinforcements. We were promised six more *gruppens* of fighters, about 500 aircraft. Without these increased fighter units we cannot stop the enemy's cross channel assault."

"You may need to do what you can with whatever is available," von Rundstedt told Junck. "We are in a state of uncertainty. The *Wehrmacht* units need arms, ammunition, and fuel for our motorized, panzer and mobile gun units, just as the *Luftwaffe* needs more aircraft. I can only say that when I call OKW in Berlin, I will press the general staff to send you the promised aircraft as I will ask them to send as soon as possible the bomber aircraft for General Peltz."

"Yes, Herr Field Marshal," General Junck said.

"You must understand that at the moment Luftflotte Reich in the homeland itself has a priority on fighter aircraft." Von Rundstedt gestured. "They are in combat almost daily against the hordes of heavy bombers that come continually over Germany. But I will do what I can."

"Thank you," the Jagdkorps II commander said.

"Do you have a completed plan in the event of an enemy invasion?" von Rundstedt looked at Sperrle again.

"Yes, Field Marshal," Sperrle said. "I have asked General Junck to supply at least two *gruppens* of fighters to escort bombers that attack an enemy beachhead. I have also asked that General Peltz send out as many fighters as possible to intercept enemy bombers that attempt to attack our Channel defenses."

"And what of anti-aircraft defenses?"

"Our Flakkorps is well supplied with 105-mm and 155-mm weapons," the Luftflotte 3 CinC answered. "Four *gruppens* of the 300th Flakregiment are assigned at posts from Antwerp, Belgium to Calais, France. The 301st Flakregiment's *gruppens* are in positions from Calais to Le Havre, and the 302nd Flakregiment units are in positions from Le Havre to Cherbourg. The four *gruppens* of the 304th Flakregiment have their batteries along a one hundred-mile front from Compiegne, northwest to Rouen, and into Montagne, southwest of Paris. The 304th will attack bombers that fly beyond the beaches in attempts to disrupt communications systems. We also have flak batteries about most of the important railroad and highway bridges, since the enemy has been attacking these spans of late. Of course, we could always use more flak units."

"If it is possible, I will try to get you more," von Rundstedt said.

"I would appreciate that," Field Marshal Sperrle answered.

Field Marshal Gerd von Rundstedt pawed through the papers on the table again and then once more addressed the high officers of his AOW command. "If there is no other business, we can conclude this conference."

No one answered.

Von Rundstedt nodded. "I leave all of you with this parting comment. Remember, the enemy is unusually strong in men, arms, aircraft and supplies. The Allies would not even consider an invasion of the continent unless they believed they could succeed in such an endeavor. Though we do not have the military power of our enemy, we have enough strength to repel an amphibious landing if every man in every staffel, flak battery, panzer battalion and infantry company does his duty with dedication and loyalty."

The AOW chief looked at Rommel before he spoke again. "I am sorry if I offended you, Herr Field Marshal, but I must consider the defense of the entire western front and not only the Normandy beaches. No matter what our differences, you can be sure that we will send you whatever is necessary to hurl back an Allied invasion attempt, whether such attempted landings come at Calais, the Cotentin peninsula, or on the Bayeux beaches. I promise you that the three reserve panzer divisions will be the first units to move; they will proceed with all speed to fill whatever gaps you feel must be covered."

"Thank you, Herr Field Marshal," Rommel said.

Von Rundstedt sighed again. "Of course, mobility is the key in defeating an enemy invasion force. Troops from Army Group G must move quickly from their bases in northern France, Belgium, Holland and northwest Germany. Troops from Army Group H must act just as swiftly in moving across France, and those forces in the south of France must move swiftly north to bolster shoreline defenses. I will ask the transportation chief of the Armies of the West to make a thorough tour of all highways, railroads, marshalling yards and bridges to make certain that men and arms can travel quickly by road or by rail." He looked at Sperrle. "You must make certain that your *Luftwaffe* units are also on alert."

"Of course," Field Marshal Sperrle said. "I have already told General Peltz and General Junck to inspect all fighter and bomber *gruppens* to make certain they can take to the air on a half hour's notice. We will also make sure that all airfields are well prepared: smooth runways and taxiways, ample stocks of supplies, bombs and ammunition, and combat-ready aircraft and flyers. Luftflotte 3 will not fail you, Herr Field Marshal."

"Good," the AOW chief said. Then he sighed yet again. "I have ordered refreshments and they should be here soon. I suggest that within the next day or two you meet with your own individual staffs and acquaint them with our proposed plan to repel an enemy invasion. If we are alert and dedicated, we can stop an invasion of the continent."

But the Allies knew they would need more than men and arms to wrest *Festung Europa* from the Germans, and they too would draw up a plan to assure a successful invasion at Normandy.

CHAPTER TWO

The headquarters for the U.S. Strategic Tactical Air Force (USSTAF) was located at Bushy Park, England, just outside of London. USSTAF maintained its offices and quarters at Pinetree Estate, a beautiful complex on a sprawling acreage that had once served as an exclusive girl's school. The airmen assigned to this headquarters, from CinC Gen. Carl Spaatz to the lowest corporal clerk, enjoyed excellent living quarters, good food, and frequent trips into London on off-duty hours. The complex included everything from Spaatz' ornate oak-paneled office to a full-stocked PX, where USSTAF personnel could buy anything from cigarettes to cameras at drastically reduced prices.

Nowhere overseas did GIs enjoy such excellent duty as at Pinetree.

By mid May of 1944, General Spaatz and his staff had prepared an aerial strategy to aid Operation Overlord, the plan for the cross-Channel invasion of France. The knowledge of an impending invasion had aroused an air of confidence and expectation among everyone in England, including London civilians. Residents now moved about the ancient Anglo-Saxon capital with faster steps and with broader smiles. Everybody in the British Isles knew that more than a million soldiers, along with countless tons of armor, guns, ammo and supplies, had been massed at Plymouth, Weymouth, Portsmouth and Shoreham along the lengthy English Channel coast.

The streets of London became more crowded as soldiers roamed through England's capital city in larger numbers and with more frequency before they embarked on the big show. The pubs in the Soho district had experienced a huge increase in trade as American GIs and British Tommies jammed the bars more frequently to drink stout and strong liquor. English women spent more time with their soldier and airman sweethearts, for they knew that some of them would never come home. Shopkeepers, businessmen, families, and hostess organizations offered more services and hospitality to Allied soldiers because they also knew that these soldiers would be off on the biggest offensive mission of World War II.

In camp sites, GIs wrote letters home or left prized mementos to those who would not cross the Channel with them with the instructions. Be sure this gets to my mother (or wife or sister or sweetheart) back home.

At scattered U.S. airfields in southeast and eastern England, ground crews kept the fighters and bombers of USSTAF in good condition, with arms and bombs on the ready. U.S. pilots and crews waited for the day they would fly across the Channel by the thousands to lace German defenses during the massive Operation Overlord.

Soldiers and airmen in England, British and Americans alike, knew that the invasion would be the most important undertaking of the European war. Gen. Dwight Eisenhower, CinC of SHAEF (Supreme Headquarters, Allied Expeditionary Force) in the ETO, had planned Operation Overlord for months with Allied staff officers. Combat troops had spent weeks practicing landing tactics on British beaches, and moving inland against simulated German defense positions. Air crews had flown over coastlines to practice low-level ground support tactics.

The Allies knew the nature of the German defenses almost as well as the AOW staff themselves, because SHAEF intelligence men had received a constant flow of coded radio messages from the underground in France during the past months. French partisans had given the Allies the location of gun emplacements on the Channel coast, the site of the enemy's defenses, and the deployment of German units in France, including infantry, panzer, and *Luftwaffe*.

The SHAEF staff had especially familiarized themselves with defenses on the Normandy beaches, the Cotentin peninsula and the Calais port area. Ironically the excellent intelligence reports had dismayed Eisenhower because the information told him that the Germans had prepared well. No matter where the SHAEF CinC sent his amphibious troops, he would likely meet stiff resistance from German defenders and major obstacles in mines, hedgehogs and stakes. He had decided to land on the sixty-mile stretch of smooth beaches at Normandy.

Eisenhower, of course, enjoyed a vast superiority in planes, with more than eight thousand combat aircraft at his disposal for Overlord. They would face a mere twelve hundred German planes according to intelligence reports, but even this estimate was much too high. Luftflotte 3 actually had about eight hundred planes on the western front.

Yet the German Channel defenses and the *Luftwaffe* did not worry Eisenhower half as much as the vast number of enemy troops in France and the low countries. The SHAEF CinC had learned that the Germans had at least fifty divisions of troops, of which at least fourteen were armored. He knew that only six divisions, including one mere panzer division, protected the Normandy beaches.

Eisenhower reached a simple conclusion: if he could immobilize the mass of German infantry and armored divisions in France before the invasion, he would need to deal only with the seven German divisions at Normandy itself. In conjunction with the USSTAF, Eisenhower and his military leaders planned Operation Chattanooga Choo Choo to destroy the rail and road transportation system in France and the low countries. When they completed these plans, Eisenhower and Spaatz called a conference at USSTAF headquarters at Pinetree in Bushy Park to discuss a vital air operation before the Operation Overlord Normandy landings.

On 21 May 1944, an array of SHAEF brass arrived at Bushy Park. USSTAF clerks watched curiously as the VIPs came into the beautiful main building: Gen. Dwight Eisenhower; his chief-of-staff, Gen. Walter Smith; Field Marshal Sir Bernard Montgomery, CinC of the Twenty-first Army Group that would make the Normandy landings; Gen. Omar Bradley, commander of the First Army; Gen. Miles Dempsey of the Second Army; Sir Leigh Mallory, CinC of Allied European Air Forces (AEAF); and Gen. Lewis Brereton, commander of the U.S. Ninth Tactical Air Force. General Spaatz greeted each man individually. At 1020 hours, as aides passed out stapled sheets to those present, Eisenhower opened the meeting.

"The invasion plans for Operation Overlord

are complete," Eisenhower began. "Men, supplies, arms, planes, naval vessels—they're all ready. We'll make the invasion next week on 6 June, as weather conditions are expected to be favorable on that date. As planned, General Bradley's First Army troops will land in two areas designated Utah and Omaha. The Second Army forces under General Dempsey will land to the north on the stretches of beaches known as Gold, Juno and Sword. The First Army has as its objective the road center at Carentan, and the Second Army's objective is the rail center at Caen."

Ike paused, looked at a sheet in front of him, and then continued. "We know from intelligence, reconnaissance, and French underground reports that the Germans have about fifteen divisions along the Channel coast between Calais and Cherbourg, with six divisions facing our planned landing sites in Normandy. The Germans have forty more divisions in reserve at various locations in west Germany, Holland, Belgium, and France. At least fourteen of these are panzer divisions. The Germans have scattered their forces all over Western Europe because they do not know when or where we'll make our landings. They can only guess that they will be somewhere between Cherbourg and Calais, a two hundred-mile stretch of coastline. However—" the SHAEF CinC gestured—"all of their forces are poised to move swiftly, and they can reach the Normandy beaches within twenty-four hours."

"If the enemy stalls us on the beaches, for, say, ten to twelve hours," chief-of-staff Gen. Walter Smith now spoke, "we could be facing massive German infantry and panzer units that come to the aid of the Normandy defenders."

"So," Eisenhower said, "we will mount an operation that is designed to stop the enemy from sending heavy reinforcements quickly to Normandy." He looked at Gen. Carl Spaatz. "Carl?"

The USSTAF commander nodded and gestured to an aide who pulled down a huge map on the wall. "With the approval and help of Air Marshal Leigh-Mallory," Spaatz said, "we've drawn up a series of proposed air strikes in a strategy called Operation Chattanooga Choo Choo." The officers at the table broke into laughter and Spaatz, grinning, waited for the guffaws to subside before he continued.

"Chattanooga Choo Choo" . . . the name of a very popular American song of 1944 in the repertoire of the equally popular Glen Miller and his big band. The lyrics of the song take the listener on a passenger train ride between Penn Station, New York and Chattanooga, Tennessee.

"The code name is quite appropos," Spaatz said, "because the purpose of this aerial plan is to stop German choo choo trains from operating in France and the low countries. It is our intent to isolate the Germans in Normandy from their other units in France, while our amphibious forces break through the beach defenses and move inland."

"This operation," Leigh Mallory said, "will entail the destruction of major railroad marshalling yards, railroad bridges, road and rail centers, highway bridges, and the principal German airfields in Western Europe. Please look at the front page of the operational plan in front of you. As you can see, the American Ninth Tactical Air Force will carry out attacks on the rail systems, the RAF Second Tactical Air Force will attack road networks, and all air units will attack airfields. The American targets will be primarily in France and the RAF targets primarily in the low countries." He looked at the Ninth Air Force commander. "Perhaps General Brereton should explain as you look over the sheets in front of you."

"Thank you, sir," Brereton said. The Ninth Air Force commander then walked to the map. "We know several things about the German plans to defend Western Europe. They have troops of their Army Group B stationed in bases through northwest France, Belgium, Holland and into northwest Germany. This group numbers about twenty divisions, including several panzer units."

Brereton moved the pointer down the map before he continued. "Army Group H is scattered in bases from Poitou inland from the Bay of Biscay across central France and into Freiburg, Germany. The overwhelming majority of these forces would move by rail over the Nancy-to-Brest rail line. The Germans to the north of Army Group G—" he moved the pointer again—"would probably move through the Paris area to the coast along the Paris-to-Cherbourg railroad line, making extensive use of the Seine River bridges along the way. It is our intent to put these three main east-west communication routes out of business."

"We see that," General Bradley said. "What are you proposing?"

"We've selected a number of strategic targets, bridges and marshalling yards, along these potential German routes to the Channel coast," Brereton said. "If the Germans attempt to move troops from the northern areas, they would need to cross the Letripad, Hasselt, Gent, and Louvain bridges in northwest France and Belgium. They would muster their forces at Lille marshalling yard. Army Group B units moving through the Paris area over the Paris-to-Cherbourg rail line would need to cross the Juvisey, Courcielles and Vernon bridges while they mustered men and supplies at the Verdun, Lesnil, and Limidan marshalling yards."

"That seems obvious," Field Marshal Mongomery said.

Brereton gestured. "Now, troops and supplies from Army Group H would no doubt move across central France over the Nancy-to-Brest rail line. We therefore believe we should destroy the Le Fitte, Orival, and Denan bridges, while we put the Dijon and Meziere marshalling yards out of business. Of course, we have other targets that we'd also like to destroy and we'll have RAF and American units attacking those."

"Lew," General Bradley asked, "aren't you taking on an impossible job? Most of those bridges are steel and concrete framed, and I've heard that our air forces have never been good at knocking out such bridges. British railway experts say that you would need twelve hundred tons of bombs just to knock out the Seine River bridges. You'd need to expend an awful lot of bombs which will be needed for invasion air support."

"Omar," Brereton said grinning, "we've discovered a few things in recent months. There was a time when we needed too much tonnage to destroy a bridge. And, worse, the Nazis always had hordes of AA guns around their important bridges. But we've taken advantage of what we learned from the Strangle operation in Italy. We intend to use B-26 medium bombers, A-20 light bombers, and P-47 fighter bombers in low-level tandem strikes. We'll use delayed fuse bombs so the bombardiers and pilots can get right on top of a target to make sure they hit it. With a few good, well-placed thousand-pound bomb hits in rapid succession, we'll weaken the bridge quite badly and following bombers can finish it off."

"Does that system really work?"

"It worked in Italy," Brereton said. "When the tactical wings of the Fifteenth Air Force finished Operation Strangle, the Germans were unable to get any troops within fifty miles of Naples to stop the U.S. Fifth Army's northern drive up the boot of Italy."

"What about road junctions?" General Dempsey asked.

"That will entail mostly the use of Typhoon and Mosquito light bombers from the RAF," Leigh Mallory said. "The Second Tactical Air Force will carry out the same kind of tactics on highway bridges and road junctions that the American air units carry out against railroad bridges and marshalling yards. After we have completed these operations, we'll send out massive air units to destroy stalled trains and motorized columns."

"Let's hope the operation succeeds," General Dempsey said, looking at the stapled sheets in front of him. "It would be pleasant to know that we have no worries about German reinforcements pouring into the Normandy beaches."

"It'll work, General," Brereton insisted.

"What are the other aspects of this operation?" Dempsey asked.

"German air power," Brereton said. "We intend to start Choo Choo with the German airfields in France to eliminate as much of their air power as possible before we hit the communications systems. We know the Germans have some major air bases in the Paris area at Cormeilles, Conflants and Lesnil. They also have major bomber bases here along the western part of France at Lamar, Beaumont, Edex and Orival, with fighter bases at Lille-Nord and Abbeville. In central France, their major bomber base is at Ambria-Epinoy and their big fighter base is at Chartres. It is our intent to knock out these airfields and as many *Luftwaffe* aircraft as possible."

"How about bases in Belgium and Holland?" Field Marshal Montgomery asked.

"That will be the responsibility of the RAF," Leigh Mallory said.

"We'll begin Operation Chattanooga Choo Choo on 2 June with air strikes on the airfields," Brereton continued. "B-26 medium bomber groups will attack three of the west coast fields along with the Cormeilles field outside of Paris. Two more B-26 groups will attack the fields on north and western sectors of France, especially at Chartres. Then fighter bomber groups will conduct massive raids on the Conflants field outside of Paris and the two major airfields of Lesnil and Ambria-Epinoy in central France. We may strike these fields again if reconn reports indicate we did not do a thorough job the first time."

"What about the bridges, marshalling yards and road junctions?" Gen. Omar Bradley asked.

"Those, of course, are the main objectives,"

the Ninth Air Force commander said. "All USSTAF and RAF bombers and fighter bombers will begin these attacks on 3 June. As we indicated, we've pinpointed thirty-four bridges and fourteen marshalling yards for Ninth Air Force units alone. We believe that with the use of the delayed fuse bomb we can destroy these bridges, both railroad and highway, with a minimum of difficulty. Again, if reconn reports show we did not do a thorough job on these spans, we'll make followup bombing attacks."

Brereton paused and then gestured. "If we successfully destroy the bridges in the low countries and northwest France, the Germans will not be able to send troops over these highways and rail lines. As I said, we'll conduct followup raids on 4 June if necessary."

"Won't that still leave some bridges intact?" Dempsey asked.

"Yes," the Ninth Air Force commander said. "But, on the fifth, we'll send out bombers again to attack the bridges at Orival and Denain, along with the Meziere-Charleville marshalling yards. If we succeed here, we'll stop any chance for the Germans of sending reinforcements over the the Paris-to-Cherbourg line. Also on the fourth, the B-26 units will hit the big Juvisey and Elbeuf bridges in central France. That would cut almost completely the Nancy-to-Brest rail line. And to make certain, we'll do a complete job on the Dijon marshalling yards."

"General—" Dempsey pointed—"the targets you've named are not the only bridges, airfields, marshalling yards and roads in Western Europe. In fact, these objectives are really only a small percentage of such targets. Isn't that correct?"

"Miles," Leigh Mallory answered the Second Army commander, "no matter how many groups we use, we could not possibly knock out every bridge, freight yard, airfield and road junction on the continent. But, after a thorough study by the AEAF staff, we selected those targets which we considered the most important. While there may still be many bridges, airdromes and transport points that escape attack, the Germans could not possibly move the bulk of their reinforcements without using the targets that General Brereton outlined. They would never get enough armor, infantry troops or mobile guns to the Normandy beaches in time to stop our troops."

"This will be especially true as we expect to have only Allied planes over the beachheads," General Spaatz said. "Our fighter planes will be over France and the low countries continually to intercept any German aircraft that attempt to attack our forces on the landing beaches. I can assure all of you, there will be little interference from the German air force." He scanned the assembly before he spoke again. "Are there any questions?"

No one had any.

"I can assume then that all of you understand clearly the objective to destroy the German communications network and major airfield sites," Eisenhower now spoke. "I have every confidence in the air commanders. Our air units have done an excellent job over Germany. Agents have sent us glowing reports that continual bombing attacks have left the Nazis short of ball bearings, aircraft and, most of all, fuel. We can expect General Brereton and Air Marshal Leigh Mallory to do an equally good job in this operation."

"We will, of course, continue our heavy bombing missions over Germany and the enemy's defenses at Normandy," General Spaatz said.

Eisenhower scanned his officers and spoke again. "As we've already discussed, the invasion is planned for 6 June and we need not dwell anymore on Operation Overlord. The three airborne divisions will jump behind the German defenses shortly before dawn and the six combat divisions will hit the Normandy beaches at about 0800. All commanders will follow implicitly the instructions from Field Marshal Montgomery who is the OTC for Operation Overlord."

The officers at the table looked at the field marshal, who rose from his chair, tilted his red beret, and then addressed the group. "I would remind all of you that we have reached an emotional and strategic climax in this global war. For Britain and our wonderful American allies we have come to the end of the beginning after five years of struggle, frustration and hardship. For our friends in France, our efforts in this operation will mean their return to freedom. We will drive our Nazi enemies out of France and the low countries and send them on the low road to *Gotterdammerung,* a road to ruin, a twilight for the Nazi gods who will suffer inevitable destruction."

General Eisenhower then spoke again. "This cross-Channel attack has been a dream since the beginning of this war. We Americans, from the time we first entered this conflict, have been obsessed with one goal—the liberation of Europe. The time has now come to begin this liberation. This operation will be the first massive blow towards the heartland of Germany. Our soldiers have sweated in training, and our staff has toiled for endless hours. This will be the biggest military operation in history, and its success depends on a willingness by every one of the million or more men involved to carry out his duty. Please return to your units and meet with your commanders. Make certain that every man in every company and in every squadron is prepared to fulfill his role."

As Eisenhower paused, and no one said anything, the SHAEF CinC spoke softly. "OK, the conference is over. We'll retire for lunch."

Thus had the Allies completed their plans for the invasion of the continent and the subsidiary aerial operation that was designed to stop the flow of reinforcements and any interference from the *Luftwaffe*.

Operation Overlord was immense in its size and scope. The invaders would move from a half dozen Channel ports in Britain, using 5,300 ships and craft, the largest flotilla in history. The AEAF would mount 12,000 aircraft, the greatest air armada that ever took to the skies. The planes included paratroop transports and gliders, hordes of fighter planes to escort the airborne soldiers, swarms of bombers to attack the Normandy defenses, communications and enemy positions behind the beaches.

The six infantry divisions—three American, two British and one Canadian—would assault a sixty-mile stretch of beaches in the first wave between Caen and Cherbourg. 107,000 troops, 14,000 vehicles, and 15,000 tons of supplies would land on the beaches during the first twenty-four hours.

The Allies would bring with them artificial ports, portable docks, bombardons and gutted ships that would be sunk to serve as improvised piers. The U.S. and Royal Navies would supply a hundred men-of-war—battleships, cruisers and destroyers—to plaster the enemy defenses before the troops hit the beaches.

But the Germans had known for weeks that an invasion was coming and Gen. Dwight Eisenhower realized this fact. The SHAEF CinC was certain the Germans would spare no effort to hurl back his troops from the beaches. But, without reinforcements, the Germans on

Normandy could not possibly throw back the invaders. And once the Allied troops had firmly established a beachhead and moved inland, there would be no chance of chasing the Americans and British off the continent.

Gen. Lewis Brereton had prepared thirty-six air groups of the Ninth Tactical Air Force and Leigh Mallory had prepared twenty-two air groups of the Second RAF Tactical Air Force, over twenty-five hundred planes, for the Choo Choo operation. General Spaatz was confident, certain the enemy could not do much to deter these tactical air raids. But if the Germans had inferior forces in numbers, they did not lack courage, ability or determination. The men of Luftflotte 3's *geschwaders* and flakregiments would do all they could to stop Operation Chattanooga Choo Choo.

CHAPTER THREE

Without a doubt, the glory boys of the ETO during World War II were the airmen of the U.S. Eighth Air Force. By late spring of 1944, the B-17 and B-24 groups of the Eighth had conducted countless raids over Europe, including 11 raids in Berlin, and another 167 raids over other targets in Germany.

Among the bomber groups of the Eighth, the Third Air Division's One-hundredth Bomb Group, the Ninety-fifth Bomb Group, and the Ninety-first Bomb Group had attained renown. These B-17 units had already won nine D.U.C.s among them. In the Eighth Air Force fighter units, the pilots of the Fifty-sixth and Fourth Fighter Groups had become the darlings of the ETO. These airmen in the P-51s and P-38s had shot down more than four hundred German aircraft since they began operations over Europe. The two groups had flown mostly escort missions for the B-17 formations into Fortress Europe, so the fighter pilots of the Fourth and Fifty-sixth continually met German interceptors that tried to stop the Flying Fortresses. Between the two groups, they had won five D.U.C.s.

Each new Eighth Air Force mission had brought higher kill scores with fewer losses because by mid-1944, the German Air Force had lost many of its aces. The *Luftwaffe* had been forced to send more and more inexperienced and hastily trained airmen against the Americans. Further, the FW 190s and ME 109s, once the best fighter planes in Europe, were not superior to the speedy P-51 Mustang and durable P-38 Lightning.

Gen. James Doolittle, CO of the Eighth Air Force, got a request for some important missions from General Eisenhower only two days after the meetings for Operation Chattanooga Choo Choo. Eisenhower wanted Eighth Air Force heavies to neutralize the German synthetic oil industries as the Ninth Air Force Tactical Air Force units would attempt to stop troop movements in the Choo Choo operation. The SHAEF commander felt that if Germany could be deprived of fuel, the Germans would be further hampered in moving troops into the French coast during Operation Overlord.

Eisenhower had singled out five particular targets: the major synthetic oil plants at Ruhland and Magdeberg, and the lesser synthetic plants at Zeitz, Merseburg-Leuna and Lutzendorf.

"I want to put them out of business," Eisenhower told Doolittle.

"We'll hit those plants hard," the Eighth Air Force commander promised.

Doolittle prepared 23 heavy bomb groups and 24 fighter groups, 864 B-17s and 1040 P-38 and P-51 fighter escorts for the bombing missions. He scheduled the raids for 28 and 29 May 1944.

On the evening of 27 May, Doolittle met with air division and wing commanders at High Wycombe, England, the U.S. Eighth Air Force headquarters. "D-day is about a week away," he told his commanders. "USSTAF has already planned the tactical operation to neutralize communications systems and air bases in Western Europe. Our Eighth Air Force missions are designed to destroy five German synthetic oil plants. No matter how successful the USSTAF missions, they cannot possibly knock out the entire rail and road system in France and the low countries; nor can they knock out every German air base. But—" the Eighth Air Force commander gestured—"if we deprive the enemy of fuel, he can't fly his planes, operate his tanks, or drive his motorized columns."

"When do we leave, sir?" Gen. Earl Partridge of the Third Air Division asked.

"We'll send out the First and Second Air Divisions tomorrow and the Third Air Division on the twenty-ninth," Doolittle said. He gestured to an aide who lowered a map on the wall behind him. Then Doolittle took a pointer and pointed to several areas on the map.

"As you can see, these synthetic oil plants are pretty much bunched together in this area. The First and Second Divisions will hit Ruhland and Magdeberg tomorrow, while the Third Air Division hits the smaller Zeitz, Merseberg-Leuna and Lutzendorf plants on the twenty-ninth. The Eighth Fighter Command will furnish fourteen groups to escort the two air divisions tomorrow and they'll furnish ten groups to escort the Third Division on the twenty-ninth."

"What about interceptors?" General Partridge asked.

"We can expect opposition, but our fighter pilots are good and they should keep most of the *Luftwaffe* fighters off the backs of the B-17s during the bomb runs." He nodded to Gen. William Kepner of the VIII Fighter Command.

Kepner approached the dais, looked at the officers and then spoke. "If you'll check the FO, you'll see the details of this operation. The First Air Division will get off first from their bases at Bassingborn and Alconbury. Gen. Bob Williams will lead the 28 May mission. The Second Air Division will take off from their bases at Thorpe Abbott, Horsesham, and

Ketteringham to rendezvous with the First Division at Dover. Escorts from the VIII Fighter Command will pick up the bomber formations over the Channel. Route in will be the usual course through the Dummor Corridor: northern France, Belgium, and into Germany."

"We understand," General Williams said.

"On the twenty-ninth," General Doolittle said, "the Third Division's B-17s will follow the same pattern. The groups will turn east at Dover and pick up escorts over the English Channel. These bombers will also follow the Dummor Corridor route. General Partridge will lead this second air mission." He looked at the Third Air Division commander.

"I'll hold a briefing with group commanders tomorrow to explain full details of the FO," Partridge said.

Doolittle nodded and scanned the high-ranking wing and division officers again. "Any questions?"

None.

"OK, get back to your units and prepare your own FOs."

The 864 heavy bombers—550 on the 28 May mission and 314 on the 29 May mission—would carry a total of 1718 tons of heavy GP bombs. They would bomb at altitudes from twenty-eight thousand feet down to seventeen thousand feet, coming over target in the usual box patterns.

Bomber crews of the Eighth Air Force had

already made several deep penetrations into Germany, including missions to Berlin. Still, the flights into Germany had never been routine. Almost always, FW 190s, ME 109s, and ME 110s rose up to meet them. For months, Eighth Air Force leaders had been saying the *Luftwaffe* was dead, but Flying Fortress crews continued to experience heavy and aggressive opposition from German fighter pilots. Thus, the order that called for another deep penetration into Germany left the B-17 crews uneasy.

Dawn of 28 May broke clear and dry, with only small puffs of white clouds scattered in the sky. Visibility would be easy for takeoff and excellent for a flight across the English Channel. Although meteorologists had predicted good weather over all the Europe, American combat crews had often found weather forecasts inaccurate. Clear weather over England and the Channel had often given way to dense cloud cover after flying 750 miles into Germany, necessitating bomb drops by radar. And worse, the crews could not observe results, and flew back to England with a question in their minds—had they hit and hurt the target? And, as always, some of the U.S. B-17 crews did not come back.

At 0700 hours, at Bassingborn Field in England, thirty-eight B-17s of the Ninety-first Bomb Group lumbered over taxiways towards the runways. The big engines screamed in the early morning, awakening residents of the nearby village. But the Britishers had become accustomed to these thousand-HP Wright engines. In fact, many of the civilians often came to the field to watch the B-17s take off.

In the lead plane, Gen. Bob Williams sat in the pilot's seat. Behind him, Col. Henry Terry, CO of the Ninety-first Group, taxied his plane towards the runway. At 0710 hours, a flare shot up from the control tower and General Williams revved the four big engines of his B-17. Then, he released the brake and the B-17 roared down the runway and hoisted itself skyward into the clear morning sky.

Behind Williams, Colonel Terry also zoomed down the runway and lifted his heavily loaded Fortress into the sky. Thirty-six more B-17s of the Ninety-first also roared down the runway for nearly a half hour before all were airborne.

At the large American airbase in Thorpe Abbott, thirty-eight B-17 pilots of the One-hundredth Bomb Group also tore down a runway and hoisted their B-17s skyward, with each Fortress carrying six GP five hundred-pound bombs. Some thirty miles away, at Alconbury, forty-two Flying Fortresses of the Ninety-second Bomb Group lumbered over taxiways towards the airstrip. In the lead Fortress, Col. Bill Reid swung his B-17 to the head of the apron and, at precisely 0720 hours, revved the engines of the heavy bomber. The big plane vibrated and strained against the brakes. A moment later, a flare went up and Reid released the brakes to roar down the apron and into the air. Forty-one more B-17s followed him.

At eleven other airbases, other B-17s of the First and Second Air Divisions also roared down runways and soared skyward. Soon, the fourteen heavy-bomb groups from the Middlesex County air bases were airborne, jelling into formation and heading towards Checkpoint I at Dover, on the English Channel coast. By 0850 hours, the formation of B-17s, 550 planes, turned eastward and droned towards the continent.

Earlier, at 0745 hours, in the U.S. fighter base at Boxted, Col. Hubert Zempke led the first 54 Mustang fighters of the Fifty-sixth Fighter Group to the head of the runway. Few fighter groups in the U.S. Air Force had scored as many kills and produced as many aces as the Fifty-sixth Wolfpack Group. Zempke himself had downed 11 German planes and the group had downed 221 more enemy aircraft, and had an excellent possibility of adding to that score today. As soon as the flare arced out of the control tower, Zempke and his wingman zoomed down the apron and shot skyward. Within twenty-five minutes, 52 other Mustangs of the Wolfpack group had also roared into the sky.

Less than ten miles away, at Derben Field, the P-38s of the equally renowned Fourth Fighter Group also rolled over taxiways toward the head of the runway. Col. Don Blakeslee, the group commander, had already scored seven kills over Europe and his group had run up a total of 173 kills since entering combat. By 0750 hours, all fifty-two Lightnings were airborne and heading for the Channel.

On twelve other airfields, 518 more P-38s and P-51s of the Eighth Fighter Command took off for the flight towards Germany. By 0845 hours, the 624 U.S. fighter planes were heading southeast by east. The P-38s would take on interceptors as far as the German border before returning to England; the long-range P-51s would accompany the B-17s all the way to target and then back to the British Isles.

By 0900 hours, the fighters had joined the long line of bombers crossing the English Channel, a column of B-17 diamonds stretching for nearly fifteen miles and flying at 225 miles mph at five thousand feet. In the early morning, British fishermen watched for more than ten minutes as the parade of American planes crossed the water on the way to Fortress Europe. The Britishers knew that the Yankee bombers would be hitting another major target inside Germany. They also knew that some of these American airmen would not come back.

Before the Flying Fortresses reached the coast of Belgium, American fighter planes from the Sixty-fourth and Sixty-seventh Fighter Wings settled either alongside the B-17s or above the Fortress groups. The nearly one thousand planes then droned over the English Channel. At 0945 hours, they crossed the coast of northwest France and headed for Belgium. The huge

American formation would drone over Western Europe for three hours. But the Germans would not let them fly over their conquered continent unmolested.

"Achtung! Feindliche flugzenge!" Enemy aircraft. At 0950 hours, the cry of approaching planes came from the warning controller of the Jagdfuhrer Belgium radar station in Liege. The controller had caught the first elements of the American bomber fleet as the B-17s passed over Belgium toward Germany. The radar operator quickly sent his report to Luftflotte 3 headquarters in Paris, where personnel quickly passed on the information to JG fighter units in Holland and to Luftflotte Reich in west Germany. At the Cormeilles air base in north central France, Col. Hans Assi Hahn of the JG 2 Richthofen Geschwader mounted seventy-six FW 190s and roared northward to intercept the American formations.

At 1025 hours, Col. Hubert Zempke of the Fifty-sixth Fighter Group got a call from one of his scouts on the flanks of the U.S. air armada. "Colonel, bandits coming in at three o'clock."

"OK, Captain," Zempke answered. He then called Col. Don Blakeslee of the Fourth Fighter Group. "Don, we're going after some bandits to the south. Your group should stay with the Forts."

"Will do, Hubie," Blakeslee said.

The crews of the B-17s watched the P-51s peel off and roar southward while the Flying

Fort gunners fingered the triggers of their guns gingerly. They would need to take on any FW 190s that escaped the fighter escorts.

Moments later, high over Belgium, the chatter of machine gunfire and the *whoosh* of twenty-mm shells streaked through the blue sky. But the American fighter pilots stopped most of the JG 2 pilots from reaching the American bombers. In a ten-minute running dogfight, the Americans shot down twelve of Colonel Hahn's planes, while the U.S. fighter group lost three of their own. Only twenty of the German FW 190s broke through the gauntlet of P-51s to reach the bombers.

Now, the B-17 squadron leaders tightened their formations while Fortress gunners sent blistering machine gunfire into the attacking German planes. The *Luftwaffers,* as usual, attacked viciously, in pairs, chopping holes in many of the Flying Fortresses with raking wing fire and twenty-mm shells. The Germans damaged seven B-17s, four of them badly enough to force an abort of the mission and a return to England. The Germans also downed three of the big bombers. In return the B-17 gunners downed nine of the FW 190s.

Soon, the long American air fleet had cleared this first run-in with German fighters. The tight B-17 formation crossed the German border and headed east, southeast towards their targets, the Ruhland and Madgeberg synthetic oil plants. The B-17s met heavy anti-aircraft fire along the Dummor Corridor. The ack-ack knocked down an additional two B-17s and damaged several more, but the bombers escaped serious trouble. However, a swarm of ME 109 German fighter planes soon headed for the formation.

Col. Hubert Zempke called General Williams. "Keep the formation tight, sir. We're in for another donnybrook."

"We read you, Colonel," Williams said.

Soon, the whine of arcing, diving planes, the thunder of twenty-mm shells, and the chatter of machine gunfire once more rumbled through the sky. But, again, the U.S. pilots of the Fifty-sixth and other P-51 groups kept most of the *Luftwaffe* fighters at bay, while knocking down twenty-three of the German planes against a loss of only six U.S. planes. The few German fighters that reached the B-17 formations caused minimal damage to the Flying Forts, failing to knock down any of the big bombers. In turn, the German staffels lost another six planes to the Flying Fort gunners.

Then the huge U.S. air fleet, despite losses to German fighters and ack-ack, continued through the Dummor Corridor. Finally, at 1215 hours, General Williams cried into his radio.

"All units! IP in ten minutes. First Division aircraft will continue on 105 course to 375 target (Ruhland), and Second Division aircraft will alter course to 133 degrees to attack 379 target (Magdeberg)." He paused. "Good luck."

Heavy anti-aircraft fire greeted the B-17 formations as the Flying Forts approached target at twenty-eight thousand feet. Flak downed another three B-17s and damaged sixteen more Fortresses, ten of which were forced to turn back. But the others continued through the dense puffs of black ack-ack that now darkened the sky like huge, ebon dust particles.

At 1305 hours, the first whistling bombs dropped from the B-17s of the Ninety-first Bomb Group and struck the Ruhland Synthetic Refinery in a staccato of numbing concussions. Two smokestacks toppled, a pair of buildings collapsed, and an array of fuel lines and tubing erupted into a mass of twisted metal. The Ninety-first had hit its target perfectly.

"OK," Col. Henry Terry cried, "let's get out of here."

Immediately behind the Ninety-first, the Ninety-second Bomb Group also dropped a confetti of bombs on Ruhland. Then came the other five groups of the U.S. First Air Division, the B-17s dropping their loads from twenty-six thousand to twenty-two thousand feet. All total, the First Division bombers dropped over five hundred tons of bombs on the Ruhland complex. Most of the bombs hit within a quarter mile of the plant's center, macerating seven large buildings, one smaller one, eight oil tanks, and miles of pipelines. Fires raged through the complex and smoke rose to ten thousand feet.

As the bombers left target, more ME 109 German fighters pounced on the big American Forts. But, again U.S. pilots of the Fifty-sixth

Fighter Group and other American fighter units successfully staved off most of the interceptors, and downed another seventeen German planes. Col. Hubert Zempke of the Fifty-sixth Group got two ME 109s himself.

Meanwhile, the B-17s of the Second Air Division droned southward to Magdeberg. These Flying Forts also ran into a wall of anti-aircraft fire. The black puffs were so thick that Flying Fortress crewmen could not even see fellow B-17s during much of the time. But the bomber pilots flew grimly on and bombardiers aimed at drop points without wavering.

At 1325 hours, Col. Bob Kelly in the lead One hundredth Bomb Group B-17 sighted the target. He cried into his radio. "IP in one minute; one minute. All pilots hold course; all bombardiers prepare for drop."

"Yes, sir, Colonel," somebody answered.

Before the first B-17 of the Second Air Division reached target, the heavy AA fire downed four of the Flying Fortresses and damaged six more badly, forcing them to abort. Still, the B-17s droned on, in their tight box pattern formation. At 1320 hours, five hundred-pound GP bombs tumbled out of the lead diamond of bombers from the One-hundredth Group. The explosives fell squarely on one of the refineries. A shattering staccato of concussions followed. Twelve of the sixteen bombs hit a building squarely. The roof collapsed, machinery inside the structure jerked loose in warping clanks, walls tumbled down, and barrels of synthetic oil ignited. Within seconds the building was a mass of wreckage, fire and smoke.

"We got her good, Colonel," the co-pilot told Kelly.

"Right on the button." The One-hundredth Bomb Group commander grinned.

Thirty-six other B-17s of the One-hundredth Group also droned over the oil complex to drop heavy loads of bombs. More buildings were shattered; more fires erupted; more pipelines were wrenched into twisted metal; more storage tanks ruptured before erupting in flames.

The other six bomb groups of the U.S. Second Air Division now came over the Magdeberg Refinery to destroy still more of the synthetic oil complex. The B-17s left in their wake a square of destruction. Seven large buildings destroyed or badly damaged; seventeen large and small storage tanks wrecked. Dense, black smoke spiralled upwards to twelve thousand feet.

As the B-17s of the Second Division left the area, German fighters also jumped these Flying Forts. But American fighter pilots answered the challenge from sixty FW 190s. Fighter pilots from four P-51 groups raced into the formations of *Luftwaffe* interceptors. Once more, chattering machine gunfire and swishing twenty-mm-shells streaked across the sky. The Germans quickly lost five planes, but others managed to break the Mustang screen and reach the bombers.

Despite heavy fire from B-17 gunners, the Germans shot down four B-17s. As the Fortresses roared out of the Dummor Corridor and over northern France, Col. Hans Hahn again took off with fifty FW 190s from his JG 2 unit. A new dogfight erupted, with the adept Hahn, who had already scored more than 150 kills during four years of combat, getting still another kill. Hahn knocked off two engines of a B-17 and shattered the left wing. The Flying Fort upended and fell erratically downward to crash and explode. The JG 2 airmen also shot down two more Forts and a P-51 before the American air armada flew out of range. But these successes were little compensation for the vast destruction at the Ruhland and Magdeberg Refineries.

Late in the afternoon, almost dusk, the American bombers and their fighter escorts finally returned to England. Seventeen B-17s and fourteen P-51s had not returned. However, the American fighter pilots and bomber gunners had claimed the destruction of thirty-four German FW 190s and ME 109s. The day had been hard and bloody, as had almost every run through the Dummor Corridor into Germany.

At dawn the next morning, 314 B-17s of the Third Air Division took off from their airfields in England to hit the Zeitz, Merseburg-Leuna and Lutzendorf synthetic oil plants. Three groups of B-17s would hit each of the three targets. 416 P-51 and P-47 fighters of the Eighth Fighter Command furnished escort.

29 May became a replay of the day before. Gen. Earl Partridge of the Third Air Division led the bomber groups, with the Ninety-fifth Bomb Group in the lead. The long formations of B-17s once again crossed the Channel and then droned across northern France and Belgium and into Germany. And, again, German fighter staffels, swarms of FW 190s and ME 109s, rose from a dozen air bases on the continent to challenge the American formations. All along the eight-hundred-mile route from the English Channel, American fighter pilots and B-17 gunners fought furious battles with *Luftwaffe* pilots. By the time the American air units crossed the German border, the Third Air Division had lost twenty-seven B-17s to German fighter pilots and anti-aircraft shells. The Americans had also lost six P-51s while downing twenty-eight German fighter planes.

At 1245 hours, General Partridge cried into his radio. "This is Sparky Leader; please assume course for targets."

The nine B-17 groups then broke away from each other. The Ninety-fifth and two other groups headed for Zeitz on a straight easterly course. The Ninety-sixth Group and two other Fortress groups headed southeast to Merseburg-Leuna; the 303rd and two more B-17 bomb groups droned southward toward the oil refinery at Lutzendorf. The American fighter groups also broke off in three groups, each escorting three groups of bombers.

At 1310 hours, General Partridge sighted the Zeitz refinery. Despite the dense, black puffs of ack-ack bursting in the sky, he called his pilots. "Keep the formations tight. All bombardiers prepare for drops. Ninety-fifth will drop at twenty-eight thousand feet and the other two groups will drop at twenty-four thousand and twenty thousand respectively. Route out will also be in box formation."

"Yes, sir," Col. Karl Truesdale of the Ninety-fifth Bomb Group answered.

At 1315 hours, the first five hundred Gp bombs fell on the sprawling Zeitz refinery. Again, the American bombardiers showed excellent accuracy with more than seventy percent of the bombs landing within the target area. Storage tanks exploded into huge balls of fire. Buildings collapsed and pipelines ruptured. The three bomb groups had knocked out half of the target area. However, the Americans did lose six B-17s and two P-51s over the target area.

Yet the assault on the German synthetic oil plants continued unabated. At 1325 hours, the second trio of bomb groups from the Third Division droned over the Merseburg-Leuna plant to drop another 260 tons of bombs on this complex. The weather had remained clear allowing the bombardiers could bomb visually, and thus hit with relatively good accuracy. Nearly half the bombs struck the complex to cause extensive damage. The last trio of B-17 groups enjoyed similar success at the

Lutzendorf oil complex. But here, too, German anti-aircraft gunners and aggressive fighter pilots downed nine of the B-17s and six P-51s to a loss of fourteen *Luftwaffe* fighter planes.

The successful but battered Third Division heavy bombers were harassed all the way back to England by both anti-aircraft fire and German fighter planes. Even as the formations crossed western Belgium, fighter staffels tried to knock them down. Among the most fierce interceptors were the pilots of the renowned JG 26 Schlagetor geschwader based at Abbeville, France.

Col. Joseph "Pips" Priller, commander of JG 26, was one of the most experienced and canny pilots of the *Luftwaffe*. He had already scored over two hundred kills in a six-year combat career, having first served with the German Condor Legion in Spain during that country's civil war in the mid-30s. He took off with fifty-six fighters from Abbeville and Lille-Nord in northwest France to lash out at the Flying Fortress formations.

"Attack in pairs; in pairs!" the JG 26 commander cried.

"We will do so," Maj. Herman Graf of the Schlagetor's II Gruppen answered his colonel.

The JG 26 fighter pilots then engaged American P-51 pilots and B-17 gunners in a running fight for almost a half hour, over more than a hundred-mile stretch of Belgium. The aggressive Priller knocked down two P-51s and then got himself a B-17 when he knocked off the tail of the Flying Fort with three solid twenty-mm shell hits. The Schlagetors downed twenty-one planes, thirteen Forts and eight Mustangs before the American formations finally reached the Channel. The JG 26 *geschwader,* however, lost nineteen planes of their own.

General Partridge had seen his air division suffer another traumatic day, no matter how successful the attacks on the three synthetic oil refineries. The Third Air Division commander sighed in relief as he finally led his B-17 units across the English Channel.

"We're home, General, we're home," his co-pilot said.

Partridge shook his head. "God only knows how many planes didn't make it back. Goddamn it, they keep telling us the *Luftwaffe* is dead, but they aren't dead, Captain, they aren't dead."

"No, sir," the co-pilot said.

Partridge was tired when he finally returned to his quarters at Third Air Division headquarters on Horsesham Field in England. He should have fallen asleep quickly, but he did not. No matter what they told him, he always agonized when he lost so many young airmen on these vicious bombing missions into Germany.

CHAPTER FOUR

Adolf Hitler reacted furiously when aides informed him of the serious damage to five synthetic refinery plants. He called an immediate conference of high-level military chiefs at the Reich Chancellory in Berlin. He stood slightly stooped over, shaking from his palsy condition. His neck had reddened and a fiery anger beamed from his dark eyes. He threw cold stares at everyone around him before he pointed to his military chief, Gen. Wilhelm Kietel, head of the OKW (Oberkommando der Wehrmacht).

"Incompetents! That's what we have for military leaders, incompetent fools. How could we let this happen? How, when there is every evidence that the Anglo-Saxon enemies may attempt an invasion of the continent?"

Those in the room remained silent, with Field Marshal Hermann Goering rubbing the perspiration from his neck to alleviate his uneasiness. The *Luftwaffe* OKL knew that Hitler's rage would soon be directed at him. Gen. Alfred Jodl, the OKW chief-of-staff pursed his lips nervously, and the Oberkommando der Luftwaffe Reich, Gen. Joseph Kammbuber, only stared soberly at the Fuhrer. Gen. Reinhold Gehlen, the Kommando der Flakregiments, tightened his face to await an expected malediction from the Fuhrer. Production Minister Albert Speer stood rigidly.

"We need every gallon of fuel that came from those refineries." Hitler wagged a finger angrily. "Why did not the *Luftwaffe* stop these enemy bombers? Why did not the flakregiments shoot them down? We promised the German people that the enemy would never succeed with air attacks on Germany, but they have succeeded, and they have caused much damage." He scowled contemptuously before he spoke again. "What do you have to say for yourselves? What?"

"Mein Fuhrer," Albert Speer spoke, "the damage to the refineries is not as bad as we first thought. We can still turn out fuel at thirty percent to forty percent capacity. Within two months, they will be fully repaired and back to full production."

"Two months!" Hitler screamed. "In two months, if we do not have fuel for tanks and aircraft, the enemy may be on the continent and all the way across France."

Albert Speer did not answer.

Hitler now glared at Hermann Goering. "This was your responsibility. Your *geschwaders* were supposed to stop these aircraft. You assured us that enemy bombers would never fly over German soil. Yet the enemy comes over every day with impunity. Why has this happened? Why?"

Goering lowered his head slightly and then glanced at General Kammbuber. "The defense against these air attacks was the responsibility of Luftflotte Reich." He passed the buck.

"Well?" Hitler barked at Kammbuber.

"Mein Fuhrer, we unfortunately underestimated the strength of the enemy, and the introduction of their long-range, superior P-51 fighter plane that they use for escort."

"Superior!" Hitler screamed again. "What of our own aircraft? We should have the superior aircraft, not the decadent Anglo-Saxons. We have the best scientists in the world. How dare you speak of a superior aircraft on the part of the enemy? No, the enemy's P-51 is not a superior aircraft. The *Luftwaffe* fighter units are manned by cowardly pilots who have no plan because bumbling officers are commanding these *geschwaders*."

Kammbuber did not answer.

Hitler now looked at General Gehlen. "And what of the anti-aircraft gunners? We know that the Americans always send their bombers through the Dummor Corridor, the shortest route into Germany. We have stationed flakregiments all along this route. Yet, most of these bombers get through. How can this be? The flakregiments should have shot down all of these bombers before they reached targets deep into Germany. But these gunners are also inefficient because they were badly trained and they have poor leadership."

"The enemy sends over aircraft by the hundreds," Gehlen said. "We cannot possibly shoot them all down."

"Nonsense," Hitler retorted irritably. "Do not we have more anti-aircraft shells than the enemy has aircraft? If your gunners were efficient, each shell would knock down one Anglo-Saxon aircraft."

Now it was General Gehlen who did not answer.

"Must I do everything myself?" Hitler raged on. "Is it necessary that I make all the decisions to assure the effectiveness of our flak gunners, our soldiers, and our airmen? Why do I have an OKW chief?" He now glowered at Kietel. "And why do I have an Oberkommando der Luftwaffe?" he huffed at Goering.

"Please, Mein Fuhrer," Field Marshal Kietel said. "It is as General Gehlen said, the enemy now sends his bombers over the Fatherland by the hundreds, and with hundreds of fighter escorts. No matter how efficient our flak gunners and no matter how capable our fighter pilots, we cannot possibly shoot down this many aircraft. Our defenders damaged or destroyed nearly half of the attack force in these refinery raids, but that still left several hundred American bombers to strike the five targets."

"Then why have we not destroyed the enemy's English bases?" Hitler asked Goering. "I told you months ago that we needed a new bomber force that would annihilate the enemy air force at its source. Yet, Herr Field Marshal, you have not carried out my wishes." He then scowled at Speer. "You told me that you would produce one thousand aircraft a month, of which at least half would be bombers. If you had followed my instructions, the *Luftwaffe* would have the means to destroy the enemy's air bases in England."

No one in the conference room answered Hitler during this tirade. How could they tell him he was indulging in deranged thinking? Heavy Allied air attacks had cut down German aircraft production drastically. And how could the *Luftwaffe* possibly destroy Allied bases in England? The Americans and British had nearly three hundred air bases on the British Isles and more than ten thousand planes to defend these bases if necessary. Even if the *Luftwaffe* could mount a thousand plane bomber force with an equal number of escorts to attack these bases, the Germans would meet so many interceptors on the way that the hordes of Allied planes would blacken the skies over the English Channel.

And, realistically, even if Speer could produce one thousand planes a month, the *Luftwaffe* had neither the pilots nor crews to fly them; nor enough gasoline to fuel even the training aircraft needed to instruct new airmen. The *Luftwaffe* could barely keep half of its already assigned *geschwaders* in the air for lack of gasoline and the attacks on the five refineries would not help the situation.

The leaders at the chancellory conference had long ago stopped giving Hitler advice. The Fuhrer would not listen to any problems, needs, reports of shortages, or reports of the overwhelming enemy strength. Hitler had only disparaged those who had spoken in negative terms. He had refused to hear that a *geschwader* of *Luftwaffe* planes often met ten or twenty times their number in enemy planes over Europe, or that a single tank battalion on the Eastern front often faced a full division of enemy tanks, or that a single company of German infantry defenders might need to stop an attack force of several regiments.

In recent months, German military leaders had allowed Hitler to rant and rave, and they then carried on as best they could against superior Allied strength. Almost all of the generals now believed that the British and Americans would successfully gain a foothold on the continent, although none of them dared to express this opinion to the Fuhrer.

"I have personally drawn up a new plan—" Hitler wagged a finger at his subordinates—"and I want this plan carried out without fail." He shuffled through some papers in front of him with trembling fingers and then looked at those about the room. He first addressed Albert Speer. "You will have the refineries repaired within the week, so that the flow of needed fuel will not be interrupted."

"A week?" Speer gasped. "But, Mein Fuhrer—"

"I want no excuses," Hitler cut him off. "They can be repaired if you use all available labor and if you take steps to ship necessary material."

Speer said nothing more. The German production chief knew he could not reason with the irrational Third Reich dictator.

Hitler now looked at Gehlen. "I want the flakregiments strengthened about the refineries. Use as many guns as necessary. You will make certain that in the future all enemy aircraft will be shot down before they reach any of these refineries. Do you understand?"

"Yes, Mein Fuhrer," Gehlen said.

The flak OKF chief, although answering positively, also knew that Hitler's instructions were ludicrous. All the anti-aircraft guns in Germany could not shoot down a thousand planes droning over a target. The B-17 flew high and it could take plenty of punishment. No matter how much flak they threw into the sky, most of the Flying Fortresses would reach targets and drop their bombs. And, worse, the

Americans had the ability to bomb accurately with H2X radar.

Now, Hitler looked at Goering. "Herr Field Marshal, there must be a new effort on the part of the *Luftwaffe*. Your pilots must rededicate themselves to the Fatherland. They must show total aggressiveness against these enemy bombers. You must match the enemy aircraft for aircraft. If they send over five hundred bombers, five hundred fighters must meet them. If they send over a thousand bombers, one thousand German fighters must rise to attack them. In this way, each German fighter pilot can shoot down one plane and none of the enemy aircraft can reach target."

Goering did not answer, but General Kammbuber, too astonished to remain silent, did. "Mein Fuhrer, what you suggest is impossible. We would need to muster every aircraft from every German airfield and bring them into Luftflotte Reich. Besides, we could never find enough pilots to fly enough aircraft to destroy the huge formations of Allied aircraft that come over the continent."

"Ridiculous," Hitler scoffed. "It can be done. If we can produce one thousand new aircraft each month, we will not need to pull even one fighter plane from the Eastern front, the Mediterranean front, or the Western front. As for pilots, we have thousands of young, loyal Germans who would gladly fly these aircraft. You have only to enlist them into the *Luftwaffe* and train them with able instructors. Even if some are not as experienced as the enemy pilots, what our airmen lack in such experience, they will make up in their sense of duty to the Third Reich. Such devotion will compensate for their lack of experience."

Goering and Kammbuber only pursed their lips in dismay. How could they or anyone else in this room respond to the distorted ramblings from their Fuhrer? German pilots had not found any lack of devotion in American pilots. In every aerial clash during the past several months, even where the odds were even, the U.S. P-47, P-51 and P-38 fighter pilots had fragmented JG fighter units most of the time because the Americans did not lack courage or aggressiveness. But who could explain this fact to Hitler, who had refused to believe anything except his own head-in-the-sand delusions?

Hitler scanned his commanders once again before continuing. "I have given you an excellent plan to restore oil production and stop further Allied air incursions into Germany. It is now up to you to carry out these plans." He looked at Speer. "I will expect daily reports on the progress of repairs to the five refineries and the output of new aircraft."

"Yes, Mein Fuhrer."

Hitler now looked at Goering. "I expect you to train new pilots, hundreds of them if necessary, so we can successfully stop any more Allied air attacks on our vital industries."

"I understand," Goreing said.

The Fuhrer now looked at Kietel. "You will see to it that Field Marshal von Rundstedt has prepared an adequate plan to repel a possible Allied invasion of the continent."

"The field marshal has completed such plans for defending western France," Kietel said. "Strong positions have been constructed along the Atlantic wall and these defenses can surely stop an Allied invasion." Kietel then looked at some papers in his hand. "We have also established a plan to rush reinforcements in armor and infantry to any area on the Western front where the enemy may attempt to land troops."

Hitler nodded and then looked at Goering. "What of the Luftwaffe?"

"Field Marshal Sperrle has assured us that he has considerable aircraft, both fighters and bombers, to deal with any invasion force," Goering lied. "Be assured, Mein Fuhrer, the enemy will meet strong and aggressive Luftflotte 3 units during any invasion attempt."

Hitler nodded again, his face now softening. "At least there is some favorable news. Now, you will carry out my instructions. I want no more excuses and no more incompetence. If any *Wehrmacht* or *Luftwaffe* commander does not carry out his duties loyally and efficiently, he is to be relieved of his command at once."

"Yes, Mein Fuhrer," Kietel said.

"Good," Hitler answered. He looked at the wall clock and then gestured. "I believe the business of this conference is over. You are all dismissed."

Goering, Jodl, Kietel and the others left the room in silence. Once more they had heard their Fuhrer give instructions that were impossible to carry out. They would need to lie to him again when the inevitable misfortunes struck the German *Wehrmacht, Luftwaffe* or industry. They had only one consolation—at least things looked good on the Western front. The Army of the West had prepared itself well for an invasion, with strong defenses and a strategy of mounting planes and deploying troops when such an invasion came.

But the Germans were not aware of the impending American strategy: Operation Chattanooga Choo Choo.

At his headquarters in Bushy Park, England, on the morning of 30 May, 1944, Gen. Carl Spaatz, CinC of USSTAF (U.S. Strategic Tactical Air Forces) met with Gen. James Doolittle of Eighth Air Force. Gen. Lewis Brereton of the Ninth Air Force, Gen. William Kepner of the Eighth Fighter Command, and several air division commanders. Spaatz had studied the mission reports against the German synthetic oil plants and he felt quite perturbed. While the reports indicated that the B-17 groups had done considerable damage to the quintet of targets on 28 and 29 May, he was quite appalled at the losses. A total of fifty-seven B-17s and twenty-four P-51s had been shot down, with varying amounts of damage and personnel injury to at least another one hundred aircraft and nearly a thousand men.

"Gentlemen," Spaatz said, "the bomb runs over Germany are still costly. It's now evident that the major reason for these losses is the long hours of flight through eight hundred miles of heavy anti-aircraft batteries and enemy fighter interceptors. Our crews and fighter pilots are undoubtedly weary and tense by the time they reach targets deep inside Germany and that has hurt their effectiveness."

"It's rough," Gen. Earl Partridge said, "but our airmen go out every day anyway and they do the best they can. They do perform quite well."

"We'd like them to do even better and without so many losses," Spaatz said. "I think the answer is obviously Operation Overlord. Once we've established air bases in France, we'll not only cut down drastically on the flying time into Germany, but we'll also eliminate much of the anti-aircraft and interceptor resistance."

"That would sure be nice," General Williams of the First Air Division said.

"The attacks on the refineries will no doubt cut down the German fuel capacity," Spaatz gestured, "and it will take them at least a couple of months before they can get those five plants back to full production. That should impair their movement of ground reinforcements and restrict their air flights during the invasion." He looked at General Brereton.

"Lew, what about Operation Chattanooga Choo Choo?"

General Brereton shuffled through some papers in front of him. "Plans for Choo Choo are all set. We've prepared about three thousand aircraft from our Ninth Tactical Air Force and the RAF's Second Tactical Air Force to hit airfields, marshalling yards, railroad pikes, bridges, highways and road junctions. Most of the Ninth Air Force targets are in France, including airdromes, highways, and specific rail and bridge targets. Air Marshal Mallory has assigned his RAF units for assaults on highways and highway bridges in Belgium, Holland and northwest Germany. The RAF will also hit airfields in that area."

The Ninth Air Force commander gestured and then continued. "The attacks on the airfields will be carried out on 2 June as outlined in the Choo Choo plan, and the attacks on the bridges and marshalling yards will commence on 3 June, the next day. That will give us at least a couple more days before D-day to carry out any more necessary air attacks."

"What about air opposition in France?" Spaatz asked.

"We've had reconn planes flying over France continually," Brereton said, "but we really have no concrete information on the strength of Luftflotte 3. Our best estimate is that the Germans have about five hundred fighters on their French bases, mostly FW 190s, and they may have as many as five hundred bombers.

But Luftflotte Reich has been drawing planes from France as well as from the Eastern front and Italy to deal with our heavy bomber attacks in Germany. So Luftflotte 3 may not even have this many planes."

"With our resources, we can certainly deal with a few hundred German planes," Spaatz said. "We've prepared nearly ten thousand aircraft for air operations during the D-day landings."

Brereton nodded.

Spaatz looked at a map on the wall behind him before he spoke again. "Starting today, we will launch RAF and Eighth Air Force attacks on the German Atlantic wall. We'll be hitting the coastal defenses for the next three days, all the way from Calais down to Cherbourg. That should confuse the Germans as to where the landings will take place. Meanwhile, Ninth Air Force will carry out Operation Chattanooga Choo Choo." He paused. "Any questions?"

None.

"Okay, then let's get the air shows moving."

When the conference ended, Gen. Lewis Brereton went immediately to his own headquarters in Bushy Park and called an aide into his office. "I want a meeting of all B-26, A-20, P-47, P-38, and P-51 group commanders in my office tomorrow morning."

"Yes, sir," the aide said.

By 1000 hours, 31 May, the commanders of sixteen medium bomb groups, six light bomb groups, twelve fighter bomber groups, and twenty-four fighter groups had arrived at Bushy Park. The Ninth Air Force CinC wasted no time before assembling them in the huge conference room, a former auditorium of the onetime exclusive girl's school.

"By this time," Brereton began, "all of you have the FOs for Operation Chattanooga Choo Choo. The air groups of the Ninth Air Force will be responsible for destroying thirty-four major railroad bridges, twenty-six French airfields, and fourteen marshalling yards. We'll have three days to carry out these strikes, the second, third and fourth of June. Each air group will have its assigned target, time of TO, date of mission, and expected bomb load. I cannot overemphasize the importance of succeeding on these missions."

Brereton gestured to the map on the wall before he continued. "The green lines on the map are the principal rail routes the Germans would use to bring reinforcements to the Normandy beachheads. The red pins represent the major marshalling yards where the Germans would likely make up trains for the movement of tanks, troops and supplies to the Atlantic wall. The yellow pins are the major railroad bridges on these rail lines, and the black pins represent the major German airfields in France. Those are your targets, gentlemen, seventy-four of them. If we knock them out by dawn of 6 June, Operation Overlord can go a whole lot easier."

"We'll do it, sir," Col. Glen Nye of the 322nd Bomb Group said.

Brereton looked at the 322nd commander and grinned. "Your group will be initiating this plan, Glen. As you can see from the FO, the 322nd and 387th Groups will hit the German airfields at Lamar, Beaumont, Edex, and Cormeilles on 2 June. You'll be carrying one thousand-pound bombs so you can dig huge holes in the runways. In fact, on all the airfield attacks, the B-26s and A-20s will be using HE thousand pounders. The P-47 fighter bombers will use five hundred pounders."

"Is this right, sir?" Col. Tom Seymoure of the 387th Group looked up. "The 354th Fighter Group will furnish escort for these missions?"

"Yes," Brereton answered. "All three squadrons from the 354th Group and one squadron from the 367th Group will cover the 322nd and 387th Groups. Each bomb group will have two squadrons of fighters for escort. The other two squadrons of the 367th Group and two from the 474th Fighter Group will be escorting the 391st and 416th Groups that hit the airfields at Abbeville, Orival, Lille-Nord and Chartres."

"My god, sir, three of those airfields are German fighter bases," Col. Jerry Williams of the 391st Group said. "Will four squadrons of fighter escorts be enough?"

"We've got a lot of territory to cover, Tom," the 9th Air Force commander answered the 391st Group commander. "So, our escort will be spread a little thin." He looked at the sheet in front of him before he spoke again. "As you can see, the fighter bomber groups will also be hitting some of the airfields. The 365th, 366th, and 368th Groups will attack the fields at Conflants, Lesnil, and Ambria-Epinoy, one group to each airfield."

"As I see from this FO," Col. Norman Holt of the 366th Group said, "only a single 474th Squadron of P-51s will be escorting our entire group."

"Yes," Brereton said, "about twenty fighters for each P-47 fighter bomber group. You would not need escorts as badly as the B-26 and A-20 groups because the P-47s could jettison their bombs if necessary and fight off interceptors yourselves."

General Brereton then went through the remainder of the FO sheets, pointing out other targets for the other B-26, A-20 and P-47 groups. He also outlined the escort duties for the other P-38 and P-51 fighter groups of the Ninth Air Force for these Chattanooga Choo Choo missions. All total, nearly eight hundred medium bombers, light bombers, and fighter bombers would conduct air attacks over the three-day period, with nearly seven hundred fighter planes acting as escort, or conducting strafing runs if the opportunity arose. Brereton felt confident that fifteen hundred planes were sufficient to carry out successfully these tactical air operations.

"Remember," Brereton said, gesturing to his

group commanders, "for every piece of rolling stock and every passenger car you knock out, the Germans will have that much less armament and that many less soldiers to kill American GIs on the Normandy beaches. Every crater on a German airfield and every German plane destroyed will mean that many less GIs getting hit by *Luftwaffe* bombs or strafing fire. So, I cannot overemphasize the importance of these missions, not only for the success of Operation Overlord, but for the saving of American lives." He paused and scanned the group commanders. "Any questions?"

"I guess not, sir," Colonel Holt of the 366th Fighter Bomber Group said.

"Everyone understands his particular assignment?"

"It's pretty clear, sir," Col. Lance Call of the 365th Fighter Bomber Group answered.

"Good," Brereton nodded. "I expect the bomber groups to perform in their usual aggressive fashion, and I expect the fighter groups to deal effectively with interceptors, so that the bombers can carry out attacks with a minimum of interference. Get back to your units and brief your airmen." Then he pursed his lips. "Good luck to all of you!"

The Ninth Air Force commander stood motionless as the colonel and lieutenant colonel group commanders left the briefing room. When they were gone, an aide turned to the general. "If they succeed, sir, we'll prove once and for all the worth of a tactical air force."

"They'll succeed, Captain, they'll succeed," Brereton said.

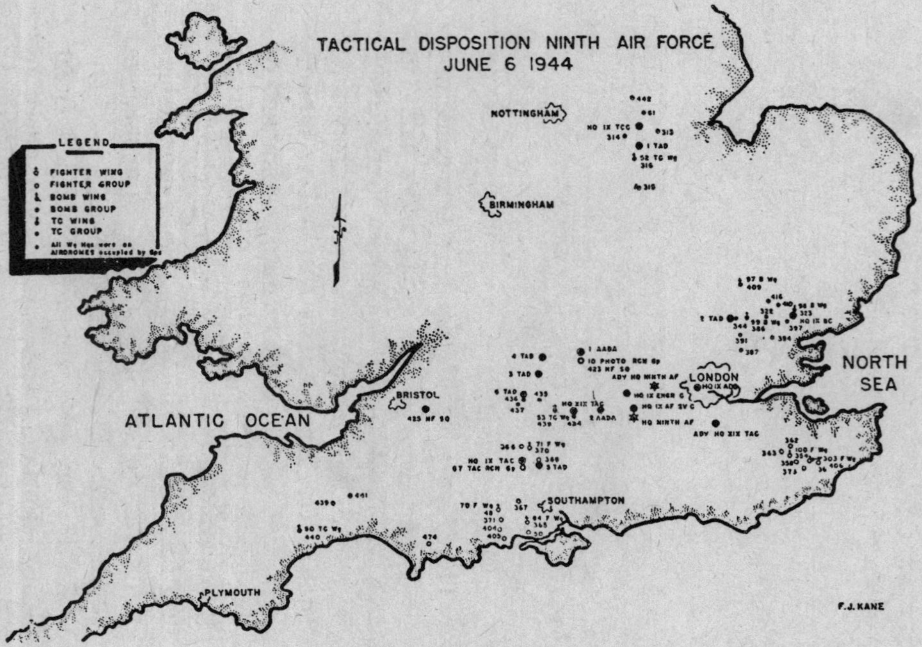

TACTICAL DISPOSITION NINTH AIR FORCE
JUNE 6 1944
LEGEND
FIGHTER WING
FIGHTER GROUP
BOMB WING
BOMB GROUP
TC WING
TC GROUP
NOTTINGHAM
BIRMINGHAM
BRISTOL
LONDON
SOUTHAMPTON
PLYMOUTH
ATLANTIC OCEAN
NORTH SEA
F.J. KANE

CHAPTER FIVE

The 322nd Bomb Group, Nye's Annihilators, had been in England for a year and a half. The USSTAF had activated the unit in June of 1942, and the 322nd had moved overseas from their Drane Field, Florida airbase only seven months later. Col. Glen Nye had assumed command of the group in May of 1943. Since the group began combat operations out of England, they had been hitting airfields, power stations, shipyards, rail systems and bridges from medium altitude in the B-26 Marauders.

On 17 May 1943, the 322nd had left Great Saling, England with eleven Marauders to attack and finish off a power plant in Holland that had been damaged earlier by other U.S. planes. One B-26 had aborted and the other ten went on without fighter escorts. However, aggressive German pilots from the JG 54 Green Hearts *geschwader* had shot down all ten B-26s, destroying the aircraft and fifty crew members. The disaster prompted the Eighth Air Force to pull the group out of action for more training before sending them out again on combat missions over the continent. Not until July of 1943 did the 322nd go out again, this time with P-47 fighter escorts.

By early 1944, the group had switched to low-level tactics with the delayed fuse bomb, specializing in attacks on bridges, motorized columns and other tactical targets.

By May of 1944, when the 322nd Group celebrated its first anniversary of combat, the group had flown 187 missions, with 5,008 individual sorties, unloading 6100 tons of bombs on enemy targets. They had earned a bumper crop of awards during the period: 2 DUCs, 2 Silver Stars, 493 DFCs with 87 clusters, 909 Air Medals with 398 oak-leaf clusters, 2 Legions of Merit, a Soldiers Medal, and a British DFC. They had also earned the name Nyes Annihilators because of their vast destruction of enemy targets.

The 322nd's air base at Great Saling in rural northeast England lay outside the small village of Swaffham in Norfolk County. The eight hundred-man complement, the only American military men within a dozen miles, had established an excellent rapport with the villagers and Swaffham residents often came to the field and watched the B-26s take off on missions to Europe, just as they often returned in the afternoon to count the Marauders landing on the runway. They expressed sorrow if all of the medium bombers did not make it home.

The rural English villagers came again to the field on the pleasant morning of 2 June to await the takeoff of B-26s.

At 0700 hours, Col. Glen Nye, the group commander from Raleigh, N.C., called fifty-six B-26 crews to order in the 322nd's operations quonset hut. He waited until the men had settled on their benches before he leaned over the podium.

"Gentlemen, for the next three days we will be involved in a new operation that includes the destruction of airfields, bridges and marshalling yards in France and the low countries. The invasion date is only a few days off and SHAEF headquarters wants to disrupt the Nazi rail and road system as much as possible to stop reinforcements from reaching the beaches, and also to minimize German air attacks on the Allied invasion forces." He cocked his head and the operations officer pulled down a map of Western Europe on the wall behind the podium.

"Today," Nye said, "dozens of air groups from the Ninth Tac will hit some special airfields in France." He picked up a pointer and tapped the map. "Our targets are the Lamar bomber base near the west coast of France and the larger air base at Beaumont, also near the west coast. Intelligence believes that a full *gruppen* of Dornier light bombers are in Lamar and perhaps two *gruppens* of Junker 88 medium bombers are at Beaumont. These aircraft are reportedly in reserve to hit the invasion sites. So our mission is to destroy as many of these planes as possible while we chop up the runways. Each aircraft will carry four thousand-pound bombs, two GPs and two HEs."

"Who's going where, Colonel?" Lt. Col. Charles Olmstead of the 452nd Squadron asked his commander.

"The 449th and the 450th will hit Lamar; the 451st and 452nd Squadrons will hit Beaumont. On the first pass, in pairs, we chop up runways with GP bombs, and on the second pass we knock out aircraft with our HE bombs."

"What about escorts?" Maj. Hank Newcomer of the 450th Squadron asked.

"P-51s from the 354th Fighter Group's 353rd and 355th Squadrons will accompany us." Nye looked at the map again. "This is not a very long mission, only about two hours away, so we shouldn't be airborne more than four or four and a half hours."

"Yes, sir," Maj. Howard Doolittle of the 451st Squadron said.

"Any questions?" Nye asked.

"No, sir," somebody answered.

"OK, let's get breakfast before we mount up."

At 0815 hours, Col. Glen Nye and his lead

B-26 Marauder *Sandra Ann* turned into the head of the runway. He waited for the green light to blink. When it did, the colonel revved his engines once more, released the brake, and roared down the runway with his big bomb load. Ground crews of the 322nd as well as civilians watched anxiously and then sighed in relief when the medium bomber hoisted itself skyward.

After Nye, thirteen more B-26s of the 449th Squadron were soon airborne. Then twelve more planes of the 451st Squadron took off. Next, Maj. Howard Doolittle led fourteen B-26s of the 450th Squadron down the runway and into the air. Then came the thirteen Marauders of the 452nd Squadron under Lt. Col. Charles Olmstead, who would lead the attack on the Beaumont airfield. Soon, the fifty-six Marauders jelled into four-plane diamonds and droned southwards towards the English Channel.

Sixteen miles away, at Stoney Cross Drome, on the outskirts of the village of Fakenham, also in Norfolk County, Col. Tom Seymoure of the 387th Bomb Group also held a briefing in a group operations quonset hut. Here, fifty-four Marauder crews sat and listened as the group operations officer also pulled down a map of France and the low countries. Seymoure waited until the chatter of his airmen subsided before he spoke.

"Today, USSTAF will begin a three-day

operation known as Operation Chattanooga Choo Choo."

"Choo Choo, sir?" Capt. Sam Monk of the 556th Squadron laughed before an explosion of guffaws erupted through the quonset hut. Seymoure grinned and waited for the din to abate before he continued.

"I know the code name is strange," the 387th Group commander said, "but the name signifies our objective—the destruction of the enemy's transportation system in Western Europe, especially the rail networks. Oh, I know, we've been making rail cuts, hitting bridges, and knocking out rolling stock for months. But, this operation is especially designed to destroy particular marshalling yards, bridges, airfields and road networks so we can stop German reinforcements from reaching the Channel coast during Operation Overlord."

"Do we have a bridge target today, sir?" Maj. Jim Keller of the 558th Squadron asked.

"No, today we go after airfields. Tomorrow we hit bridges and marshalling yards." Seymoure picked up a pointer, turned to the map, and slapped several points on the chart. "We're going here, today—to the Cormeilles airfield outside of Paris and to the Edex airfield near the west coast. I will personally lead the 558th and 559th Squadrons to the Paris field, and Maj. Jim Keller will lead the 557th and 556th Squadrons against the Edex airdrome. Takeoff will begin at 0735 hours."

"What about our bomb load, sir?" Capt. Ed James of the 556th Squadron asked Seymoure.

"Every aircraft will carry four thousand-pounders, two GPs to chop up the runways, and two HEs to ignite parked aircraft. We believe there's a full group of medium bombers at Edex and as many as two *gruppens* of fighters and fighter bombers at Cormeilles. Our route in will be straight south to Canterbury where we'll rendezvous with the 322nd Group at eight thousand feet. We'll pick up our escorts of P-51s and P-38s from the 354th and 367th Fighter Groups at Folkstone and then fly across the Strait of Dover to Mareghem at a point of forty-nine degrees north by four degrees east. Then we split up. My units will go on to Cormeilles and Major Keller's units will go to Edex."

"Will escorts be with us all the way?" Captain Monk asked.

"Yes. The 367th Group's 392nd Squadron will accompany Major Keller to Cormeilles and the 354th Group's 356th Squadron will escort our other squadrons to Edex. We'll be going in low, maybe below two thousand feet, and we'll attack in pairs. Stay at least thirty seconds apart to avoid damage from preceding bomb drops. We'll make two passes. The first drop will be with GPs on the runway, and the second drop with the HEs will be on parked planes." He paused and scanned the men. "Any questions?"

None.

Seymoure nodded. "OK, we've got about twenty minutes before we board aircraft. Get yourselves some quick cups of coffee. The motor pool has vehicles waiting to take us to the field."

The fifty-four crews of the 387th Pathfinder Bomb Group chattered in large and small groups as they drank coffee and ate rolls. Then, they left the quonset hut for a ride to the field. By 0735 hours, the combat crews were inside their aircraft. Pilots revved engines, co-pilots checked instrument panels, bombardiers examined sights, engineer gunners inspected equipment, radio gunners checked frequencies, and tail gunners tested their weapons. In fifty-six Marauders, crews answered positive to pilot requests on readiness.

By 0740 hours, the long line of B-26s were on the taxiways and lumbering towards the main runway. Col. Tom Seymoure swung his B-26 to the head of the apron. He waited impatiently, revving his engines, while the Marauder vibrated and strained against the brakes. At 0745, when the green light blinked, Seymoure released his brakes and the medium bomber lurched forward. As soon as the lead plane rose from the apron, Capt. Sam Monk of the 556th Squadron zoomed down the runway and took off.

Then, Maj. Jim Keller whirled his B-26 to the head of the runway before he too released his brakes and zoomed down the runway with a heavily laden B-26. Behind him, thirteen more Marauders of the 558th Squadron took off. Finally, the fourteen medium bombers of the 559th Squadron took off.

By 0830 hours, the 54 B-26s of the Pathfinder group had reached Canterbury, the first check point, and settled behind the 56 Marauders of the 322nd Bomb Group. Then the 110 B-26s droned towards Folkstone on the coast.

At 0730 hours, Col. George Bickel of the 354th Fighter Group completed his briefing with sixty-four P-51 pilots. "This Chattanooga Choo Choo operation will be very important. If we can knock out the enemy's important French airfields and his road and rail communication system, the Nazis can't send many planes and reinforcements to the Normandy beaches against our GIs." He turned to a map on the wall. "OK, one last time. We pick up the B-26s at Folkstone and then cross the channel to the French town of Mareghem, about a hundred miles inland. "I'll be leading the 353rd Squadron to accompany the B-26s going to Lamar. Major Weldon's 355th Squadron will accompany the B-26s going to the enemy airfield at Beaumont, and Major Howard's 356th Squadron will take the B-26s of the 387th Group going to Edex."

"I understand, Colonel," Maj. Howard said.

"I must warn you," Bickel cautioned, "that enemy fighter planes are at Chartres and they might come out to intercept. So we'll have to stay alert."

"We'll be alert," Maj. Bob Weldon said.

Bickel nodded and then continued. "OK, if there are no more questions, you can get yourselves some doughnuts and coffee at the rear of the quonset hut. We'll mount up in twenty minutes."

The fighter pilots of the 354th Valor Group ad-libbed like excited hounds as they moved about the two tables to get coffee and doughnuts. These pilots had enjoyed considerable success since coming into combat six months ago. They had come to England in October of 1943, after extensive training with P-39s at the army air force base in Portland, Oregon. However, upon arrival at Greenham Common in the British Isles, they had found P-47s waiting for them. So the pilots spent six months acclimating themselves to these heavier, speedier Thunderbolts. When they finally entered combat, the 354th pilots had directed most of their efforts to escorting 9th Air Force tactical bombers in attacks on German targets in France. During the six-month period, Valor pilots had shot down 121 German planes, an astonishing score for their relatively short tour. But the 354th pilots had been well trained and their Thunderbolts could take severe punishment. Then, two months ago, the 9th Air Force had assigned the new, sleek P-51 fighter plane to the group, an aircraft that was totally superior to the enemy's fighters. The Mustang could outrun, outclimb and outdrive any ME 109 or FW 190.

The 354th airmen, while scoring the 121 kills, had lost only 23 planes, of which 12 pilots had been rescued by the French underground and returned to England.

By 0935, as sixty P-51s of the 354th Fighter Group approached Folkstone, tail gunner George Morse, aboard Major Keller's *Flak Bait* of the 387th Group's 557th Squadron, saw the dots behind him. He could not make them out clearly as P-51s, but he assumed they were Mustangs since they were still over England. He called the pilot.

"Sir, I think our escorts are coming on."

"OK, Sergeant," Major Keller said.

Co-pilot Lt. Ed Cook craned his neck to look out of the starboard cabin window and he too could see the dots in the distance. In the nose, bombardier-navigator Lt. Tom Clark squinted from his plexiglass bubble and also saw the P-51s coming on. In his waist section, gunner Tom Davis listened over the intercom, but he did not look up from his charts. He could not see anything from his windowless compartment. In the bubble, engineer-gunner Sgt. Tim Snyder squinted from his blister and watched the P-51s zoom past them. The Mustangs would be escorting other bomb units and not the trailing 387th Group's squadrons. P-38s from the 367th Group would escort Keller's two squadrons to Cormeilles.

Meanwhile, at 0945 hours, Col. George Bickel of the 354th called Col. Glen Nye of the

322nd Group. "This is Spotlight Leader. Spotlight 1 and 2 will accompany all Mayflower squadrons to Lamar and Beaumont. Spotlight 3 will accompany Pallidin 1 and 2 to Edex. Brightlight 1 is on the way to escort Palidin 3 and 4 to Cormeilles."

"We read you," Colonel Nye answered. "All Mayflower squadrons will remain in formation as far as Checkpoint 2."

In Lt. Alton Ottley's B-26, behind Colonel Nye's lead Marauder, the pilot stared from his cockpit at the two P-51s that soon hung off his port. Co-pilot Bob Grosskopf looked at the pair of Mustangs off his starboard window. Then he turned to Ottley and grinned.

"They look beautiful, Al, just beautiful."

"They'll take good care of us." The pilot nodded.

In the nose, navigator-bombardier Sgt. Tom Anderson darted his eyes in several directions, looking at the Mustangs all about him. He then looked at his single .50-caliber machine gun and he wondered if he'd need to use it with these sleek Mustangs to protect them.

In the top turret, gunner Sgt. Joe McDonald stared up at the diamonds of P-51s about him, counting and re-counting them to occupy his time. In the waist, radio gunner Sgt. Jim Bradford toyed with his radio dials, but looked up occasionally to stare at a hanging P-51 beyond the starboard window. And finally, in the tail, gunner Sgt. Floyd Sapp squinted in his cramped compartment to look at the Mustangs around his formation.

Only five minutes later, the P-58s of the 367th Group's 392nd Fighter Squadron, under the group commander, Col. Ed Chickering, jelled around the 387th Bomb Group's 558th and 559th Squadrons that were going to Cormeilles. "This is Brightlight 1," Chickering said. "We'll be taking Pallidin 3 and 4 to target and back."

"Glad to see you, Brightlight," Maj. Jim Keller answered.

The B-26s and their escorting fighter planes soon droned across the Strait of Dover and then inland over France beyond Calais. At 1010 hours, they reached Checkpoint 2 and then split up. Lieutenant Colonel Olmstead took his twenty-eight bombers and headed for Beaumont. Twenty P-51s accompanied him. Twenty Mustangs under Col. George Bickel hung next to the Marauders under Col. Tom Seymoure that headed for the German bomber base at Lamar. A moment later, Maj. Jim Howard led his twenty P-51s of the 356th Squadron southeast to accompany the two B-26 squadrons under Col. Tom Seymoure that droned toward the German bomber base at Edex. And finally, Col. Ed Chickering took his twenty P-38s straight east with the two Marauder squadrons under Maj. Jim Keller who was heading for the Cormeilles air base outside of Paris.

* * *

At 1020 hours, air raid sirens wailed throughout northwest France as German radar teams picked up aircraft in the skies. The operators followed the various flights of American planes before sending reports to Luftflotte 3 headquarters in Paris. Technicians in the huge tracking room were soon shuttling blocks about a huge map and then reporting the movements to Capt. Peter Heindroff who directed the Luftflotte 3 tracking station. After calculating the potential route of the American bombers, Heindorff got a good idea of the destination of these American air units.

"Enemy bombers seem to be heading for Lamar Airdrome," the captain told his aide, Col. Heidi Schroeder. "A second formation appears to be heading for Beaumont. Another formation seems to be approaching Edex, and the fourth enemy is coming eastward, possibly to the Paris area. You will notify interceptor units at once."

"Yes, Herr Heindorff," Corporal Schroeder said. She then called several *geschwader* units in France, the JG 1 at Argentan and the JG 26 at Lille-Nord. JG sent off twenty-four FW 190s from its II Gruppen. The FW fighters broke into two formations to intercept the Americans heading for Lamar and Beaumont. At Lille-Nord, Col. Joseph "Pips" Priller mounted forty FW 190s to attack the B-26s heading for Cormeilles and Edex. Priller took twenty planes towards Cormeilles, while Maj. Herman Graf took the other twenty FWs after the two 387th Group squadrons that were heading for Edex.

Meanwhile, AA from flak batteries along the routes of the U.S. aircraft sent booming 105- and 155-mm flak into the air. Big black puffs soon saturated the sky. But although some B-26s caught shrapnel hits, none of the Marauders went down, and none of the airmen were killed or seriously injured.

Col. Glen Nye reached Lamar at 1105 and ogled at the field below. Some twenty Dornier 17 bombers were lined up on both sides of the runway. "OK," he cried to his pilots, "in pairs! Hit the runway first and then the planes."

"We read you, Colonel," Maj. Howard Doolittle of the 450th Squadron said.

Despite AA fire, the twenty-four B-26s from the 322nd Bomb Group went in low, in pairs, and at thirty-second intervals. They dropped nearly thirty tons of GP bombs on the runway. Within minutes the airstrip became a heavily cratered ribbon; dust rose a hundred feet into the air, while exploding concrete and earth showered the parked German Dorniers along the airstrip. By the time the B-26s had left the field, the runway did not have a square yard of smooth area.

"Okay, let's go back after the planes," Nye cried.

Moments later, the B-26s swooped over the field again, this time dropping their HE thousand peunders. The explosions struck plane after plane, igniting some Dorniers, smashing apart more, and turning other German bombers into twisted wrecks. By the time the Marauders left the field the second time, they had completely destroyed fourteen bombers and seriously damaged four more. Only two Dorniers were operable and they could hardly take off on the damaged field.

Some distance away, Lt. Col. Charles Olmstead took his 451st and 452nd Squadrons over Beaumont, where once more Nye's Annihilator units met heavy AA fire. The flak knocked down one B-26 and damaged two more. But still, the American airmen swooped over the field in pairs to puncture the runway into shreds with their heavy GP bombs. Within ten minutes they came back on a second pass to lay a string of HE thousand pounders over some forty-odd Junker 88 medium bombers, igniting fires, twisting metal, and smashing wings and fuselages. By the time Olmstead and his crews left the area, only smoke and fire rose from the airfields. The Americans had destroyed twenty-two of the German bombers and seriously damaged eleven more.

"OK," Olmstead cried into his radio, "let's go home."

Meanwhile, fighter pilots from the 354th Group under Col. George Bickel dealt effectively with the enemy interceptors out of Argentan. The twenty P-51s of the U.S. 353rd Squadron waded into the first staffel of JG 1

FW fighters that had hoped to stop the attack on Lamar. Within several minutes the Americans shot down six of the twelve German planes and damaged the others. The Germans in turn had damaged just three Mustangs, only one of them seriously. Not a single JG 26 plane had interfered with the American attack.

Twenty-four fighters from the 355th Fighter Squadron clashed with the second staffel from JG 26 that had tried to intercept the B-26s over Beaumont. The Americans hit the FW 190s in pairs before the German planes could reach the Marauders. The U.S. pilots quickly downed five of the German fighters with heavy .50-caliber wing fire, while damaging four other JG 1 fighter planes. The Germans damaged only two P-51s. As at Lamar, the B-26s roared over Beaumont to carry out their attacks without interference from any German fighter planes.

To the north, Col. Tom Seymoure led the 556th and 557th Squadrons of the Pathfinder 387th Group into the Heinsel bomber base at Edex. Here again, AA fire greeted the Americans, but Seymoure kept his planes low for the first run over the airfield. Despite the loss of a B-26 and damage to a second Marauder, the American medium bombers quickly chopped up the runway with whistling bombs. As soon as they B-26s arced away, Seymoure called his pilots.

"Good job, now let's go back after those parked aircraft."

"Lead the way, sir," Capt. Sam Monk said.

The crew aboard Monk's plane ogled at the rising dust from the airfield as the pilot veered the plane to come back for a second run. They stiffened as the pilot dropped a pair of thousand-pound HEs on the parked aircraft. As the B-26 arced away, the Pathfinder airmen peered in awe at the raging fires and spiralling smoke that now enveloped Edex. At least twenty of the close-support German bombers were aflame, and they would not be used against American GIs on the Normandy beaches. The German airbase itself was in ruins.

Meanwhile, Maj. Jim Howard, leading the 354th Fighter Group's 356th Squadron, had hung high over the airdrome until he spotted the FW 190s coming toward the field. He picked up his radio and called his pilots. "Bandits at nine o'clock; nine o'clock. Hit them in pairs."

"Yes, sir," Lt. Glen Eggleston answered from his P-51 *Cisco*.

A moment later, the twenty 356th Squadron pilots waded into the twenty 190s under Maj. Herman Graf of JG 26. The Americans, making full use of the P-51's speed and climb, downed six of the FW 190s against a loss of three of their own. The Germans suffered further damage to four planes, but also hit five P-51s. The U.S. pilots had run into a tough fight. However, the Americans had stopped the Germans from reaching the B-26s that were plastering Edex Drome. Before the dogfight ended, the B-26s had completed their two runs and had scooted away.

Finally, Maj. Jim Keller led the Marauders of the 558th and 559th Squadrons over the Cormeilles Drome outside of Paris. Fortunately, German fighter planes at the field had not taken off before the B-26 pilots laced the runway with thirty tons of GP bombs. Keller and his airmen then knocked out some thirty FW 190s of JG 2 destroying or damaging them. The Pathfinder airmen had completed their second run before Col. Pips Priller arrived to intercept with twenty FW 190s from JG 26.

Col. Hans Hahn, the *geschwader* commander at Cormeilles, had cowered in a shelter during the attack, while he cursed vehemently because he had not gotten his fighters off before the U.S. attacks on his airfield. He blamed the radar teams that had failed to send out alarms soon enough. But Captain Heindorff and Cpl. Schroeder had been so swamped with enemy air formation detections that they had simply not found time to notify JG 2 soon enough.

Meanwhile, in still another dogfight, the squadron of P-38s under Col. Ed Chickering from the 367th Fighter Group took on the twenty FW 190s under Col. Pips Priller. Again the Germans from the Schlagetor unit proved tough and capable. They shot down five of the P-38s while losing five planes of their own. Priller himself got two of the planes, Lt. Walter

Schuck shot down two, and another JG 26 pilot had shot down the fifth American plane. The Germans also damaged seven other American Lightnings.

Among the U.S. pilots, Colonel Chickering had downed two of the 109s, with three other pilots of the 367th Group getting one each. The Americans also damaged two other 190s.

The air battle beyond Paris had ended in a draw. But still, the American fighter pilots had accomplished their purpose. They had held off the Schlagetor airmen until the B-26s under Maj. Jim Keller had worked over the planes and runway at Cormeilles.

At his headquarters in Paris, Field Marshal Hugo Sperrle was appalled when he learned of the massive destruction to runways and planes at his airfields. He barked to an aide; "You will call JG commanders at once! Tell them to remain on full alert! Full alert!"

"Yes, Herr Field Marshal."

But if the Luftflotte 3 CinC hoped to avoid further damage to his French airfields, he was thinking wishfully. More squadrons of B-26s, along with A-20 light bombers and P-47 fighter bombers, would soon be over France to assail other major German airfields.

CHAPTER SIX

Two hours earlier, at Matching, England, Col. Jerry Williams stood on a dais in the 391st Bomb Group operations quonset hut. On rows of benches sat two hundred crew members of the Bridge Buster group, officers on one side, and enlisted-men gunners on the other side. Most of the crews had been up since dawn and had eaten by 0600 hours. Now, at 0645, they waited for their commander to speak. The American medium bomber crews were not overly concerned because they had not met heavy enemy interception or extensive AA fire during recent tactical air missions over France.

The Bridge Busters had been activated on 21 January 1943 at McDill Field, Florida, where new pilots and crewmen had trained with B-26s. The group had moved overseas in January of 1944 and they had conducted their first combat mission on 15 February 1944, when they attacked the German airfield at St. Pierre. The group had also been the first unit to hit the V weapon sites in France and the low countries. The 391st had also specialized in knocking out highway and railroad bridges for more than two months in low-level medium bomber attacks, and they had thus earned the nickname Bridge Busters.

The chattering stopped when Colonel Williams leaned over the podium. Williams, a tall, lanky air officer, had been in the air force for the past ten years, and always in bomber units. He had been assigned to the 391st Group at its inception at McDill Field, and he had led them on their first combat mission. The group had destroyed such major targets in France as the Letrant shipyards, the Meziere and Charlesville railroad centers, and the Drucat airfield.

The 391st Group had braved unusually heavy opposition from anti-aircraft fire and German interception on many of these missions and group aircraft had often returned to England with single engines, shot-up hydraulic systems, shattered landing gears, riddled wings, punctured fuselages and tattered tails. On one occasion, the 391st had returned with six of its B-26s operating on one engine, a record for a B-26 group.

During its first few months of operations, the 391st Group airmen had earned eight DSCs, 2 Silver Stars, 7 DFCs with 4 oak leaf clusters, 37 air medals with 102 clusters, 115 Purple Hearts, a Legion of Merit, 2 Soldier's Medals, and 2 British DFCs. In seventy-four missions, the group's gunners had shot down sixteen German interceptors, losing thirty-one aircraft during combat operations.

Williams looked at his crews before he spoke. "We're going to hit a couple of airfields today, Abbeville and Lille-Nord in western France, about three hundred miles from here. We'll have some P-38s from the 367th Fighter Group as escorts. Both of these airfield targets are German fighter bases, so we could have plenty of trouble from interceptors. But if we come in low and come out quickly, we may not get hurt too badly."

The colonel paused before he went on. "I'll lead the 575th and 574th Squadrons to Abbeville and Lieutenant Colonel Floak will lead the 573rd and 572nd Squadrons over Lille-Nord. We'll keep a tight formation until we reach IP, so the gunners will have heavier firepower against interceptors."

"How many planes will we have as escort, sir?" Capt. Jim Kahley of the 574th Squadron asked.

"One squadron for the two squadrons going to Abbeville and one squadron of fighters for the B-26s going to Lille-Nord."

"Damn, Colonel," Lt. Col. Bill Floak huffed. "That's not many against an enemy fighter base. They could swarm all over us."

"I'm sorry," Williams said, "but Ninth Air Force says they've got planes going all over France today to hit twenty-six airfields and they've had to spread out the fighter cover."

"Yes, sir," Floak answered in disappointment.

Among others, Capt. Jim Kahley sat nervously on his bench. Next to him, his co-pilot for *April Look,* Lt. Frank Elder, squirmed uneasily. Elder was not certain that a squadron of fighter planes could protect them against an attack on a German fighter base. He feared that 109s and 110s might swarm all over them. Sitting next to Elder, navigator-bombardier Lt. Ed Schweiter did not like going in low against a German airfield. Dreaded eighty-eight-mm ack-ack guns, powerful and accurate, usually defended such airdromes, and these eighty-eights could blow a B-26 apart with a single solid hit.

Across the aisle, in the enlisted men's section, Captain Kahley's three sergeants felt uneasy. *April Look*'s turret gunner, Ed Bonham, did not relish the idea of a low-level attack that would allow German fighter planes to dive down on him with spitting machine gunfire and streaming twenty-mm shells. Waist-radio gunner Al Mass did not know how he could cope with any German fighters from his waist position at low level. Tail gunner Larry Carr felt equally uncertain. He knew the German fighter pilots deftly avoided coming in at six o'clock so he didn't know if he'd get any shots at *Luftwaffe* planes before such aircraft pounced on him. Carr looked up when Colonel Williams spoke again.

"Everything is outlined in the FO orders," the 391st Group commander said. "Are there any questions?"

"I guess not, sir," Captain Kahley said.

Williams nodded. "OK, let's mount up."

By 0715 hours, the long line of B-26s, forty-eight of them, lumbered toward the runway. As on other U.S. air bases, nearby English villagers had come out to the field to watch the planes take off. The screaming aircraft engines echoed across the English countryside in deafening dins. The engines whined furiously or settled to near-idleness as the planes awaited takeoff. Finally, at 0720 hours, the green light blinked from the control tower and Colonel Williams roared down the runway and into the air in the lead plane, a Marauder of the 575th Squadron. Behind him came the eleven other B-26s of this squadron.

Now came the twelve planes of the 574th Squadron. After the first three planes took off, Captain Kahley turned into the head of the runway. When the control tower light blinked green, Kahley zoomed *April Look* down the runway. Co-pilot Frank Elder tensed up as he watched the plane eat up countless yards of runway before hoisting itself into the air. In the nose, bombardier-navigator Ed Schweiter relaxed after the plane got off the ground. In the waist, gunner Al Mass knew they were safely off when he felt the feathery feeling. Inside the top turret, Sgt. Ed Bonham saw the other planes still coming into the head of the runway, as his own *April Look* arced upwards. And in the tail, Sgt. Larry Carr watched the next B-26 roar down the runway.

Then Lt. Col. Bill Floak led the second element of 391st Group aircraft that would hit Lille-Nord. He wheeled his twin-engine bomber into the head of the runway and waited for the green light while he revved the engines. A moment later, Floak released the brakes and the Marauder zoomed down the runway, the engines straining from the heavy bomb load. But, the lieutenant colonel hoisted the plane safely into the air.

Behind Floak came eleven more planes from the 572nd Squadron and then twelve aircraft from the 573rd Squadron. In his A/C 625, Capt. Larry Fogoneri zoomed down the runway, but his plane could not seem to pick up speed. He grew tense, as did his co-pilot. But at the last moment the Marauder jerked quickly forward and Fogoneri got the B-26 safely off the runway.

By 1740 hours, all forty-eight Marauders from the Bridge Buster group were airborne. They jelled into formation before heading south for the first checkpoint at Dover, and then picked up their escorts over the English Channel.

Earlier, at 0700 hours, forty-eight A-20 crews had assembled in the briefing hut of the 416th Bomb Group at Wethersfield, England. Col. Harold Mace, the group commander, stood on the podium and spoke to his three-man light bomber crews on today's mission.

"Our targets include two enemy airfields in France, the fighter base at Chartres and the bomber base at Orival. The 668th and 669th Squadrons will hit Orival; the 670th and 671st Squadrons will hit Chartres. I'll lead the first element against the bomber base and Maj. Dan Willits will lead the squadrons attacking the fighter base. We'll be quite heavily loaded, carrying a pair of thousand-pound GPs, as we want to dig good craters on those runways. These targets are only three hundred miles away, so we should have ample fuel, even with these heavy bomb loads. As usual, we'll go in low, in pairs, with each duet of aircraft at least thirty seconds apart."

"Colonel, sir," Maj. Dan Willits of the 669th Squadron said, "isn't that Chartres base loaded with German fighters?"

"It might be," Mace said.

"Won't they swarm all over us?"

"You'll have a squadron of escorts from the 474th Fighter Group. Those pilots are good, especially in their P-51s. They'll keep most of the interceptors off your backs. Our squadrons going to Orival will also have a squadron of P-51s from the 474th as escorts. Still, I can't guarantee that some German fighters won't attack you. That means gunners will need to be exceptionally alert on this mission, especially the ones going to Chartres."

"Yes, sir," Major Willits answered, but he felt no assurance from his group commander.

Willits's turret gunner, Sgt. Ozzie LeNave, and the major's radio gunner, Sgt. Henry Lempke, squirmed uneasily on their benches. They did not like this low-level attack over an enemy fighter base anymore than did the B-26 gunners. German early-warning systems had improved drastically during the past year and the two gunners of the A-20 *Sentimental Journey* knew that enemy planes could be on top of them before they reached target.

Perhaps Willits's two gunners would have felt even worse had they known that the German unit at Chartres was the III Gruppen of the JG 54 Green Hearts, one of the most successful fighter *geschwaders* in World War II. The Green Hearts had counted at least fifty aces among its complement of pilots during five years of war, of which more than fifteen pilots had scored more than 100 kills. The JG 54 commander, Col. Erich Rudorffer, had himself already downed 197 planes, including 3 B-17s. Under him, Lt. Otto Kitell, a man with an Iron Cross and cluster, had already downed an astonishing 243 enemy planes.

Other high-scoring aces of JG 54 included Capt. Erwin Flieg, who had 106 victories and had flown as wingman for the renowned Werner Molders, and Lt. Reichold Hoffman, with 166 kills, including 6 four-engine bombers. Also in this unit was Capt. Werner Schroer, a triple Iron Cross holder with 144 victories that included among his kills an astonishing 26 four-engine bombers. Maj. Franz Eisenach, another Green Heart ace, had 144 kills to his credit.

The U.S. A-20 airmen and their P-51 escort pilots would indeed have reason to fear Chartres.

But if it was any consolation to the 416th Bomb Group crews, their escorting P-51 pilots from the 474th Group had already downed more than a hundred German planes. Capt. Bob Milliken of the group's 492nd Squadron that would escort the A-20s to Chartres had already destroyed five German planes in his short combat career. Capt. Joe Miller of the same squadron had six kills since coming into combat only four months ago, and Lt. Ed Best had destroyed seven German fighter planes as a member of the U.S. 492nd Squadron.

By 0800 hours, the forty-eight planes of the 416th A-20 Group had reached their checkpoint at Dover and then turned eastward over the English Channel. Less than five minutes later, a swarm of P-51s from the 474th Fighter Group loomed from the northwest. The twenty Mustangs of the 492nd Squadron would escort the A-20s to Chartres, and the twenty-two Mustangs of the 428th Squadron would escort the A-20s to Orival.

"This is Flashlight Leader to Shannon Leader," Col. Clinton Wesem, the 474th Fighter Group commander, cried into his radio.

"We read you, Flashlight," Colonel Mace of the 416th Group answered.

"Flashlight 1 will accompany Shannon 1 and 2 to Orival. Flashlight 2 will accompany your Shannon 3 and 4 to Chartres," Wesem said.

"We read," Colonel Mace said again.

The forty-eight A-20s roared across the channel in tight formations of four-plane diamonds with the P-51s over and around them. Maj. Don Willits looked at the Mustangs, happy to have them with him. But as the Havoc light bombers approached the coast, the 669th Squadron commander became uneasy. They could get jumped by bandits at any moment. He called his turret gunner, Sgt. Ozzie LeNave, who had also been staring at the protective chain of Mustangs.

"Sergeant, any sign of bandits?"

"No, sir," LeNave answered.

"Stay alert."

"Yes, sir."

Willits then called Henry Lempke. "Sergeant, are you picking up anything on the radio? Anything from German UHF or VHF channels? Any sign of detection?"

"No, sir, not yet," the radio gunner answered.

"As soon as you hear anything, let me know."

"Yes, sir," Lempke answered his *Sentimental Journey* pilot.

The Havocs and their forty Mustang escorts droned on. When they reached the French coast, the 416th Group would split, with two squadrons under Colonel Mace going to Orival and the other two squadrons under Major Willits going off on a southeast path to the Chartres airfield.

Some miles to the north, Col. Terry Williams in the lead B-26 medium bomber of the 391st Bomb Group stared ahead at the looming coast of Belgium. Around him and behind him were the other forty-seven Bridge Buster Marauders. Meanwhile, a squadron of P-38s from the 367th Fighter Group, twenty Lightnings under Maj. Ron Gray, and a squadron of P-38s from the 367th Group's 393rd Squadron under Capt. Henry Brown had surrounded the Bridge Busters. Since the 391st Group Marauders were heading for fighter bases, they would need all the escort they could get.

In his *April Look,* Capt. Jim Kahley caught sight of the French coast and he stiffened slightly in his pilot's seat as co-pilot Frank Elder licked his lips. Kahley called his crew. "French coast ahead; stay alert."

"Yes, sir," tail gunner Larry Carr answered.

Then waist gunner Al Mass and turret gunner Ed Bonham tightened the grips on the triggers of their twin .50-caliber machine guns.

They peered hard out of the plane, trying to spot any German fighters that might come from the east to meet them.

Kahley now called his bombardier navigator. "Lieutenant, we'll be turning southeast pretty soon. IP is about ten minutes away. Stay alert for bomb drop."

"Yes, sir," Lt. Ed Schweiter answered.

Meanwhile, German radar teams at Calais in northwest France picked up this new formation of American aircraft, only five minutes after detecting the 322nd and 387th Bomb Groups that had flown on to attack airbases in Lamar, Edex, Beaumont, and Cormeilles. Once more the radar stations sent quick reports to Luftflotte 3 headquarters in Paris. "More enemy bombers crossing the coast; medium bombers just south of Calais."

"What is their destination?" Capt. Peter Heindorff asked.

"We do not know yet. We will check their course and report as soon as we are sure."

"You must do so swiftly," Heindorff said, "for we must mount interceptors."

Even as the radar teams in northwest France calculated the possible destination of the B-26s from the 391st Bomb Group, the radar men at Antwerp, only seven minutes later, picked up the A-20s of the 416th Group and their P-51 escorts north of Calais. Once more reports went quickly to Paris.

"More enemy bombers, light bombers, heading due east along the Belgium-French border. We will give you an estimate of their destination as soon as possible."

Heindorff scowled as he looked at the table chart to track these new American formations. He made changes on his chart as quickly as new reports came in from radar stations. Finally, at 1040 hours, only ten minutes after guessing the destination of the 322nd and 387th B-25 Bomb Groups, the charting officer drew a conclusion.

"It appears these new medium bombers are flying to Abbeville and Lille-Nord," Heindorff told his aide, Cpl. Heidi Schroeder. "They will divide into two formations, with each *gruppen* striking one of those airfields."

"Yes, Herr Hauptman," the aide said.

Moments later, the radar sergeant at Antwerp also called the Luftflotte 3 tracking station. "We now have an excellent idea of the destination of the enemy light bombers. It appears they are flying to Orival or Chartres, or both."

"As I suspected," Heindorff said. He turned to Corporal Schroeder again. "It appears the Americans intend to attack all of our French airfields today. You will notify all *geschwader* units in central and northwest France to mount staffels of fighters at once for interception."

"Herr Hauptman," the aide said, "we have already notified aircraft units at Lille-Nord and Argentan to intercept the first stream of enemy medium bombers that crossed the coast. I shall notify the JG 54 headquarters at Chartres to intercept these new intruders."

"Please do so," the captain answered.

At Chartres, a JG 54 aide soon got Corporal Schroeder's request to intercept. He immediately called Col. Erich Rudorffer. "Enemy bombers heading for the airfields at Chartres, Orival, Lille-Nord and Abbeville."

The JG 54 commander frowned. He had less than a hundred FW 190s based at Chartres, hardly enough to take on two full groups of bombers and several squadrons of escorts. And, worse, since the enemy formations would break off and fly to four different targets, he would need to spread his units quite thin, and he might then be ineffective. Rudorffer was tempted to forget three of the potential targets and only defend his own Chartres base. But he knew that JG 1 and JG 26 fighters had already taken off to intercept the American bombers that had crossed the coast earlier. So the JG 54 commander could hardly leave these other bases exposed.

Rudorffer sent off twenty-four FW 190s under Maj. Franz Eisenach to attack the bombers heading for the Abbeville airfield. He sent off twenty-five planes under Maj. Horst Adameit to attack the B-26s going to Lille-Nord. He ordered twenty-two fighters under Lt. Otto Vincent to hit the A-20s droning towards Orival. He himself would take up the last twenty-four Folkwolfe fighters of his Green Hearts *geschwader* to defend Chartres itself.

By 1045 hours, all ninety-six Green Heart fighter planes had taken to the air. Three staffels peeled off to race after three of the attacking U.S. bomber formations, while Colonel Rudorffer hovered over Chartres to meet the Ninth Air Force bombers coming toward his own airfield.

At 1205 hours, the 574th and 575th Squadrons of the 391st Bomb Group under Col. Jerry Williams approached Abbeville, whose own German fighter planes of JG 26 had already taken off to intercept the B-26 bombers from the 322nd Bomb Group. As Maj. Franz Eisenach approached Abbeville, Capt. Henry Brown of the 367th Fighter Group's 393rd Squadron saw the enemy planes and called Williams.

"Bandits ahead, Colonel. We're going after them while you attack the field."

"I read you," Colonel Williams said.

Moments later, the twenty Lightnings clashed with the twenty-four FW 190s high over northwest France. Though the Germans did have a few good pilots, including staffel leader Franz Eisenach, the Americans were generally more aggressive and more capable. In a ten-minute dogfight, the Americans successfully kept the German pilots at bay, while the Marauder bombers continued toward target.

The American fighter pilots shot down six FW 190s to a loss of four P-38s. They also damaged several other German fighter planes while suffering damage to a trio of their own Lightnings. The Green Heart pilots from JG 54 were tough and determined, as expected, but the American pilots had accomplished their mission—keeping the Germans off the B-26 bombers while the Marauders made their bomb runs.

At 1210 hours, Colonel Williams cried into his radio. "OK, in pairs; attack in pairs."

"Yes, sir," Capt. Jim Kahley of the 374th Squadron answered.

A moment later, despite intense ack-ack fire, the B-26s came down to three thousand feet to lace the Abbeville runway. They dropped a total of forty-four tons of high explosive thousand-pounders along the apron, gouging huge holes in the runway, and setting afire several buildings on either side of the strip. Unfortunately, they had not found many planes to destroy on the field because the JG 26 units had already taken off from Lille-Nord and Abbeville to attack the B-26s of the 322nd and 387th Bomb Groups.

A few FW 190s from Eisenach's staffel did reach the B-26s with chattering machine gunfire and thumping twenty-mm shells. They shot down two of the Marauders. The 391st gunners, in turn, destroyed two FW 190s, with Sgt. Ed Bonham on Captain Kahley's *April Look* getting one of the kills.

Meanwhile, the other two squadrons from the 391st Bomb Group droned over the fighter base at Lille-Nord, where again the Bridge Buster crews found few parked German planes, since most of the FW 190s had also gone off from this base to intercept other 9th Air Force medium bombers.

"Make your drops count," Lt. Col. Bill Floak cried into his radio. "In pairs; attack in pairs!"

"Yes, sir," Capt. Larry Fogoneri of the 573rd Squadron answered.

The two squadrons of bombers from the 391st zoomed over Lille-Nord to unleash dozens of thousand-pounders on the long runway. Shattering explosions erupted, shaking the ground, while German ground crews cowered inside shelters. For more than twenty minutes the B-26s came over the base. When the last duet of planes finally zoomed away, Lille-Nord lay in rubble. The airstrip was utterly potted with countless holes, some of them up to fifty-feet deep. Several buildings had also been set afire.

Meanwhile, the 394th Squadron escorts of the 367th Fighter Group under Maj. Ron Gray quickly pounced on the German JG FW 190s that had come out of Chartres to intercept the bombers. The P-38 pilots quickly shot down seven German planes, with Major Gray in his Lightning *Just Lazy* getting two of the kills. Again, only a handful of the FW 190s reached the bombers. The Germans shot down two Marauders over Lille-Nord, one from the 572nd Squadron and one from the 573rd Squadron. But the U.S. B-26 gunners shot down two German planes.

And still the destruction against German air bases in France continued on this 2 June 1944 day. The 668th and 669th Squadrons of the

416th Bomb Group struck the German bomber base at Orival. The Havocs came in at almost deck level, low and suddenly, so that German anti-aircraft gunners were caught completely by surprise. The A-20s roared over the field in pairs, with most of the planes finishing their runs before the German ack-ack gunners had even gotten into position to shoot back at the Havocs. The A-20s chopped out sixteen holes in the runway with their thousand-pounders and destroyed a repair shop, an engine shop and a fuel-storage building.

But, worse, many of the bombs caught parked fighter bombers parked about the runway. The crews of the 416th Group's 668th and 669th Squadrons set afire at least ten of the German light bombers, smashed six and damaged at least eight more Hershels.

By the time the A-20s roared away, dense smoke and blazing fires prevailed about the Orival air base in western France.

Meanwhile, a squadron of P-51s under Col. Clint Wesem of the 474th Group had quickly engaged the staffel of FW 190s under Lt. Otto Vincent of JG 54, twenty Mustangs against twenty-two FW 190s. The American pilots battled the German pilots for nearly a half hour, shooting down five planes against three losses of their own. Wesem got one of the Green Hearts and Lt. Ed Best shot down two Folk-wolfes to raise his score to nine. In turn, the renowned Otto Vincent got two Mustangs with adept maneuvers that put him on the tails of his two victims. Vincent's accurate twenty-mm shellfire and blistering machine gunfire got both P-51s.

Yet, even if the Germans held their own against the American fighter pilots, the Green Heart *Luftwaffers* had failed to stop or even disrupt the A-20 attacks on the Orival airdrome.

Meanwhile, the other two A-20 squadrons of the 416th Bomb Group were roaring over the German airdrome at Chartres, headquarters of the JG 54 Green Hearts. Fortunately for the Americans, most of the *geschwader's* planes were away, attempting to stop the attacks at Abbeville, Lille-Nord and Orival. Only Colonel Rudorffer with twenty-four FolkWolfe fighters was aloft to meet the oncoming A-20s and their P-51 escorts.

Most of the JG 54 pilots were determined and experienced. But the P-51 pilots, twenty of them from the 474th Group's 429th Squadron, were just as determined. The U.S. airmen quickly flew into the Germans, clashing high over Chartres in a heavy dogfight. Whining engines, bursting cannon shells, and chattering machine gunfire reverberated across the sky. Both German military and French civilians squinted up at the melee. They saw both Mustangs and FW 190s falling out of the sky, for the two sides were virtually even in ability and strength.

However, strategically, the dogfight became another American victory, because few of the

FW 190s broke through the U.S. escort defense while the A-20s of the 416th Group's 670th and 671st Squadrons roared over Chartres drome in pairs. The Havocs sent bomb bay loads of thousand pounders atop the runway and atop some of the service buildings. By the time the last Havoc left target, not a single German fighter plane had reached them. The two squadrons under Maj. Don Willits had left a swath of destruction at the enemy base. In Willits' *Sentimental Journey*, gunner Sgt. Ozzie LeNave peered from his turret and radio gunner Sgt. Henry Lempke stared from his small compartment in the waist at the extensive fires and smoke that covered the Chartres air base.

At 1305 hours, Major Willits cried into his radio, "OK, let's go home."

Ten minutes later, the A-20s were droning westward with their ring of P-51s from the 474th Fighter Group around them in a protective chain—in case the Germans sent up more interceptors. Uncannily, the Americans had not lost a single A-20 over Chartres, one of the most feared German fighter bases in all of France.

As the 2 June day wore on, more American B-26 and A-20 groups from the Ninth Air Force attacked other airfields. By 1400 hours, American medium and light bombers had walloped twelve more *Luftwaffe* bases. But if the Germans hoped that the rampant destruction was over, they were thinking wishfully. They would barely digest the reports of damage to airfields and losses in aircraft before the radar stations in northern France and Belgium again reported enemy planes on the way.

The fighter bomber groups of the U.S. Ninth Tactical Air Force now took their turn against the other six airfield targets in France.

CHAPTER SEVEN

Even as B-26 and A-20 groups of the U.S. Ninth Air Force took off from England to hit German airfields in France, group commanders of the P-47 fighter bomber groups held briefings to acquaint pilots with their targets.

At Beaulieu, England, Col. Lance Call had assembled fifty-one airmen of the 365th Hellhawk Group in a quonset operations hut. These P-47 pilots had not felt any particular uneasiness because they had generally done well against German pilots in aerial dogfights when the necessity arose.

The 365th Fighter Bomber Group had been activated in May of 1943 under their commander Lance Call. After nine months of training in the States, they had moved to

England's Gosfield drome in December of 1943 to train with P-47s. The group completed its first combat mission in February of 1944, a dive bombing attack on a bridge in northwest France. They subsequently struck airdrome, rail facility, and gun emplacement targets as well as V weapon sites in northwest Europe. The Hellhawks had also escorted medium bombers of the 9th Air Force on several missions.

The 365th had been among the P-47 units that had escorted the first American bombing mission to Berlin on 4 March 1944, covering the Fortresses as far as the German border before the P-51 groups took the Forts in and out of Germany.

Call referred to a map on the wall behind him as well as to papers in front of him before he spoke. "A horde of B-26 and A-20 groups, as well as hordes of P-47 groups, are going out this morning with us to hit German airfields in France. Our own particular target this morning is the Conflants air base outside of Paris. That's a long way from here and we could be airborne for seven or eight hours. But even worse, Conflants is a *Luftwaffe* fighter base, so we can expect stiff opposition."

"Will we have escorts, sir?" Capt. Vince Beaudrit asked.

"Yes," Call replied, "a squadron of P-38s from the 370th Fighter Group. They'll be with us all the way and back. But if things get rough, we may need to salvo bombs and take on some FW 190s or ME 109s ourselves."

"What are we carrying, sir?" Lt. Fred O'Connell asked.

"Four two hundred fifty-pound GPs or incendiaries. Our job this morning is to destroy a runway and parked aircraft. Ninth Air Force wants as few planes as possible to hit our GIs on the beaches."

"Will this be another noball mission?" Bob Guillote asked the 365th Group commander.

"Yes," the colonel answered.

The noball mission included a new technique by the Ninth Air Force tactical groups that had been devised for better accuracy in low-level attacks. The technique included the use of delayed fuse bombs that had been so successful against ships in the Pacific. The aircraft attacked in pairs at almost tree-top level. The delayed fuse enabled the plane to arc safely away before the explosion. Getting this close to the target enabled the pilot or bombardier aboard Ninth Air Force P-47s, A-20s or B-26s to improve accuracy against targets by more than seventy percent.

The 365th commander gestured to an aide who pinned a blown-up photo of the Conflants air base on the wall. Then Call continued. "Here's the target. As you can see, it's a pretty good-size complex, with two taxiways leading to the main runway. Here on the left are service buildings. These will be the targets of the 386th Squadron, which I'll lead myself. The 387th Squadron will hit the parked aircraft, and the

388th Squadron will concentrate on the runway itself."

"What if we don't find parked aircraft, sir?" Capt. Vince Beaudrit of the 387th Squadron asked.

"If they're in the air," Call said with a grin, "you can knock them out of the sky instead. Or you can hit some of the service buildings with the 386th Squadron, or hit the runway with the 388th Squadron."

"Yes, sir," Beaudrit said.

"When we take off," the colonel continued, "we'll fly straight south and leave the British Isles at Brighton, where we'll rendezvous with other P-47 groups. We'll pick up our P-38 escorts over the Channel and cross the French coast just north of Le Havre. Then we turn south. Once inside France, the various fighter bomber groups will split and go to their own particular targets with their escorts. We'll be turning east by southeast along the Seine and head straight for Paris. Our target is just east of the city. I believe another fighter bomber group is hitting the German air base at Lesnil just north of Paris, and a B-26 group is hitting the fighter base at Cormeilles."

"Will we fly low, sir?" Lieutenant O'Connell asked.

"As low as possible," the colonel answered, "and all the way across France. We can thus avoid as much radar as possible."

"Yes, sir."

"Any other questions?" Call asked. When no one answered, the colonel looked at his watch: 0715 hours. "OK, get yourselves a quick cup of coffee and a doughnut. Take off will be at 0800 hours."

About fifteen miles away, at Thruxton, Col. Norman Holt was also holding a briefing. Fifty-one pilots sat in the group's quonset hut and listened to their commander. Holt had been an army officer for more then ten years, joining the infantry after graduating from West Point in 1933. He had served in several units in the States, but in 1939 he had transferred to the army air force and completed pilot training by 1940.

Holt's rise in rank had been quite swift because of his dedication to duty and his exceptional leadership qualities. Within a year he became an operations officer in the Canal Zone, and by 1941 he was a squadron commander. When the army air force organized the 366th Group, he became the unit's deputy commander. He had then risen rapidly to group operations officer, finally taking over as the 366th Group's commander only three weeks ago in early May. Because of Holt's ability and fairness, the pilots of the 366th had welcomed him as their group leader.

The 366th had been activated in June of 1943 and after a training period of nine months at Bluethenthred Field, North Carolina and at Richmond Air Force Base in Virginia, the group moved to Mewbury, England in January of 1944 for more training. The group had then moved to Thruxton in March to begin combat missions with fighter bomber sweeps over the French coast.

The 366th had been the first 9th Air Force fighter bomber group to conduct a noball mission when on 15 March 1944 they struck the St. Valery airfield in France with delayed fuse bombs. In their two months of combat the group had already conducted over a thousand sorties, destroying 117 German planes in the air and 200 more on the ground. The group hoped to improve its score during today's attack.

"We've got a sweet target," Holt told his flyers, "the German air base at Ambria-Epinoy in central France. Reconn reports as of yesterday say the field is loaded with Hs 129s. These Henshel light bombers are especially designed for ground support and I'd guess the Germans have readied as many 129s as possible to attack our GIs on the Normandy beaches. The 129 can do an awful job on opposing ground forces. So if we knock out these twin-engine bombers, we'll be saving a hell of a lot of lives on D-day."

"Will we use incendiaries, sir?" Capt. Zell Smith of the 390th Squadron asked.

"Incendiaries and phospherous, four 250-pounders on each plane," Holt answered. He pointed to a map on the wall behind him and then continued. "We'll be following the usual route in, south of Brighton, across the Channel, and then into France below Le Havre. We'll then turn directly southeast and head straight for Epinoy."

"How about escorts?"

"A squadron of P-38s from the 370th Fighter Group." Then Holt grinned. "They'll be carrying wing bombs, too. There's so many mediums, lights and fighter bombers going into France today that the Germans can't possibly intercept all of us. And, because Ambria-Epinoy is a bomber base, we may not see any German interceptors. In that case the P-38s will also dive bomb."

"Yes, sir," Captain Smith answered.

"We may very well reach target undetected if we drop to treetop level en route in over the French coast," Holt said. He then pinned a photo of Ambria-Epinoy on the wall. "As you can see, the Germans keep most of their 129s parked here and here." He pointed to a pair of areas on the map. "I'll take the 389th Squadron to this area on the left and Captain Smith will lead the 390th Squadron to hit parked aircraft on the right. The 391st Squadron will work over the runway."

"Did you say the P-38s will also attack the field, sir?" somebody asked.

"Only if they don't have to deal with interceptors. They can then hit anything we might have missed. Between our three squadrons and the P-38 escorts we ought to leave that enemy airfield pretty well shattered. Any questions?"

None.

"You've got about a half hour before takeoff if you want to grab yourselves some coffee," the 366th commander said. "We mount up at 0750 hours and take off is at 0810 hours."

"Yes, sir," Capt. Zell Smith said.

Ten miles to the east, Col. Gilbert Myers held a briefing with fifty-one fellow fighter bomber pilots at Chilbolton, the air base of the 368th Panzer Buster Group. The 368th had been another of the recent arrivals in England to join the relatively new 9th Tactical Air Force. For the past two months, the 368th had been attacking mostly German Panzer sites and gained its nickname Panzer Busters. However, the 368th had also made bombing and strafing runs against airfields, rail and highway bridges, trains, and anti-aircraft positions to prepare for the Operation Overlord invasion. The 368th had also been among the fighter bomber groups that had struck V weapon sites.

Colonel Myers had been an air officer for six years, joining the army air force after graduating from West Point in 1938. He had enjoyed a meteoric rise, moving swiftly from bomber pilot to flight leader to squadron commander, and then to group operations officer. He had assumed command of the 368th Group in June of 1943, when the group was activated at Hamilton Field, California. Myers was sure his unit would be heading for the

Pacific and he had been quite surprised when in January of 1944 the 368th moved to England.

The colonel pointed to a photo of the Lesnil airfield, another German airdrome outside of Paris. "We'll be flying on a route in with the 365th and 366th Groups. Then the 366th will drop southeast to hit Ambria-Epinoy, and we'll be flying on to the Paris area with the 365th that will hit the Conflants fighter base outside of the city while we hit the Lesnil bomber base south of the city."

"Do we come in at deck level, sir?" Capt. Bob Johnson of the 397th Squadron asked.

"Yes," the colonel answered. "The Germans have three or four fighter bases around Paris and they may come after us as well as anyone else. In fact, they may want to protect Lesnil quite badly because the base houses a full group of HE 110s. As you know the Germans fly these Zoresters as either fighters or as fighter bombers. No doubt the Germans intend to use these 110s against our invasion forces. They did a hell of a job on the British at Dunkirk, Dakar and Crete, and they could give our GIs a lot of grief at Normandy. So we'll have to be extremely aggressive today and knock out as many of those 110s as we can."

"Will we have escorts, sir?" Capt. Walt Mahorin of the 397th Squadron asked.

"A squadron of P-38s from the 370th Group," Myers answered. "They'll be with us all the way. If we fly at treetop in and out we might avoid much of the enemy's radar. Now—"he pointed to the photo on the wall—"the Germans have their planes parked along these three taxiways at Lesnil. So far as we can tell, most of them are camouflaged or hidden under trees. But, at low level and with noball tactics, you should be able to spot them before you make your strafing and bombing runs. I'll lead the 395th Squadron myself over the area here on the left. Lieutenant Colonel Douglas will take the 396th Squadron to hit this area, and Captain Johnson's 397th Squadron will strike this area on the right. Any questions?"

"What happens if we get jumped by bandits?"Captain Mahorin asked. "Do we salvo and take them on?"

"If necessary, yes," Myers answered, "although we hope our escorts can deal with interceptors." He looked at his watch. "OK, mount up. Vehicles from the motor pool are outside to take us to the field."

South of the three fighter bomber bases, at Aldermaston, Col. Howard Nichols of the 370th Fighter Group was briefing forty-eight Lightning pilots for the mission. "Today, we'll be escorting three groups of P-47s that are going after airdromes. We'll be carrying a pair of 500-pounders along with full machine gun belts. If we don't have to tangle with interceptors, we can hit targets ourselves. The 401st Squadron will escort the 365th Fighter

Bomber Group to Conflants airfield outside of Paris. The 402nd Squadron under Major McKee will escort the 366th Group to the German bomber base at Ambria-Epinoy, and the 485th Squadron under Capt. John Howell will escort the 368th Group to the bomber base at Lesnil, also outside of Paris."

Nichols pointed to the map before he spoke again. "We'll pick up the fighter bombers off Brighton and take them across the Channel into France below Le Havre. We'll then split up and accompany our particular charges to their targets. Route in and out will be at low level all the way to avoid radar if we can." He paused. "Any questions?"

None.

"OK, mount up."

The German radar system had vastly improved over the past year and they could detect enemy planes at any altitude. The plans by the P-47 fighter bomber groups to fly at treetop level to target had not fooled Luftflotte 3. At 1020 hours, 2 June, the operators at the radar station in Le Havre detected the formations of P-47s and P-38s coming over the French coast.

"Achtung! Feindliche Flugzenge! Feindliche!" Enemy aircraft. Once more a radar report went quickly to the Luftflotte 3 tracking station in Paris. Capt. Peter Heindorff and his team again drew frantic lines on the table map.

By now, the tracking officer was utterly frustrated. Thus far he had tracked hordes of B-26 and A-20 bomber formations in countless directions, hitting various airfields in France. The captain could not even keep up with the American air formations anymore.

Further, Jagdkorps II had already sent out almost every available fighter plane to intercept the U.S. medium and light bombers. Heindorff frantically checked his rosters to find some fighters still available. He did locate a staffel of 109s at the JG 27 base in Vire in northwest France and a JG 22 staffel at Metz south of Paris. But the two units had only about twenty-four aircraft each, not much against hordes of P-47s and P-38s droning eastward from the English Channel. Still, the tracking officer needed to do what he could.

At 1230 hours, when the 366th Fighter Bomber Group broke off from the huge formation and headed for Ambria-Epinoy, Heindorff guessed the destination of these latest intruders. "One of the American air *gruppens* is apparently flying to Epinoy and the other two are flying to the Paris area," the tracking officer told Corporal Schroeder.

"Yes, Herr Hauptman," the aide said.

"You will notify the headquarters of the JG 27 *geschwader* at Vire to intercept the enemy aircraft that are flying to Ambria-Epinoy. It is imperative that they stop an attack there for the light bombers at this base are vital to support an attack against any invaders of the continent."

"I will do so," CorporaL Schroeder said.

"You will then notify the headquarters of the JG 22 *geschwader* at Metz to mount interceptors against the other two enemy air formations that are also coming to the Paris area."

"Yes, Herr Hauptman," CorporaL Schroeder said.

At 1235 hours, Col. Norman Holt of the 366th Group reached Ambria-Epinoy, but he saw a formaation of ME 109s ahead of him. He called Colonel Nichols who was leading the P-38s of his 370th Group's 401st Squadron.

"Bandits coming in from eleven o'clock, high."

"We'll handle them, Colonel. Make your bomb runs."

A moment later, the P-47s roared over the German airfield. Heavy ack-ack fire knocked down two of the P-47s and damaged three more, but the bulk of the U.S. fighter bombers successfully laced the German air base in a noball assault. The 389th Squadron came in low, at treetop level, spewing heavy strafing fire into the camouflaged area before dropping bombs. The Thunderbolts roared in at thirty-second intervals and by the time the eighteen planes had left the area, more than twenty German Hs 129s were ablaze or totally destroyed.

At the same moment, Capt. Zell Smith led his eighteen fighter bombers over the second camouflaged area on the right side of the field.

He too brought his Thunderbolts down in pairs and the P-47s swept over the area with strafing fire before dropping 250-pound incendiary bombs on the parked German light bombers. Once more, rattling explosions, balls of fire, dense smoke and heavy debris erupted on the German air base. By the time Smith left the area with his eighteen planes, another length of the airdrome lay in ruins.

Now came the 366th's 391st Squadron to rake the main runway. Whistling bombs struck the apron in a series of staccato explosions, raising dirt and chunks of concrete into the air. The 391st Squadron left twenty huge holes in the Ambria-Epinoy runway.

Meanwhile, the staffel of planes from JG 27, sixteen of them, could not cope very well with the eighteen P-38s from the 370th Group's 402nd Squadron. The dogfight about Ambria-Epinoy had lasted little more than ten mintes before more than half of the German fighter planes went down against a loss of only four P-38s. Most of the JG 27 pilots were inexperienced. Whether they had loyalty and determination or not, as Hitler claimed, they were no match for the American fighter pilots. Not a single ME 109 got near the fighter bombers. In fact, after the U.S fighter pilots drove off the battered German staffel, they took their P-38s down on strafing sweeps over the Ambria-Epinoy drome to cause more damage.

At 1245 hours, Col. Norman Holt cried into

his radio, "We did a good job. Let's go home."

"Yes sir," Capt. Zell Smith said.

"We'll stay with you all the way Colonel," Major Seth McKee of the escorting P-38 squadron answered.

By 1300 hours, the sound of U.S. aircraft had diminished to the west. But Ambria-Epinoy was in ruins. German airmen came out of their shelters to stare at the mass of flames, smoke, and destruction. They would count thirty-seven Hs 129s destroyed and another fourteen damaged. They would need at least ten days to repair this runway, meaning no German planes would come out of this airdrome when the American GIs and British Tommies landed at Normandy only four days from now.

At 1315 hours, as the other formations of P-47s and their P-38 escorts neared their targets around Paris, civilians in the French capital stopped again on the streets to stare up at this still-new formation of American planes. The civilians inwardly gloated for they knew the Germans would suffer still another blow.

As Col. Lance Call reached the Conflants airfield, heavy anti-aircraft fire spewed up at him. But the 365th commander did not see a single German plane in the sky. He called Colonel Nichols of the 370th Group's 470th Squadron. "There's not a single bandit around, Colonel. You can bring down your Lightnings after us to hit the airfield."

"My boys will like that," Nichols said.

The few German fighter planes mounted

from the JG 22 base at Metz had apparently failed to arrive in time at the Paris area. So no *Luftwaffers* were about to stop the P-38s from also attacking the airfield. Further, the JG 2 fighters normally at this base were off to intercept the B-26s, so the 365th pilots found no planes on the airfields. Nonetheless, the P-47s punched sixty holes in the runways and taxiways with exploding GP bombs and set afire six service buildings on the field. Fire and smoke covered the airdrome by the time the fifty-two Thunderbolts had made their runs and departed.

But as German ground crews on the field started to leave their shelters, P-38s of the 370th U.S. Group swept over the airfields in pairs. Heavy strafing fire and incendiary bombs chopped up more of the airfield, wrecked more buildings, destroyed several trucks, smashed two personnel carriers and sent ground crews scurrying back to their shelters.

As with the other German bases, Conflants lay in ruins after the raid.

South of Paris, as Colonel Myers and his 368th Group pilots neared Lesnil, the staffel of 109s from JG 22 had finally arrived. However, Capt. John Howell of the U.S. 370th Group's 485th Squadron met the staffel of 109s head on. The sixteen P-38s easily dealt with the twelve German fighter planes. The dogfight lasted less then five minutes with the Americans shooting down five of the 109s and damaging at least four more. Survivors from this JG 22 staffel had no choice but to break off and run from the fight to save whatever was left of the decimated staffel.

"You can make your run, Colonel," Capt. John Howell told Gilbert Myers. "Interceptors won't bother you."

"We appreciate that, Captain," the 368th Group commander answered.

The P-47s of the Panzer Busters then roared over the airfield. Myers took the fourteen planes of his 395th Squadron over one segment of the area before the Thunderbolts unleashed strafing fire and whistling bombs on parked ME 110s. Capt. Bob Johnson in the P-47 *Little Bill* and Capt. Walt Mahorin in *Sally of Atlanta* swept over the left side of the airfield to begin the destruction of the Heinkels, erupting two fires after solid 250-pound incendiary hits.

"Goddamn," Johnson cried into his radio, "we hit them right on the nose."

"Good show, Bobby," Capt. Walt Mahorin answered.

Little Bill and *Sally of Atlanta* arced away.

The next fourteen P-47s, those of the 356th Squadron, zoomed over the airfield at deck level, spewing more heavy tracer fire and dropping more 250-pound delayed-fuse bombs. New fires erupted, as other HE 110s disintegrated from solid hits and more palls of smoke rose skyward.

Finally, Lt. Col. Paul Douglas swept over the main Lesnil runway with the last twelve planes of the 368th Group. Douglas and his pilots dropped dozens of bombs along the apron, chopping out chunks of concrete and punching holes in the airstrip. The Panzer Busters left rampant destruction in their wake, and the Germans would need ten days to two weeks to repair the runway. No HE 110s would be coming out of Lesnil to attack the GIs and Tommies on the Normandy beaches on 6 June.

By 1340 hours, the two P-47 fighter bomber groups left the Paris area, as had the 387th's B-26s less than a half hour earlier, after the Pathfinders had worked over the Cormeilles airfield.

Before the afternoon ended, three more P-47 fighter bomber groups struck three more airfields in Nazi-occupied France. All total, the American air groups had attacked and wrecked twenty-six German airfields, while destroying more than three hundred German bombers and fighters of Luftflotte 3 on the ground or in the air. The Americans had lost twenty-six bombers and fourteen fighters. The day had been profitable indeed for General Brereton's Ninth Air Force.

The JG units in France had been heavily overtaxed on this 2 June day. They could not be everywhere at once and they were unable to take on all the U.S. planes, some fifteen-hundred of them, that had swept over the German airfields.

Worse, Jagdkorps II fighter units, while off to intercept the mass of American air formations had lost many of their airfields:

Cormeilles, Conflants, Chartres, Lille-Nord and Abbeville, among others. In the Paris area, returning units of JG 2 had to land at St. Denis, badly overcrowding this field. In central France, Rudorffer was forced to take his FW 190s to Epernon, a base already covered with planes from JG 54's II and III Gruppens. And in northwest France, Pips Priller led his fighters in a confused return to the jammed St. Pierre Field because his Abbeville and Chartres field runways had been turned into potted punchboards.

By dusk, a welcome quiet had returned to France. No U.S. tactical aircraft would come over in the dark. The Germans in occupied France would at least get a good night's sleep.

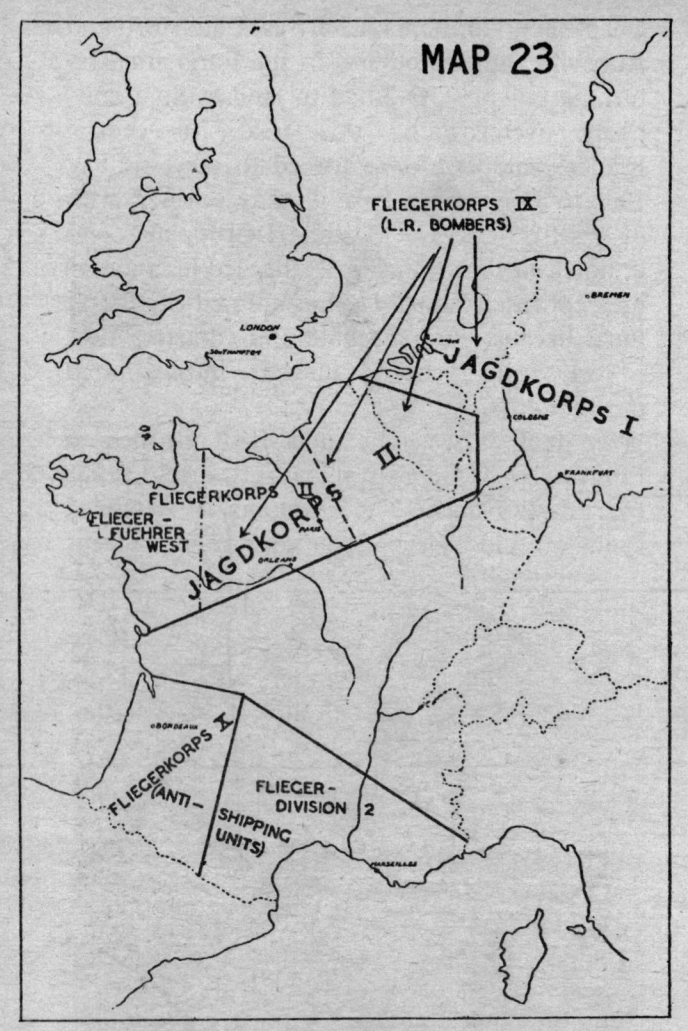

DISPOSITION OF FORCES UNDER LUFTFLOTTE 3 IN FRANCE
AT THE TIME OF THE ALLIED LANDING IN NORMANDY
(6th JUNE, 1944)

General Dwight Eisenhower, CinC of all Allied Forces in the ETO, who directed the D-Day invasion.

General Lewis Brereton, commander of the U.S. 9th Tactical Air Force that carried out Operation Chattanooga Choo Choo.

Col. Glen Nye of the 322nd Bomb Group that destroyed key bridges in France.

Enlisted airmen of the B-26 "Dolly." L to R: Sgt Mike Whitehurst, turret gunner; Sgt Al Aurelio, waist gunner; PFC Smolinski, armorer; Cpl Gorman, mechanic; PFC Bowden, armorer; Sgt Ralph Wilson, Tail gunner.

Lt. Col. Charles Olmstead who led second element of the 322nd Bomb Group B-26's.

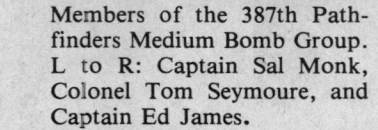

Members of the 387th Pathfinders Medium Bomb Group. L to R: Captain Sal Monk, Colonel Tom Seymoure, and Captain Ed James.

The crew of the B-26 "April Look" from the 391st Bomb Group Bridge Busters. L to R, Major Jim Kahley, pilot; Lt. Frank Elder, copilot; Lt. Ed Schweiter, navigator; Kneel; Sgt Ed Bonham, turret gunner; Sgt Al Mass, waist gunner; Sgt Larry Carr, tail gunner.

Major Jim Keller's "Flak Bait," 387th Group, that had flown nearly 200 missions during its career.

Lt. Col. Bill Floak, deputy commander of the 391st Bomb Group.

The crew of 416th Bomb Group's A-20 "Sentimental Journey." L to R: Sgt Ozzie LeNave, turret gunner; Major Dan Willits, pilot; Sgt Henry Lempke, radio gunner; and crew chief, Sgt Bill Madison.

Col. Arthur Salisbury (L) CO of the 84th Bomb Wing, pins Silver Star on Colonel Lance Call, commander of the 365th Hellhawks Fighter-Bomber Group that did well on Operation Chattanooga Choo Choo.

Lt. Fred O'Connel (L) and Lt. Bob Guillote (R) of the 365th Group recount their successful run against Vernon railroad bridge.

General Hugh Trenchard (L) congratulates Colonel Norman Holt, CO of the 366th P-47 Fighter-Bomber Group after successful destruction of the Denan Bridge.

Captain Vince Beaudrit of the 365th Hellhawks also scored well in noball low level P-47 attacks on bridges in France.

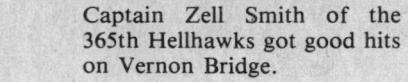

Captain Zell Smith of the 365th Hellhawks got good hits on Vernon Bridge.

Captain Bob Johnson (L) and Captain Walt Mahorin (R) of the 368th Panzer Busters P-47 Fighter-Bomber Group congratulate each other after destruction of the Ghent railroad bridge in Belgium.

Major Jim Howard (L) and Col. George Bickel (R) of the 354th Fighter Group. This unit did an excellent job in keeping German interceptors away from American bombers during Operation Chattanooga Choo Choo.

Captain Harry Brown of the U.S. 367th Fighter Group successfully led P-38 squadron against German fighter units.

Major Ron Gray of the 367th Group got three kills in course of the three day Chattanooga Choo Choo operation. Photo shows Gray when group still had P-47's.

Major Ron Gray of the 367th Group got three kills in course of the three day Chattanooga Choo Choo operation. Photo shows Gray when group still had P-47's.

Captain Bob Weldon of the 345th Fighter Group got two kills in dogfights over Beaumont, France.

Field Marshall Hugo Sperrle, CinC of Luftflotte 3 in Western Europe, was to provide air defense against an invasion. After Chattanooga Choo Choo operation, he had few planes left.

General Deitrich Peltz, commander of Jagdkorps IX, failed to scatter his bombers in France and he was hard hit in American tactical air operation.

General Werner Junck, commander of Jagdkorps II, did not have enough fighter planes in France to stem the American attacks on airfields and communications system.

Reichsmarshall Herman Goring (L) talks to young German pilot (R). He personally visited Western Front to inspire Luftflotte 3 airmen to defeat Allied air forces.

Captain Peter Heindorff (R) and his aide Cpl Heidi Schroeder (R) of the Luftflotte 3 tracking station in Paris. They were overwhelmed by massive air intruders.

Major Herman Graf of JG 26 got three kills during air battles, but it was not enough.

Lt. Walter Schuck of JG 26 also got three kills, but to no avail.

Colonel Josef Pips Priller of JG 26. He and his pilots tried hard but could not stem the massive Chattanooga Choo Choo air assaults.

Major Frank Eisenbach of JG 54, got himself four kills in air battles over France.

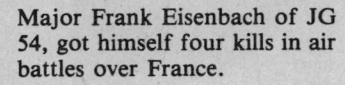

Col. Erick Rudorffer, CO of the JG 54 Green Hearts, a famed Luftwaffe air unit. He and his pilots did well against American fighterpilots, but not good enough to stop any Chattanooga Choo Choo missions.

Insignias of the famed German JG 26 "Schlagetors." (L) II Gruppen; (R) III Gruppen.

An FW 190 of the famed JG 54 Green Hearts German geschwader.

FW 190 fighter planes of the JG 2 Richthofen geschwader.

B-26's of the U.S. 322nd Bomb Group fly over the English countryside on the way to a bombing mission in France.

P-47 fighter bombers of the 368th Group taxi towards runway at Chilbolton, England, before heading for tactical air mission in France.

An A-20 of the U.S. 416th Bomb Group catches solid flak hit from German AA over France. Plane and three man crew perished.

B-26 of the 322nd Bomb Group explodes after solid hits by German fighter planes.

A-20's of the U.S. 416th Bomb Group drop their bombs on the Leshil marshalling yards outside of Paris, France.

The wrecked German airfield at Abbeville, France, after 391st Bomb Group air attack.

The wrecked marshalling yards at Lille after attack by 322nd Bomb Group on 4 June.

The pulverized marshalling yard at Verdonne, France, after 391st Bomb Group attack.

Historic Vernon Bridge in central France became reluctant but necessary target. P-47 fighter bombers of the 365th Group knocked the bridge to pieces.

The important Seine River bridge at Courceilles was destroyed by the U.S. 391st Medium Bomb Group's B-26's.

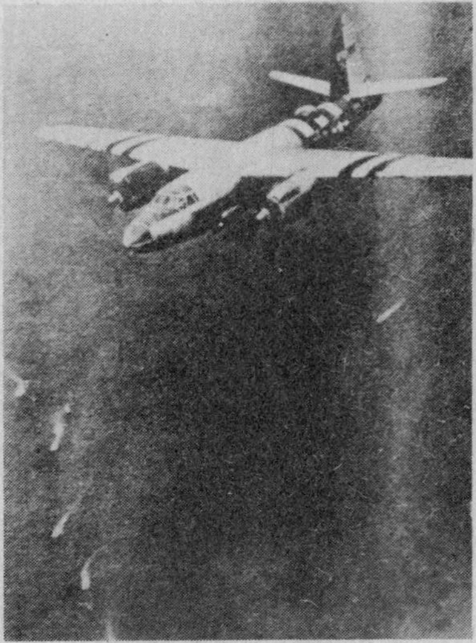

B-26 of the 391st Bomb Group flies over the English Channel, with English fishing boats below the plane.

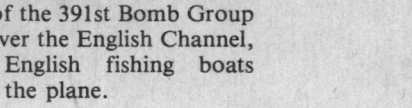

The important Gent railroad bridge in Belgium was destroyed in low level P-47 attack by the 368th Panzer Buster fighter-bomber group.

CHAPTER EIGHT

After the attacks on the German airfields had ended, Field Marshal Hugo Sperrle called a conference of his bomber and fighter commanders at Luftflotte 3 headquarters in Paris. "I want every *geschwader kommando* here by 2100 hours," he told an aide. "I don't care how they get here. They will stay here all night if necessary to conclude plans for an air defense in France."

"Yes, Herr Field Marshal," the aide answered.

Radio messages went out to all *geschwader* headquarters: JG 2 in Paris, JG 54 at Chartres, JG 26 at Lille-Nord, JG 27 at Vire, JG 1 at Argentan and JG 22 at Metz. Luftflotte 3 aides also sent radio instructions to the bomber unit headquarters: ZG 26, the HE 110 light bomber unit at Lesnil; ZG 4, the DO 17 unit at lamar; ZG 11, the JU88 unit at Beaumont; ZG 34, the Hs 129 unit at Ambria; and ZG 16, the Hs 129 unit at Rouen. Sperrle also asked that Gen. Deitrich Peltz of Jagdkorps TX bomber command and Gen. Werner Junck of Jagdkorps II fighter command also attend the meeting.

These JG and ZG commanders in the Paris area easily drove to Luftflotte 3 headquarters, but others, like those in central and western France, flew to the St. Denis airfield, the only drome in the Paris area that had not come under attack today. Every *geschwader kommando* reached Luftflotte headquarters within a couple of hours, on time for the conference at 2100 hours.

The *Luftwaffe* officers sat silently and quietly as Field Marshal Sperrle entered the conference room and scanned his subordinates. He stared at them for a full minute before he spoke, prompting the officers to squirm uneasily in their chairs.

"We have suffered severe losses in France today. I do not know who will tell our Fuhrer of this unfortunate day. Who will explain to him that twenty-six of our airfields were left in ruins and three hundred of our Luftflotte 3 aircraft have been destroyed or damaged? I have already spoken to Field Marshal von Rundstedt and he was utterly dismayed by reports of the heavy destruction."

Sperrle leaned forward and smirked. "I also called *Luftwaffe* OKL in Berlin and asked for aircraft replacements. Do you know how they responded? They laughed. They said we must make do with what we have, and that we must repair our airfields and runways with only the equipment we have in France. Obviously this will be quite difficult when so many of our repair facilities have also been put out of commission. That also means we will be seriously hampered in our attempts to provide an aerial defense against an Allied invasion of the continent, an invasion that could come within the next month or even sooner."

The Luftflotte 3 officers only listened soberly.

"I hold you responsible, all of you," Sperrle gestured sharply. "The fighter *geschwaders* failed to contain the American interlopers today and anti-aircraft gunners failed to destroy enough of the attacking aircraft. As for the bomber *gruppens*—I cannot understand why the aircraft were not hidden more effectively to thwart these American airmen."

"They have developed a new mode of attack, Herr Sperrle," General Peltz answered. "They now bring even their medium bombers into a target at extremely low altitudes and drop delayed fuse bombs. They can attack so closely to their targets that they can destroy parked aircraft even through the most elaborate camouflage."

"Then something must be done about the problem," the Luftflotte 3 commander said. "You must scatter your parked aircraft over dozens of acres so the enemy cannot possibly do the kind of damage he did today."

General Peltz did not answer.

Sperrle now looked at General Junck. "I must tell you that the efforts of the fighter units today were a disgrace. In the Paris area, JG 2 failed to protect the air bases. Three of the Paris airfields sustained heavy damage to the airdromes and to parked aircraft."

"You must understand our position," General Junck defended himself. "We have only limited resources and the Americans no longer come over France with a mere *gruppen* or even a wing of aircraft. They now send their bombers over the continent by the hundreds and they send hundreds of fighters to protect them. I strongly protest the implication of cowardice or inefficiency on the part of our fighter pilots. My JG airmen did the very best they could. In all of the engagements today against enemy escorts, our pilots did well. We have reports that we shot down over a hundred American aircraft. But what good was that when the enemy sends over a thousand planes or more? Our pilots cannot possibly shoot them all down. We simply do not have the aircraft to engage the Americans in twenty-six places at once. And, worse, because we mounted every available fighter, some of the airfields today were left without air protection."

"Please, Herr Field Marshal," Colonel Rudorffer said, "in our sector alone we had only a hundred fighters available to intercept wave after wave of American aircraft. We could send out only four staffels from JG 54 to intercept heavy air formations that attacked four different airfields. We simply had no fighters left to battle both the enemy's escorts and his attacking bombers."

"The same was true in northwest France," Col. Pips Priller now spoke. "How could 120 fighter planes of our JG 26 attack nearly 600 American fighters and bombers that attacked the ten airfields in our sector? While we were defending some of the airfields, the enemy was destroying our own bases at Abbeville and Lille-Nord. We needed to land all of our returning aircraft at St. Pierre, which fortunately was not attacked by the Americans."

Col. Hans Assi Hahn, his neck red from the earlier criticism by the Luftflotte 3 CinC, stared hard at Sperrle before he spoke to him. "Herr Field Marshal, our position in Paris was the same as that of Colonel Priller and Colonel Rudorffer. We simply did not have the aircraft. In fact, most of the JG 2 fighters were defending airfields in central France when the Americans attacked the Paris airfields. We must accept a horrible truth: the Americans now have the means to mount countless aircraft to make simultaneous attacks on multiple targets in France. Today, they used anywhere from seventy to eighty aircraft against each of the twenty-six airfields, all under attack at about the same hour. In God's name, where could we get the number of fighters necessary to defend ourselves against such massive, widespread attacks?"

"Something must be done," Field Marshal Sperrle said.

"We are willing to listen," General Junck said, "if you have a plan that will enable us to defend the French airfields against such huge aircraft formations. We will be happy to follow such a plan."

Field Marshal Sperrle squeezed his face and sighed, softening his earlier harsh attitude. "Perhaps you are right," he told his officers. "Still, we must take steps, and I do have some suggestions." He gestured to an aide who pulled down a huge map of France on the wall behind the field marshal.

"As you can see by the notations on this chart," Sperrle said, gesturing, "although the Americans did extensive damage today, they did not attack all of our Luftflotte 3 airfields. There are still three airdromes intact in the Paris area, six in central France, six in western France, and ten in the south of France. Over half of these are bomber bases that contain a staffel or even two staffels of aircraft. Ten of them are fighter bases that hold up to a full *gruppen* of aircraft."

The officers listened.

"It is the opinion of the Luftflotte 3 staff and myself that the Americans will return tomorrow to attack these other airfields," Sperrle said. "It is obvious they do not want any aircraft in France to interfere with their invasion attempts which could come at any time within the next month."

General Peltz studied the map, stroked his chin, and then spoke to the field marshal. "Herr Sperrle, the Americans attacked our major air bases today and left the small airdromes intact. I am not sure the Americans will bother with these fields."

"The enemy has a definite plan in mind," Sperrle answered, "a plan to stop even a single *Luftwaffe* aircraft from attacking their invasion forces."

"They have succeeded well enough today," Peltz answered, "and they have ample air resources to deal with anything we have left. It is my opinion that they will not expend the effort on these minor airfields as they did on the major airfields today."

"Then what would they strike next?" Sperrle asked.

"Possibly our Wehrmacht and armor unit encampments, perhaps heavy attacks on the Atlantic wall, or perhaps on our communications system—road junctions, marshalling yards, bridges and railroad lines."

"They have been attacking such targets as a matter of routine," Sperrle said. "I cannot believe that the enemy will ignore our remaining airfields; nor do I think they consider these airdromes unimportant."

General Peltz did not answer.

"I believe we must take every precaution to stop further damage," Sperrle continued. "First, the bomber *kommandos* will scatter all aircraft at their bases, so the Americans cannot make concentrated attacks. Also, at least one staffel of fighter aircraft should be assigned to each of these twenty-five undamaged airfields." He looked at Junck. "Is that possible?"

"We have twenty-five staffels among our JG *geschwaders*."

"Good," the Luftflotte 3 CinC said. "You and General Peltz will meet with *geschwader kommandos* to draw up detailed plans that will enable you to carry out my suggestions. Are there any questions?"

"No, Herr Sperrle," General Peltz said.

Sperrle gestured. "Then you will work out plans before the *geschwader kommandos* return swiftly to their units so they can prepare staffel and *gruppen* leaders for new enemy attacks tomorrow."

After a fifteen-minute break, in which the Luftflotte 3 officers drank schnapps and ate cakes, Junck and Peltz held their own private meetings. When Junck assembled his JG leaders, he looked first at Hans Hahn. "How many aircraft do you have available for combat?"

"Less than a hundred among my three *gruppens* in the Richthofen *geschwader*," Colonel Hahn said.

"And what of JG 26?" Junck now looked at Priller.

"We have about fifty serviceable aircraft," the Schlagetor commander said.

"And JG 54?" Junck now turned to Erich Rudorffer.

"Perhaps we can mount thirty-five or forty fighters," the Green Heart commander said.

Junck also learned that he had about 125 other fighters available in the JG 27, JG 22 and JG 1 units. He could thus mount between 300 and 350 fighters. Therefore, he could only assign 12 to 15 aircraft to each airfield that might come under attack tomorrow. He asked that the fighter commanders assign a particular staffel to a particular air base.

"However," the Jagdkorps II CinC said, "you should assign larger staffels to the larger fields, such as Vire, Rouen, St. Pierre and St. Denis. You will not need as many aircraft for the small airfields in the south of France that may not even come under attack."

"We will do our best, Herr Junck," Colonel Priller said.

"I know that you may not get back to your JG headquarters until quite late this evening," Junck said, "but you must meet with staffel leaders before daylight to make certain they understand clearly their responsibilities. All fighter pilots must be ready for interceptor duty by dawn, so they can fly off as soon as we receive reports of approaching enemy aircraft."

"Yes, Herr Junck," Colonel Hahn said.

"We cannot predict, of course, how many aircraft the enemy will send to these airfields, but let us hope that between our staffel pilots and anti-aircraft gunners we can cut to a minimum the damage to our airfields and aircraft."

"If they plan to attack the airfields," Colonel Hahn scowled.

"You do not think they will, Colonel?"

"I am inclined to agree with General Peltz," Hahn said. "I believe the enemy is more likely to concentrate on communications in the next massive, simultaneous attack as he conducted today."

"The field marshal believes otherwise," Junck said, "and we will follow his instructions."

"Yes, Herr Junck."

Gen. Dietrich Peltz, meanwhile, had assembled the commanders of his Zorester bomber units. "I need not remind you that the Heinkel, Dornier and Henshel aircraft are in France to attack enemy troops that may attempt an invasion somewhere along the Atlantic wall. We have suffered badly today in the air attacks on Lamar, Beaumont, Edex, Orival, and the other bomber bases. The field marshal made a wise suggestion when he asked that we scatter our bombers as much as possible. If more attacks come, the enemy will be hard pressed to destroy such scattered aircraft."

"But is it possible, as you yourself said, that

the Americans will attack other targets tomorrow instead of the airfields?"

"That is my personal opinion and I could be wrong. Field Marshal Sperrle is the OKL of Luftflotte 3 and we must abide by his judgment. It is my understanding that at least one fighter staffel will be assigned to defend each airfield. We can make their jobs easier if we force the enemy pilots to fly their attacking aircraft over a wide area to search for our parked bombers."

"Yes, Herr Peltz."

The CinC of Jagdkorps IX now took stock of his aircraft. He had seventy available Hs 129s, 105 HE 110s, and less than 50 DO 17s at his sixteen bomber bases still intact, not much to stop any massive Allied invasion. Still, 200-plus light and medium bombers could be easily scattered since they represented about a dozen planes on each airfield.

Not until 2300 hours did the meetings at Luftflotte 3 in Paris finally end. *Geschwader* leaders could not even remain here until morning, but needed to return to their headquarters for meetings with *gruppen* and staffel leaders. Such conferences would last until well after midnight because all German air units had to be ready by dawn of 3 June.

Enemy airmen in Luftflotte 3 agreed with Field Marshal Sperrle on at least two points. They did not want any more aircraft losses and they wanted no more damage to French airfields.

But, Sperrle had guessed wrong. The U.S. Air Force had been content with the damage today to Luftflotte 3's major airfields in France. Thus, while the Germans worked far into the night to prepare defenses for their remaining airfields and aircraft, no American planes would come over these airbases tomorrow.

The hordes of U.S. 9th Air Force airmen gabbed endlessly during evening chow. At a cost of only forty planes out of nearly fifteen hundred aircraft, the Americans had badly damaged twenty-six German airfields and destroyed or damaged hundreds of aircraft. B-26 combat crews recounted their wanton destruction at Lamar, Beaumont, Abbeville and other bases. A-20 and P-47 pilots detailed their excellent attacks on airfields like Orival, Conflants, and Lesnil. Pilots from the 354th, 367th, 474th, 370th and other P-51 and P-58 fighter groups spoke of their heavy kills against German FW 190s and ME 109s.

But even as these returning Ninth Air Force airmen ate their evening meals at dozens of English airfields, their ground crews were preparing aircraft for new sorties tomorrow— bridges and marshalling yards along the main routes from east to west across France to the English Channel. Group commanders had found orders waiting for them to report at once to Bushy Park to complete plans for initiating the next aspect of Operation Chattanooga Choo Choo.

Almost an hour before Sperrle called his meeting in Paris, Gen. Lewis Brereton had called his group commanders into conference. But most of the Ninth Air Force airfields were within two hours driving distance or a mere half hour flying distance to Pinetree. Many of the group commanders flew to Bushy Park in Piper Cubs or Beachcrafts, while others simply drove. All thirty-two group commanders arrived on time for the scheduled 2000 hours conference. Brereton waited until the men had settled into their chairs before he spoke.

"Gentlemen, we don't know the exact damage we caused today. We'll need to wait for reconnaissance reports. But, if the preliminary information from pilots and crews are half accurate, we can be sure you did an excellent job. Unfortunately, there can be no rest. The landings begin three days from tomorrow morning and we've still got plenty of work to do."

Brereton cocked his head at an aide who lit a lamp over a huge map of France that hung on the wall behind the podium. "You've already seen this map," the Ninth Air Force CinC said, "and in fact, you have a copy of it. We'll go over it again just to make sure that each group knows its mission."

The group commanders listened.

"Take off tomorrow will begin at 0700 hours, with the 391st Group and the 416th

Group going to the Paris area. They'll hit the Seine River bridges at Verdun and Courcielles and the marshalling yards at Lesnil and Limidan. The 368th, 366th and 365th Fighter Bomber Groups will take off next to hit the Vernon and Le Fitte bridges in central France and the Gent railroad bridge in Belgium. The 322nd and 387th Bomb Groups will start taking off at 0800 to hit the railroad bridges at Letripad and Louvain in northwest France, the Hasselt bridge in Belgium, and the marshalling yard at Lille in northwest France."

"We're hitting a bridge in Belgium, sir?" Colonel Myers of the 368th Group asked. "I thought that all the targets in Belgium and Holland were assigned to the RAF."

"Well, Gent and Hasselt are pretty close to the Ninth Air Force theatre of operations, so they've given us these two Belgium targets."

"Yes, sir," Myers answered.

"Take another look at the map. You can see the green line to the north that runs east to west and slightly southwest out of northwest Germany, through Holland and Belgium, and then into the Normandy beach area. We must destroy fourteen bridges and six marshalling yards along this route. This red line is the potential route through the Paris area and along the Seine River to eastern France. We've got several major bridges and two big marshalling yards in that area that must be destroyed. And down here—" Brereton pointed at the map—"the blue line is the potential route the Germans would use through central France to reach the Normandy coast. There are sixteen bridges and a half dozen marshalling yards that should be destroyed along this route, especially the LeFitte and Vernon bridges."

"What about escorts?" Col. Norman Holt of the 366th Fighter Bomber Group asked.

Brereton grinned. "I think our fighter pilots knocked down half of the German Air Force in France today, so I don't know what the *Luftwaffe* can send up against us tomorrow. However, we'll have the usual two squadrons of fighters to escort each B-26 and A-20 group and one squadron of fighters to escort the P-47 fighter bomber groups."

General Brereton then pointed to the other bridge and marshalling yard targets for the other Ninth Air Force tactical units. All total his air groups would assail thirty-four bridges and fourteen marshalling yards. Meanwhile, the RAF Second Tactical Air Force, which had already struck twenty airfields in Holland and Belgium, would be out tomorrow to hit fifteen bridges and twelve marshalling yards in the low countries.

"Get back to your units as soon as this meeting is over so you can brief your squadron and flight leaders on tomorrow's series of missions. Also, make sure you check with group and squadron commanders on your particular escort."

"What about armament, sir?" Colonel Myers asked.

"The units attacking bridges will use noball delayed-fuse bombs so they can get right on top of the spans and trestles before letting go. The units attacking marshalling yards will use HE five hundred and thousand pounders to tear up as much trackage as possible and to destroy as much rolling stock as possible."

The General paused and then sighed. "Any questions?"

"I guess not, sir," Col. Glen Nye said.

"Okay, get back to your units. Hold briefings as soon as you're home, even if such meetings continue until after midnight. I want every squadron off on time as listed on the FO sheet. We want planes crossing the French coast in one continuous formation before breaking off to particular targets. This will give the Germans no rest and they won't be able to mount enough fighters to take on all of you."

The meeting ended at 2100 hours and the various group commanders returned quickly to their own headquarters. From the 322nd Bomb Group base at Great Saling, Col. Glen Nye would personally lead the 449th and 450th Squadrons against the Lille marshalling yards, while Lieutenant Colonel Olmstead led the 451st and 452nd Squadrons against the Letripad Bridge. From Stoney Cross, Col. Tom Seymoure would lead the 556th and 557th Squadrons of his 387th Group to attack the

Hasselt Bridge, while the Pathfinders' 558th and 559th Squadrons under Maj. Jim Keller would hit the Louvain Bridge.

When Col. Jerry Williams of the 391st Group reached his headquarters at Matching, he decided to personally lead the 575th and 574th Squadrons against the Verdun Bridge, while Lieutenant Colonel Floak led the Bridge Busters' 573rd and 572nd Squadrons against the Courcielles Bridge. At his 416th A-20 Group headquarters in Wetherfield, Col. Harold Mace assigned the 670th and 671st Squadrons to Maj. Don Willits to hit the Limidan marshalling yard, while Mace himself led the 668th and 669th Squadrons against the Lesnil marshalling yards.

Both the 391st and 416th Group aircraft would have a long flight tomorrow, so the two 9th Air Force units would be the first to cross the French coast. Both Colonel Williams and Colonel Mace hoped they did not catch the brunt of fighter interceptors. But then, they would have two squadrons of P-38 fighters from the 367th Fighter Group and two squadrons of P-51s from the 474th Fighter Group and the pilots of these groups were good.

At his Beaulieu headquarters, Col. Lance Call of the 365th Fighter Bomber Group studied photos of the railroad bridge at Vernon, deciding how to hit the spans and trestles for best results. At Thruxton, Col. Norman Holt of the 366th Group studied photos and reconn reports of the Le Fitte Bridge. He too looked for the best places to strike the bridge with delayed-fuse bombs. And finally, at Chilbolton, Col. Gilbert Myers of the 368th Fighter Bomber Group studied pictures of the Gent railroad bridge, a principal artery through Belgium. Myers worried about heavy interceptors in the area. The Panzer Buster Group commander did not know if a single squadron of P-38 escorts would be enough to contain German fighter planes while he and his P-47 fighter bomber pilots hit the bridge.

In other B-26, A-20, P-47, P-38 and P-51 groups of the Ninth Air Force, group commanders were also awake until well after midnight to brief squadron and flight leaders on tomorrow's missions. Some of the groups would be hitting highway bridges instead of railroad bridges.

But dawn of 3 June broke dark and dreary over England, with dense gray clouds leaving a near-zero ceiling over the English airfields of the Ninth Air Force. The massive weather front extended far to the east, across the English Channel, across France and the low countries, and into Germany. Group commanders of the Ninth Air Force did not know if they could fly out today. But, since no word had come from Bushy Park, they planned to take off.

Most of the bomber crews in the 322nd Bomb Group operations quonset hut chattered furiously. They did not mind flying another mission to France, but not in this kind of weather. They quieted down when Colonel Nye entered the hut and mounted the podium. The colonel leaned over the dais and spoke. "So far as we know, we're going out today."

However, Glen Nye had only been speaking to his airmen for a couple of minutes when a sergeant came into the briefing hut and handed Nye's operations officer a message. The captain read the communication and then walked to the dais. "I'm sorry, sir, but I think you'd better read this."

The 322nd Group commander read the message, grinned and then looked at his airmen. "New instructions from Bushy Park—all mission for today are scrubbed; postponed until tomorrow. You can go back and sack out for the day."

A rousing cheer erupted from the two-hundred-odd crew members of Nye's Annihilators. The colonel allowed his men to work off their elation before he spoke again. "Just be sure you're back here at 0600 tomorrow."

"Yes, sir," somebody answered.

Similar messages of cancellations reached the other group commanders of the Ninth Air Force throughout the eastern England airbases.

In Paris, an aide brought a meteorologist report to Field Marshal Sperrle's chief-of-staff. The colonel read the message in satisfaction. "It appears the weather has taken a severe turn. I suspect the Americans will not send their tactical bombers over today. This is welcome news. Our *geschwaders* will have a respite to better prepare themselves for new American intrusions tomorrow."

"Yes, Herr Colonel."

Thus, with no U.S. air attacks, a quiet prevailed over France on this dreary 3 June day. German *Luftwaffe* and *Wehrmacht* troops appreciated the rest. But the respite would only last one day. The Americans would be back in France tomorrow to lace German targets again.

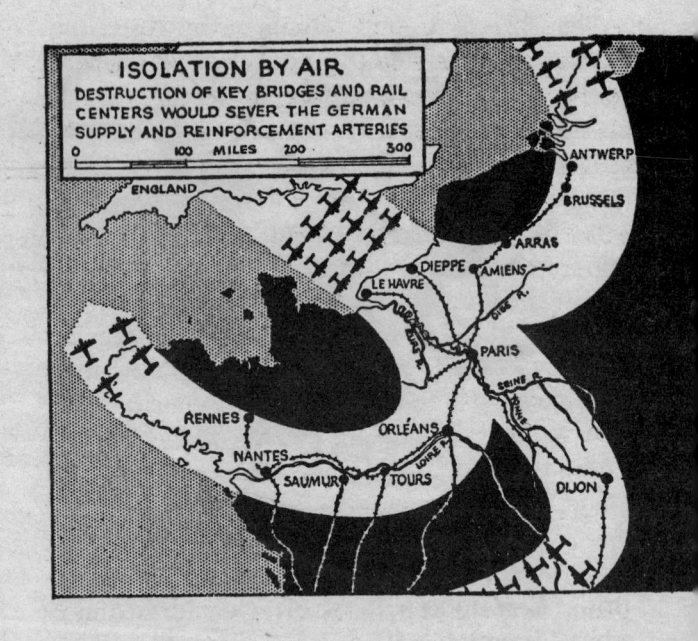

ISOLATION BY AIR
DESTRUCTION OF KEY BRIDGES AND RAIL CENTERS WOULD SEVER THE GERMAN SUPPLY AND REINFORCEMENT ARTERIES

CHAPTER NINE

A slight drizzle had dampened the Matching, England air base on the morning of 4 June, when Col. Jerry Williams of the 391st Bomb Group swung his lead B-26 to the head of the runway. The morning was as dreary as yesterday, but General Brereton believed they were too close to D-day to postpone further. Bad weather or not, the planes of the 9th Air Force must get off its Choo Choo missions. All planes would bomb at relatively low altitude, so pilots could fly under the clouds to attack their targets. When the forty-two planes from the Bridge Buster Group took off, they formed into a box formation, with a Pathfinder leading each squadron. By 0730 hours, all aircraft were airborne and droning south, slightly southeast.

The 391st would fly deep into France to hit the Seine River bridges at Verdun and Corcielles.

Aboard *April Look,* co-pilot Frank Elder stared at the low, dense clouds overhead then glanced at the other Marauders hanging next to his own B-26. He turned to pilot Jim Kahley. "I don't like this. The weather's too bad. Half of these Marauders may abort before we reach Paris."

"We've got to knock out those bridges," Kahley answered. He looked at his instrument panel and then at Elder. "Pressure looks OK The engines sound OK. We'll make it to Verdun, Frank, we'll make it."

"If bandits don't jump us first."

"Our fighter guys gave those Nazi fighter units a good working over a couple days ago, and we gave their airfields a good pasting. We may not run into much trouble."

"Maybe," Elder said, but there was still doubt in his voice.

Capt. Jim Kahley stared at the other planes in his box formation before he peered down at the English countryside. Then he called his crew.

"Lieutenant," he spoke first to his bombardier navigator, "How's it going in the nose?"

"Everything OK, Captain," Ed Schweiter answered.

"Stay alert," Kahley said. "If you have any problems, let me know. You've got to be accurate with your bomb hits."

"Yes, sir."

From his nose position, Lt. Ed Schweiter enjoyed an excellent view of the terrain under him, the dense clouds overhead, and the other B-26s of the 391st Group. But, like co-pilot Elder, Schweiter did not like this flight through a drizzle and low clouds. The overcast could worsen before they reached France, deepening even more. He checked his bomb sight and then swung his single .50-caliber machine gun to keep his mind off the long flight to the Paris area.

"Sergeant," Kahley now called his turret gunner, "what does it look like upstairs?"

"Thick, sir, thick," Sgt. Ed Bonhman answered, "but the cloud cover isn't getting any worse. If it stays like this all the way to IP, we should't have much trouble."

"If you note any change, call me."

"Yes, sir."

Bonham checked his guns, fingering the triggers of his twin fifties and swinging the weapons to make certain they moved freely. Then the gunner looked up at the clouds again and grimaced. He did not like the overcast. Over France, German fighter planes could come out of these clouds unexpectedly to rake their B-26 with machine gun and cannon fire before the American airmen knew what hit them.

"Are you getting anything on the radio?" the *April Look* pilot now called to his waist gunner.

"No, sir," Sgt. Al Mass said, "just static. I'm trying to get something on the VHF channel, sir, but nothing is coming over. I guess there haven't been any changes in plans."

"If you hear anything, let me know."

"Yes, sir."

Mass fingered the triggers of his waist guns and then swung his weapons left and right to aim them beyond both the starboard and port windows. If bandits dipped out of the clouds and attacked, he wanted to make certain he was ready.

And, finally, Capt. Jim Kahley called his tail gunner. "Sergeant, does the cloud cover look any worse from where you sit? Are they getting lower or thicker?"

"No, sir," Larry Carr answered.

"Stay awake. We'll be reaching the Channel pretty soon."

"Yes, sir."

Captain Kahley, a lanky pilot from Story City, Iowa, then relaxed in his pilot's seat and looked at his instrument panel again. They were flying at a leisurely 190 knots at four thousand feet. On their 170 degree course, their route out would be at Checkpoint Splasher No. 8, Beachy Head, England before they crossed the English Channel at Etretat, France. They would pick up their escorts over the Channel at 49 degrees north by 0 degrees 53 minutes east. The *April Look* pilot looked at his watch: 0730. They were on schedule.

In his lead 391st aircraft, Col. Jerry Williams called his pilots. "Checkpoint I in five minutes; five minutes. All navigators please check instruments."

The forty-two Bridge Buster B-26s droned south. Soon, they left the coast and began the flight over the Channel. From this low altitude the 391st Airmen could see a relative calm in the water today, a sharp contrast to the Channel's usually choppy water. But no winds prevailed on this drizzly, gloomy morning.

At 0745 hours, tail gunner Larry Carr aboard *April Look* saw the swarm of aircraft coming towards the B-26 formation. He soon made out the twin fusilages, so he knew the oncoming planes were his escorts. He called Kahley.

"Sir, P-38s coming up."

The *April Look* captain looked at his compass reading: forty-nine degrees nineteen minutes north, by one degree forty-six minutes east. The escort was on time and at the correct rendezvous point. He grinned at co-pilot Frank Elder.

Elder looked at the approaching Lightning fighters and then turned to the pilot. "They're always on time, Jim."

Then Maj. Ron Gray of the 367th Fighter Group's 394th Squadron cried into his radio. "This is Brightlight III. We've got thirty-two Brightlights with us and we'll stick with you all the way. Brightlight II will accompany Easter 1 and 2 to Verdun and Brightlight III will accompany Easter 3 and 4 to Courcielles."

"We read you, Brightlight," Col. Jerry Williams answered. "It's good to see you."

"We all did a good job two days ago." Gray

said, "so we shouldn't have too much trouble with bandits."

"Let's hope not," Williams answered.

About a half hour earlier, at 0710 hours, Col. Harold Mace roared down the Wetherfield, England runway in his lead A-20 of the 416th Bomb Group. Behind him, forty-seven other Havocs also zoomed down the apron and took off. The same morning drizzle has also annoyed the A-20 crews; they too did not like flying over four hundred miles under this heavy overcast. By 0730 hours, the four Havoc squadrons had jelled into formation to begin the flight south. Each plane carried four five hundred-pound HE bombs, for this group would attack marshalling yards from a four thousand to five thousand feet altitude.

As the A-20s droned south in box formation, Englishmen on countryside farms, in small villages or in cities watched the planes pass overhead. Most of them looked up soberly, feeling both grateful and anxious. The Yank airmen and their hordes of planes had been a real blessing to the Britishers. The Americans had repayed the Nazis tenfold for the heavy destruction to the British Isles by German planes earlier in the war. Yank bomber crews had flattened dozens of German targets over the past year; American fighter pilots had macerated the German Air Force. Now, the *Luftwaffe* made only minor air raids over Britain. These thankful English civilians knew, however, that among the countless American airmen flying to the continent, many would never come back. The civilians could only offer prayers.

In the lead A-20, Colonel Mace studied his map. They would leave the coast at Brighton, as usual. The 416th would then cross the channel and swing southeast towards the Paris area. Mace knew from recent photos that the Lesnil and Limidan marshalling yards were jammed with loaded freight cars and packed troop cars in the yards. Warehouses were filled with stored material, including fuel, arms and hardware. Every wrecked railroad car, smashed locomotive, and destroyed supply area would reduce the casualties among American GIs who landed at Normandy. So Mace was determined to get his target today, regardless of the weather.

Behind his A-20, in the Havoc *Pink Lady,* Lt. Bill Downey studied his instrument panel and even fingered his bomb release button. He hoped his quartet of five hundred pounders caused plenty of damage to the Lesnil marshalling yard. Radio gunner Sgt. Al Neilson fingered the dials of his equipment, trying to pick up something, but thus far he did not hear anything. In the top turret, Sgt. Warren Fields stared at the other A-20s around him, and then at the dense clouds. The gunner bit his lips nervously. He did not like flying on a combat mission in this kind of weather. They would need to drop their bombs from relatively low altitudes and they could catch exploding debris that might destroy their own aircraft and three-man crew.

In the rear box of A-20s, Maj. Don Willits, piloting the lead A-20 *Sentimental Journey* of the 669th Squadron, stared at the A-20s about him. He looked at his instrument panel: a 210 knot air speed and three thousand eight hundred foot altitude. He did not appreciate flying so low, nor did he look forward to a long mission deep into France under these thick clouds. Yet the *Sentimental Journey* pilot knew that if the group scored well at the marshalling yard, they could stop plenty of German soldiers and tons of armament from reaching the French coast.

Willits called his turret gunner. "Sergeant, what does it look like?"

"Still the same, sir," Sgt. Ozzie LeNave answered. "Clouds aren't any lower and they're not any thicker."

"We'll be reaching the Channel soon; stay awake."

"Yes, sir."

Then Willits called his radio gunner. "Are you picking up anything, Sergeant?"

"Nothing, sir," Sgt. Henry Lempke answered. "I'd guess we won't hear a thing until the colonel give us new instructions, or until our escorts reach us."

"Keep alert," the pilot said.

Soon, the A-20 formations reached Brighton and then left the coast to begin the flight over the Channel. The A-20s would cross the French coast south of Calais and fly almost directly southeast to the Paris area. Now, the 416th Group pilots instinctively tightened their box formations and turret gunners became more alert, scanning the cloud-covered sky and hoping that no ME 109s or FW 190s shot out of the overcast to barrage them with machine gunfire or cannon fire.

At 0755 hours, a horde of planes suddenly emerged from the northwest and closed swiftly on the A-20s. The Havoc gunners in their top turrets stiffened momentarily but then relaxed when they saw clearly the sleek fusilages and wings of P-51 fighters. Their escort had reached the rendezvous point at the right position. Soon, Col. Clinton Wesem of the 474th Fighter Group called Colonel Mace.

"This is Flashlight Leader," the fighter group commander said. "We'll be with you all the way to targets 318 and 319."

"We read you, Flashlight," Colonel Mace said.

"Flashlight I will accompany Shannon 1 and 2 to 318 target, and Flashlight II will accompany Shannon 3 and 4 to 319 target. We finished off an awful lot of bandits the other day, so we don't expect to meet too many today."

"We didn't get them all, Flashlight," Colonel Mace said, "so make sure your pilots are alert."

"My guys are always awake, Colonel," Wesem said, "even if they have to use toothpicks to keep their eyelids apart."

Then the four squadrons of A-20s with their accompanying two squadrons of P-51s continued eastward across the Channel. Fortunately, the cloud cover had not worsened and the Americans enjoyed a minimum five thousand foot ceiling. Also, the drizzle had stopped. Maybe the Americans would find much better weather over the marshalling yards around Paris.

"Achtung! Feindliche flugzenge! Feindliche flugzenge!" Enemy aircraft. At 0900 hours, the cry came from a German radar operator at the early warning station in Letreppon. He had picked up the approaching 391st Bomb Group B-26s as the medium bombers crossed the French coast south of Dieppe. He quickly radioed the tracking station in Paris, where Capt. Peter Heindorff once more referred to his table map to estimate the course of the American bombers. A moment later, a new report came from the Letreppon station: enemy aircraft were flying east, southeast on a northern lateral paralleling the Seine River.

Captain Heindorff now suspected that the planes were flying toward the Paris area, and when he got a visual report from an air observer at Rouen, the tracking captain was certain the enemy planes were heading for the French capital.

"I am surprised that the enemy has launched a new attack in this area," Cpl. Heidi Schroeder said.

"They are intent on destroying our airfields and they are sparing no effort," Captain Heindorff said. "You will notify the headquarters of JG 2 to intercept these enemy planes, before they can destroy the airfield at St. Denis and perhaps at Maisson."

"Yes, Herr Hauptman," Corporal Schroeder answered.

Peter Heindorff had barely finished tracking the expected course of the U.S. B-26 bomber formations when he got another call from the Letreppon radar station. "Enemy light bombers have crossed the coast north of Le Havre. These aircraft are also flying south by southeast." Heindorff had barely charted the report when the Le Havre radar station sent still another report on the A-20 formations.

"There appear to be about fifty light bombers with fighter escorts," the radar sergeant said.

Captain Heindorff now drew a line over his map, waiting for more reports before he estimated the destination of these new American aerial invaders. A sighting report soon came in from visual observers at the village of Elbeau, some fifteen miles inland from Le Havre. The sky watchers reported the

A-20s flying east, southeast on a course paralleling the Seine River, but along the southern lateral. Heindorff concluded that these A-20s were also flying to Paris.

"You will send another message to JG 2 headquarters," Heindorff told his aide. "it now appears that these enemy light bombers along with the thirty to forty medium bombers are also coming to the Paris area. Both enemy air formations have escorts, so the *geschwader* pilots will need to deal with fighters as well as bombers."

"Yes, Herr Hauptman," Corporal Schroeder said.

As the two American air formations crossed into France and droned on either side of the Seine River, German airmen grew uneasy. At St. Pierre, where Joseph Priller now maintained his headquarters because of the battering to Abbeville and Lille-Nord, the JG 26 commander was tempted to mount fighters at once against these American planes. But he had his orders: his three Schlagetor *gruppens* must engage only enemy planes that went after the airfields in northwest France—St. Marie, Rouen, St. Pierre and the other bases near the Channel coast.

Maj. Herman Graf of JG 26/II was restless. "Perhaps we should intercept these enemy aircraft," he told Priller.

"They will be the responsibility of JG 2," Priller answered. "You, I, and Hauptman Emil

Lang of III Gruppen must do nothing yet. We can surely expect more enemy aircraft to cross into France today. We will ready our pilots and aircraft to intercept only such aircraft that attempt to attack the airfields in our sector."

"Yes, Herr Kommando," Major Graf answered.

By 0945 hours, the two American air formations were halfway to Paris. At Rouen, where Col. Erich Rudorffer now maintained his JG 54 headquarters because of damage to Chartres two days ago, the Green Heart commander also spoke to one of his *gruppen* leaders, Maj. Franz Eisenach. "The enemy air units have now passed Rouen, apparently on the way to the Paris area. We can be sure that enemy aircraft will also attempt to attack airfields in our area this morning. You will ready fighter staffels to intercept such American formations. I will also notify Major Adameit of our II Gruppen at Epernon."

"Yes, Colonel," Eisenach answered.

At the St. Denis airfield outside of Paris, Col. Hans Assi Hahn of JG 2 mounted two staffels of fighter planes, about thirty aircraft, to meet the oncoming American bombers. "It appears the Americans intend to attack the St. Denis and Maisson airfields," he told Maj. Heinrich Ehler. "You will take your staffel south to defend Maisson and I myself will take a staffel from I Gruppen to defend the St. Denis airfield."

"But can we be sure the airfields are their targets?"

"Kommando Sperrle believes so, and we must follow the field marshal's instructions," Hahn said. "Anyway, even if the enemy has some other target in the Paris area, we must be ready to intercept."

"Yes, Colonel."

"We will also ready two other staffels," Hahn continued, "in the event the formations split and fly to four targets instead of two."

At 1010 hours, as the two formations of American bombers approached the Paris area, the U.S. 391st Group's 575th and 574th Squadrons under Col. Jerry Williams broke sharply south. They would hit the Seine River bridges at Verdun, northwest of Paris. The 391st's 373rd and 372nd Squadrons under Lt. Col. Bill Floak, meanwhile, continued on to hit the Seine River bridge at Courcielles, just west of Paris. The 416th Group's 668th and 669th Squadrons under Col. Harold Mace continued on a direct course towards the Lesnil marshalling yards in the western suburb of Paris, while Maj. Don Willits led his twenty-four Havocs of the group's 670th and 671st Squadrons on a southeast course to hit the Limidan marshalling yards south of Paris.

Colonel Hahn took twenty-one FW 190s straight eastward and was utterly surprised to learn that two squadrons of B-26s had turned south somewhere west of Paris. There were no airfields in that area of the Seine River. Then the JG 2 commander quickly realized that the American B-26s were not heading for any airfield, but heading for the vital Verdun Bridge on the main railroad route between Paris and the Channel coast.

"We must stop them," Hahn called his pilots. "They will utterly disrupt our rail system out of Paris if they destroy the Verdun Bridge."

But the twenty-one FWs never reached the bombers. At 1025 hours, American fighters tangled with the German fighter staffels that had come out to challenge the B-26s. Capt. Henry Brown, leading the 367th Fighter Group's 393rd Squadron, cried into his radio, "Interceptors to the east. We can't let them interfere with those bombers." Then the captain banked his P-38 *Hun Flusher* and waded toward the German fighters. Nineteen Lightnings followed him.

In a quick ten-minute dogfight, Brown and his pilots knocked down seven of the German planes and damaged two others. Brown himself downed two of the FW 190s when he caught one Folkwolfe and chopped off the wing with two solid thirty-seven-mm shell hits. Brown chased a second 190 at deck level and chewed off the tail of the German fighter with blistering machine gunfire before the FW smashed into the ground.

Among the Germans, Col. Hans Hahn got a P-38 with chattering machine gunfire that shattered the cockpit and killed the American pilot. But only he and two other JG 2 pilots scored before the Americans routed the staffel of German fighters from the Richthofen *geschwader*.

Meanwhile, Colonel Williams came in low toward the Verdun Bridge. "Attack in pairs; in pairs! And stay twenty seconds apart."

Then duets of B-26s came in low and released their noball bombs, dropping the delayed fuse explosives when the Marauders were almost on top of the bridge. The Bridge Busters accurately lived up to their name as bomb after bomb from the twenty-two B-26s struck the spans and trestles before the bridge finally collapsed into the Seine.

Tail gunner Larry Carr, aboard *April Look,* stared in awe at the shattered railroad bridge. He called Captain Kahley. "She's gone, sir. All three spans gone."

"OK, let's go home," Kahley said, grinning.

Meanwhile, Lt. Col. Bill Floak approached the Corcielles railroad bridge with the other twenty B-26s of the 391st Bomb Group. When he saw the target ahead, he cried into his radio, "OK, in pairs, make every noball count. We don't want any trains coming over those spans two days from now."

"No, sir," Capt. Larry Fogoneri said.

Again the B-26s had no interference from German fighters because Maj. Ron Gray in the P-38 *Just Lazy* led twenty fighter planes towards a formation of eighteen FW 190s from JG 2 under Maj. Heinrich Ehler. Within five minutes, the Americans shot down nine of the

FWs and damaged three more. Gray, who already had seven kills during his short career in the ETO, now scored his eighth and ninth. He got his first 190 by blowing apart the fusilage with solid thirty-seven-mm hits, and the second plane when he killed the Folkwolfe's engine with chattering .50-caliber machine gunfire.

The Americans only lost two P-38s.

Now, despite heavy ack-ack fire that downed one B-26 and damaged another, Lieutenant Colonel Floak led his medium bombers toward the bridge at deck level. Again, the Bridge Buster bombardiers scored solid hits that shattered two spans and dropped them into the Seine. Nazi railroad trains would not get into Paris over the Seine River railroad bridge.

The pilots of the 416th Bomb Group also hoped to eliminate the trains that might try to roll through the Paris area. Col. Harold Mace led the A-20s of his 668th and 670th Squadrons over the Lesnil marshalling yards, crammed with freight and passenger rolling stock, as well as a dozen locomotives. From a mere four thousand feet, just under the clouds, the A-20s came over in V's to drop confettis of five hundred-pound HE bombs into the marshalling yards. A staccato of explosions erupted in the mile-square area, smashing rolling stock, wrecking locomotives, tearing up track, and destroying four service buildings, including a roundhouse. The attack put the marshalling yard out of business. No trains would organize here before the D-day invasion.

East of the A-20 bombers, the squadron of P-51 escorts quickly tangled with another staffel of sixteen ME 109s from the JG 2 Richtofen *geschwader*. Once again, the Americans prevailed. The pilots of the 474th Fighter Group's 428th Squadron downed five of the Messerschmidts and they damaged four more 109s during the ten-minute dogfight. The Americans lost but three P-51s. No German fighters reached the A-20s to disrupt the Havoc attack on the marshalling yard.

And, finally, Maj. Don Willits led the 669th and 671st Squadrons of the 416th Bomb Group over the Limidan marshalling yard. American fighter pilots of the 474th Group waded into a staffel of German fighters to protect the American bombers. The U.S. pilots downed two planes, but lost three of their own, with the renowned, experienced German fighter ace, Maj. Wilhem Baatz, getting two of the P-51s himself.

Baatz, leading a trio of fighters from JG 2/II, got his first Mustang when he made a sharp turn and came behind the American fighter plane, chopping away the tail before the American aircraft tumbled downward and crashed. The German ace got his next P-51 when he struck the cockpit with twenty-mm shellfire and killed the American pilot.

However, this second donnybrook in the Paris area also lasted long enough to stop *Luftwaffe* interceptors from reaching the A-20s as the U.S. light bombers droned over Limidan to make their bomb drops.

Maj. Don Willits, in the first V of A-20s, made the first drop when a quartet of five hundred-pound HE bombs tumbled out of *Sentimental Journey* into the marshalling yard. As he banked away, turret gunner Ozzie LeNave saw two freight cars and one locomotive explode. Willits had scored with a trio of his four bombs. The gunner called the aircraft commander.

"You got three hits, sir; three hits."

"Thank you, Sergeant," Willits answered.

By the time the last A-20 of the 669th and 671st Squadrons had made its run, the A-20 pilots had blown away at least a mile of siding, destroyed twenty pieces of rolling stock, wrecked three locomotives, and smashed the yard's repair shop. The marshalling yard was out of business, and no trains would come through here to head westward into Normandy.

By 1100 hours, the two American bomber groups and their fighter escorts were droning away from targets. Two vital railroad bridges had been destroyed and two important marshalling yards had been decimated. Even as the B-26s of the 391st Group and the A-20s of the 416th Group headed back to the English Channel, no German interceptors rose to meet them.

As Field Marshal Sperrle suspected, the Americans would be sending air formations over France all day to hit important targets, and Luftflotte 3 fighters would be needed to challenge these new formations of enemy aircraft. And, in fact, the 391st and 416th U.S. Bomb Groups were indeed only the first of countless planes from the 9th Air Force that would be crossing into France on this gloomy morning.

CHAPTER TEN

Less than a half hour after the 416th and 391st Bomb Groups took off for the continent, three P-47 fighter bomber groups were also airborne. Forty-eight Thunderbolts from the 368th Group left Chilbolton to hit the bridge target at Gent, Belgium. The 366th Group took off from Thruxton to destroy the Le Fitte Bridge in central France, and forty-eight Thunderbolts of the 365th Group took off from Beaulieu, England, to attack the Vernon Bridge, also in central France. Each P-47 carried a pair of five hundred-pound noball bombs under the wings, along with full belts of .50-caliber machine gun belts in their six forward guns.

By 0800 hours, the three P-47 groups reached

the English coastline at the village of North Foreland, where the Thunderbolts of the 368th Fighter Bomber Group veered eastward and slightly southeast to cross the lower sector of the North Sea on the way to Gent, Belgium. Col. Gilbert Myers, the group commander, led his planes over the calm waters at three thousand feet and at 210 knots. The dense clouds still hung low and the drizzle continued unabated. Myers called his pilots.

"Keep the formation tight; keep it tight. The British say the Germans have a lot of planes in Belgium and Holland. We will have a squadron of P-38s from the 470th Group to escort us into Belgium, but enemy fighters could jump us before we clear the North Sea."

"Yes, sir, " Lt. Col. Paul Douglas said.

In his P-47 *Little Bill,* Capt. Bob Johnson of the 397th Squadron stared from his cockpit at the murky waters of the North Sea below him and at the dense, gloomy clouds over him. The young pilot from Ames, Iowa had been in the U.S. Army Air Force for more than two years, but he had been overseas for only three months, flying mostly on fighter bomber missions. He had trained as a fighter pilot but in only two instances since coming to England had Johnson taken on *Luftwaffe* fighters in aerial combat while escorting B-26 medium bombers. During most of his short combat career with the 368th Group Panzer Busters, he had attacked German targets in strafing and low level bombing runs.

Johnson had enjoyed ripping up tracks,

destroying railroad cars and locomotives, wrecking airfields, chopping apart German Panzer units, and smashing motorized columns. Still, there was nothing like a good donnybrook in which he could match wits with *Luftwaffe* pilots. Capt. Bob Johnson sighed and tapped the buttons of his machine guns. He almost wished that they would run into a swarm of 190s or 109s over Belgium so he would need to salvo bombs and tangle with the Germans in a good dogfight.

In the same diamond of P-47s, Capt. Walt Mahorin in *Sally of Atlanta* stared at the two Thunderbolts alongside of him. He waved to wingman Bob Johnson to the right and the pilot of *Little Bill* waved back with a grin. Mahorin, from Atlanta, Georgia, had also joined the army air force about two years ago. After training, he too had been assigned to the 368th Group. He had also expected to fight German fighter pilots when he came overseas. But, unlike Johnson, Mahorin had relished the Panzer busting missions against tactical targets. The *Sally of Atlanta* pilot had enjoyed the attacks on Panzer tank formations and German motorized columns. He also liked the sight of exploding locomotives and burning rolling stock after low-level bombing and strafing attacks.

Mahorin had been among the pilots who first attacked bridge targets in Europe with the delayed fuse bomb that had made the job much easier and much more effective. Now, as the 368th's P-47s droned across the lower North

Sea, he looked forward to attacking the bridge at Gent.

Ten minutes after the 368th Group's Thunderbolts left the British coast-line, swarms of P-38s joined them from the southwest. "This is Monitor I, Monitor I," Col. Howard Nichols of the 370th Fighter Group spoke into his radio. Nichols was leading the P-38s of the 401st Squadron. "We'll be with you all the way to target 641."

"We read you, Monitor," Col. Gilbert Myers answered.

Soon, the sixteen Lightnings settled around the forty-eight Thunderbolts and the sixty-four planes droned on toward Belgium.

In Belgium, German radar teams at Zeebrugge soon picked up the approaching American planes. However, the blips on their screens were strange, not representative of the Mosquito or Typhoon RAF light bombers that normally came over Belgium. The Germans at first believed that the British were flying a different type of aircraft, a plane even smaller than the known British light bombers. However, as the U.S. planes crossed the Belgium coast south of Zeebrugge, a visual coast watcher was surprised to note the huge white stars on the fusilages and wings of these aircraft. As the U.S. planes did not normally come into the low countries, the Germans concluded that the Allies were changing their tactics.

But, whether the planes were American or

British, the intruders were still enemy aircraft. The Germans once again sent information to Paris where Capt. Peter Heindorff at the tracking station yet again drew a potential route on his big map table.

"Where do you believe they are going, Herr Hauptman?" Corporal Schroeder asked.

"I do not know," the tracking officer said. "We will need to wait for further reports. However, on their present course, they appear to be on their way to the airfield in Gent or Brussels."

Corporal Schroeder smiled. "I should refresh your memory. The British Typhoons have already smashed these bases."

"Then where would they be going?" Heindorff asked.

"I do not know," the aide answered.

About five minutes after the first sighting of the American formation, the next radar report came into Paris. The American planes were on a 105 degree course, speed about two hundred knots, altitude three thousand, apparently on the way to Gent.

"What would they attack in Gent?" Heindorff wondered.

"Certainly not the airfield," the pretty aide said again. "Perhaps they are after some troop concentrations or railroad pikes or ammunition dumps."

"The Gent railroad bridge," Heindorff suddenly gasped. "You will notify whatever fighter units that are available in Belgium to intercept these aircraft. They must not destroy that bridge."

"Yes, Herr Hauptman."

The American planes had come about fifty miles into Belgium when a staffel of 109s, fifteen planes, zoomed off from the small German airbase at Obier in Belgium. However, Col. Howard Nichols, leading his 401st Squadron, saw the enemy fighters and he called his pilots.

"Bandits ahead! We'll attack in pairs; in pairs!"

A moment later, the P-38s zoomed away from the P-47 fighter bombers and climbed high to take on the 109s. Again, the German fighter pilots appeared willing and aggressive, but they could not break through the American fighter screen. Nichols and his pilots kept the German planes at bay, diving, streaking, climbing and speeding through the dreary skies over Belgium. ME 109s and P-38s dove in and out of the low overcast, battling each other over and under the clouds. The whine of screaming engines, the chatter of machine guns, and the thump of shell fire echoed through the gloomy morning.

The dogfight north of Gent lasted about fifteen minutes with the Americans downing five of the German planes and losing four Lightnings of their own. The Americans also suffered damage to three more P-38s, while the Germans sustained damage to four Messerschmidts. The heavy dogfight had been a standoff but the American fighter pilots had kept the interceptors away from the P-47s now approaching the Gent railroad bridge.

"Drop to deck level," Col. Gilbert Myers cried into his radio. "Hit them in pairs, but stay at least thirty seconds apart."

The Gent railroad bridge, four spans, crossed the Muesse River on the main railroad line through Belgium and into northwest France. The pike then ran into Lille, whose bridge was also a target this morning, and then the line continued on southwest to Le Havre. The destruction of these two bridges would stop any heavy rail traffic from reaching the Normandy coastal area out of the northeast.

As Myers and the first two P-47s of his group swooped toward the bridge, heavy AA fire spewed up at the streaking Thunderbolts. Two eighty-eight-mm shells hit one of the P-47s squarely and blew apart the American fighter bomber. However, Myers continued on and released his two five hundred-pounders almost on top of the bridge. One bomb hit blasted away part of the second span and loosened the riveted trestle.

After the next two P-47s made their runs, Capt. Bob Johnson in *Little Bill* and Capt. Walt Mahorin in *Sally of Atlanta* zoomed toward the bridge side by side. Heavy ack-ack fire burst about the aircraft, but the two American pilots came on relentlessly. They unleashed their bombs on the same span, already damaged and weakened by the earlier

P-47 bomb hits. Of their four bombs, three of the noball five hundred-pounders slammed into the bridge. *Little Bill* and *Sally of Atlanta* arced safely away before the three explosions shuddered the span loose and dropped it into the Muesse River.

"One down, Bobby," Captain Mahorin said to Captain Johnson over the radio.

"We got her," Johnson answered.

For the next fifteen minutes the other forty-two P-47s of the 368th Panzer Buster Group roared into the Gent railroad bridge in pairs. The bridge suffered at least twenty-six more hits, with each succeding explosion chopping away parts of the spans, trestles, piers and girders. The continued German AA fire knocked down four more P-47s and damaged three other Thunderbolts. However, by the time the three squadrons of fighter-bombers had completed their runs, three of the spans had collapsed into the river.

"Good job, boys, good job," Myers cried into his radio.

Soon, the P-47s and their P-38 escorts turned sharply away and started back to England.

While the 368th Fighter Bomber Group was plastering the Gent railroad bridge in Belgium, the P-47s of the 366th Group and 365th Group were flying southeast. When the Thunderbolts had come halfway across the English Channel, thirty-two more P-38s from the 370th Fighter Group rendezvoused with the P-47s.

"This is Monitor II, Monitor II," Maj. Seth

McKee cried into his radio. "We'll be taking Blackbird aircraft all the way to target 381 and Monitor III will be taking Redbreast aircraft all the way to Target 382."

"We read you, Monitor," Col. Norman Holt answered.

Soon, the P-38s from the 370th Group's 402nd Squadron jelled around the P-47s of the 366th Fighter Bomber Group, while the P-38s of the 485th Squadron closed around the trailing P-47 diamonds of the 365th Fighter Bomber Group. Then, flying at three thousand feet, the 128 aircraft continued southeast toward the French coast. Fifteen minutes later, the American planes crossed into France just north of Dieppe. Once again, radar teams in northwest France sent reports to Luftflotte 3 in Paris.

By now, Capt. Peter Heindorff and his aide, Cpl. Heidi Schroeder, were totally flustered from tracking the array of U.S. air units that had already come over the continent: the 671st and 670th Squadrons of the 416th Group that were flying to the Limidan marshalling yards, the 668th and the 669th Squadrons of the same A-20 group flying after the Lesnil marshalling yards, the 573rd and 572nd B-26 Squadrons of the 391st Group heading for the Cormeilles Bridge, the 575th and 574th Squadrons of this same medium bomber group going to the Verdun Bridge, and the most recent P-47s of the 368th Group that had gone to Gent.

The Luftflotte 3 tracking officer would need

to alert still more German interceptor units.

"We do not know where these new interlopers are going, Herr Hauptman," Corporal Schroeder said.

"We will know soon enough," Heindorff answered.

And indeed, ten minutes later a visual sighting came from an early warning post at Argentan. The American P-47 unit had just passed north of the German air base on a southeast by easterly course. Heindorff checked his table map carefully and then scowled. "These fighter bombers are apparently going to some target in central France, but where?" He ordered his aide to call Col. Erich Rudorffer of JG 54 who was responsible for interception in that area.

"We will mount fighters at once," the JG 54 operations officer said.

Within five minutes, Colonel Rudorffer got off thirty six FW 190s from his JG 54 Green Hearts. The colonel himself led eighteen fighters from his I Gruppen; Maj. Franz Eisenach led the other eighteen fighters from the III Gruppen. The JG 54 commander left to alert Maj. Horst Admeit of II Gruppen.

"You will remain close to your radio for any new instructions from Paris," Rudorffer told Admeit. "I have no doubt that more American aircraft will also come into France this morning, despite the weather. You will follow any instructions from the tracking station in Luftflotte 3 headquarters as to where to make any more interceptions."

"Yes, Herr Kommando," Adameit answered.

Meanwhile, the mass of P-47 fighter bombers from the 366th Group droned on for another fifteen minutes, passing north of the Argentan air base. Then Col. Norman Holt of this group cried into his radio phone, "OK, all Blackbird aircraft will alter course to 130 degrees and head for target 381. Redbreast aircraft will remain on course to target 382. Monitor II will accompany Blackbird to 381 and Monitor III will accompany Redbreast to 382."

"We read you, Colonel," Lance Call of the 365th Fighter Bomber Group said.

"We'll hang alongside both Blackbird and Redbreast," Maj. Seth McKee of the 370th Fighter Group said.

Then, while the 365th Fighter Bomber Group's P-47s continued on their 105 degree course, the Thunderbolts of the 366th Group, under Colonel Holt, turned slightly south. They headed for the bridge at Le Fitte, while the Hellhawks of the 365th Group, under Col. Lance Hall, headed for the bridge at Vernon. The two U.S. fighter bomber units would reach their targets at about the same time.

The Le Fitte and Vernon bridges were key spans over the railroad line coming out of Nancy. The pike, south of Paris, ran almost directly across France with small yards on the line at St. Denier, Troyes, Montagne and Rennes, and a major yard at Dijon. The line then ran into the Brittany peninsula to its terminal at Brest on the Atlantic coast. The destruction of the Le Fitte and Vernon bridges would put the Nancy-to-Brest railroad route out of business.

As Col. Erich Rudorffer droned westward to intercept the P-47 fighter bombers, he got a call from his JG 54 headquarters. "Kommando, we have received word from Paris that the enemy fighter bombers have divided into two groups. One continues on its 105 degree course and the other has slightly altered course to 130 degrees. It appears they may be flying toward the railroad bridges at Le Fitte and Vernon."

"Yes," Rudorffer answered, "those would be good targets. If the Americans can destroy these bridges, the *Wehrmacht* would have extreme difficulty in moving men and equipment over the Nancy railroad line to the west coast." The JG 54 colonel then called Franz Eisenach. "Major, did you hear the report from our headquarters?"

"Yes, Herr Kommando."

"You will take the fighters of your *gruppen* to intercept the American aircraft that are now on the 130 degree course. I will take the aircraft of I Gruppen to intercept the enemy aircraft that remain on the 105 degree course."

"I will do so, Colonel," Eisenach said.

The two German fighter formations then parted, with Eisenach flying after the 366th Fighter Bomber Group on the way to the Le Fitte Bridge, while Rudorffer droned after the

365th Hellhawk Group that was on its way to the Vernon Bridge. At about 1030 hours, Rudorffer spotted the P-47s and P-38s heading for Le Fitte, while Eisenach spotted the U.S. P-47 fighter bombers and P-38 escorts that were heading for Vernon. Once more aerial clashes took place over France.

"We will come out of the clouds and dive on them," Maj. Franz Eisenach told his pilots. "We can thus surprise them."

But Maj. Seth McKee, leading the P-38s of the 370th Group's 402nd Squadron, had already picked up the oncoming German planes on radar. He had rightly guessed that the *Luftwaffers* would try to come out of the clouds, so he took most of his Lightnings above the overcast.

"Three Flight will remain below with their five planes," McKee said, "while One and Two Flights follow me above the clouds."

Then, as Major Eisenach prepared to dive through the clouds, he got jumped by eleven Lightnings under Major McKee. The German pilots now had no choice but to fight off these escorts before they could attack the P-47 fighter bombers heading for Le Fitte. The dogfight lasted only five minutes during which the Americans sent four FW 190s down in flames. The pilots in their P-47s saw these 190s tumble one after another out of the clouds, smoke trailing behind them. McKee and his pilots also seriously damaged five other German planes from JG 54/III. The battered German air formation never got a chance to dive through the clouds to attack the American fighter bombers.

Major McKee called Col. Norman Holt. "Colonel, get on with your mission. You won't have any problems."

'We appreciate that, Monitor II," Holt answered. As the pilots of the 366th Group approached the Le Fitte Bridge looming ahead of them, Holt radioed his pilots. "Okay, in pairs; in pairs! And stay at least thirty seconds apart."

Holt, in the lead P-47, came down to deck level with his wingman. They flew to within an astonishing twenty-five yards of the bridge before releasing four five hundred-pound delayed-fuse bombs. The two pilots then arced safely away before three of the four bombs struck the right pier on the right bank of the river. Numbing explosions chopped away some of the concrete and weakened the piers.

Six planes later, Capt. Zell Smith and his wingman zoomed after the same bridge and unloaded four bombs. Every one struck the battered span and ripped out the last bolts that still held the span in place. The span shuddered and collapsed into the river with a tremendous splash. The pier that held the span also crumbled and chunks of concrete fell into the river.

"One down and two to go," Captain Smith cried into his radio.

"The other two will be down for sure before all our guys make their runs," the wingman answered.

True enough. From the 391st Squadron, sixteen planes roared toward the bridge, in pairs and at thirty-second intervals. They aimed at the center span with excellent accuracy. The first pair of P-47s from this squadron walloped the span with three hits out of four bombs dropped. Succeeding pairs of 391st Squadron aircraft also scored heavily on the center span. When the last two Thunderbolts struck the target, the span broke loose from the pier and plopped into the river.

And still the P-47s came on. Pair after pair of 366th Group P-47s continued to zoom into the bridge at Le Fitte. Heavy AA fire knocked down three of the P-47s of the 366th Group, but the airmen never hesitated. By the time the forty-eight Thunderbolts had made their runs, two of the Le Fitte Bridge spans had totally collapsed into the river, and one end of the third span had also plopped into the water.

"We did a damn good job," Colonel Holt told his 366th Group pilots. "Let's go home."

"Yes, sir, Colonel," Capt. Zell Smith answered.

In the Vernon area of central France, the Germans fared no better. Col. Erich Rudorffer, commander of the JG 54 Green Hearts, was among the best fighter pilots in the *Luftwaffe*. He had been at war for more than six years and his *geschwader* included some excellent pilots. But he flew toward Vernon with only eighteen planes and he would need to deal with sixteen P-38s before he could reach the fighter bombers. Even if he did well against the U.S. 370th Group's 485th Squadron under Capt. John Howell, the American fighter pilots were likely to keep his I Gruppen engaged long enough to stop any 190s from reaching the P-47 fighter bombers.

At 1032 hours, Capt. John Howell took his sixteen Lightnings eastward toward the German FW 190s. He warned his pilots. "Stick with your wingman; stay with him. You have to protect each other."

Col. Erich Rudorffer also spoke to his pilots. "You will maintain close rottan pairs. You must look out for each other." Then: "Horrido!"

Moments later, the rattle of machine gunfire, the boom of the twenty-mm shells, and the screams of aircraft engines echoed in the sky above the dense clouds over Vernon. Rudorffer showed his prowess as a fighter pilot when he got two kills within a couple of minutes. The JG 54 commander downed his first P-38 when he tailed the American fighter and blew away the forked tail with solid twenty-mm shell hits. He got the second Lightning when he chopped apart the left wing of the P-38 with more than five-hundred rounds of machine gunfire.

Other pilots from JG 54/1 downed an additional four American planes, and damaged two more.

Conversely, the American pilots of the 486th Fighter Squadron downed six German fighters with Captain Howell getting two of them himself. Howell caught one FW 190 as the

German plane made a turn, sending withering machine gunfire into the cockpit and killing the German pilot. Howell's second kill came when he struck his victim with solid thirty-seven-mm cannon hits and almost blew the Folkwolfe apart before the tattered plane plunged downward.

Once again, despite the evenness of this most recent aerial donnybrook over France, the Germans failed to reach the fighter bombers. U.S. planes on an Operation Chattanooga Choo Choo mission made their attacks without interference from German fighters. Flak damaged two of the 365th Fighter Bomber Group P-47s, but Col. Lance Call led his Hellhawks on undauntedly. The colonel saw a long freight train going over the Vernon Bridge and he grinned. He would get a bonus kill if he and his pilots knocked down the three spans.

And yet, Call felt a little sorry. The Vernon Bridge was unique in its quaint blocks of stone and ornate concrete facing on the piers. He almost hated to destroy the target. However, the 365th Group colonel realized that any trains crossing this bridge, such as the long freight train now on the span, could bring death and destruction to the American invasion troops at Normandy.

"In pairs; in pairs!" Call cried to his pilots.

"We read you, sir," Capt. Vince Beaudrit answered.

Colonel Call and his wingman went in first, releasing a quartet of five hundred-pound noball bombs. Three hit the trestle and one struck the locomotive, igniting the engine and stopping the train dead on the bridge. Other pairs of P-47s also laced the bridge, wrecking some of the rolling stock and tearing away parts of the trestle and piers. By the time the last two Thunderbolts of the 386th Squadron slammed their bombs into the bridge, one span had collapsed into the river, taking twenty freight cars with it.

Now came the 365th Group's 387th and 388th Squadrons.

As duets of P-47s roared toward the bridge, heavy AA fire destroyed two of the fighter bombers. However, the others came on with determination. Lt. Fred O'Connell scored with both of his bombs, hitting the locomotive again and erupting more fire and smoke. Other P-47s, from the 387th Squadron, struck the middle span with at least thirteen bombs. The span finally broke loose from the shattered pier and fell into the river, taking the locomotive and ten freight cars with it in a tremendous splash.

The P-47s of the Hellhawk group continued to lace the bridge, badly weakening the third span, although they did not drop it into the water. Still, with two spans gone, no trains would cross the bridge. The Nancy-to-Brest railroad line had been cut at two vital areas, Le Fitte and Vernon, stopping any trains from chugging troops and supplies across central France to the Dijon marshalling yards and then into Normandy.

When the 365th Group completed its attack at Vernon, Col. Lance Call cried into his radio phone. "Let's go home. But stay alert. Bandits might pop out of the overcast."

However, Capt. John Howell and his pilots of the 485th Fighter Squadron had successfully dealt with the FW 190s from JG 54. No German planes would hit the P-47 fighter bombers on their way back to England.

CHAPTER ELEVEN

While the Germans tracked the many air groups of American planes that had already crossed the continent, 9th Air Force units continued to pour over the English Channel and the lower North Sea. The B-26s of the 322nd Bomb Group and the 387th Bomb Group had left Great Saling and Stoney Cross at 0800 hours and 0845 hours respectively. These two air groups would attack bridges and marshalling yards to further disrupt the German communications system in France during Operation Chattanooga Choo Choo.

Above the English Channel, in the lead B-26, *Sandra Ann,* of the 322nd Bomb Group, Col. Glen Nye peered from his cockpit at the gloomy scene ahead of him. The clouds remained low and dense, while the steady, monotonous drizzle beaded the windshield of his cabin. The day seemed more conducive to sacking out then flying off on a tactical air mission. The colonel carried a quartet of thousand-pound HE bombs in the bay of his Marauder, powerful explosives that could chop up huge segments of siding or several box cars with a single hit.

Nye's 449th and 450th Squadrons would bombard the marshalling yards at Lille, while his 451st and 452nd Squadrons would hit the Letripad Bridge. The colonel had welcomed the innovation of the noball bomb that enabled his planes to bomb on top of the target. It had improved accuracy tenfold and the 322nd Bomb Group commander was sure that his squadrons on the bridge-busting mission would do well today, just as the squadrons he led to Lille would do a good job against the Lille marshalling yard with powerful HE bombs.

In the diamond formation behind Nye's lead formation was Lt. Alton Ottley in *Mild and Bitter*. He had seemed uneasy this morning when he reached his B-26. His ground crewmen could not determine whether Ottley felt a premonition of disaster or whether he simply did not like flying in this poor weather at such a low altitude. The other members of *Mild and Bitter* had appeared just as sober when they boarded the plane.

Co-pilot Bob Grosskopf had a faraway look in his eyes when he boarded the B-26. Perhaps Grosskopf did not like flying in this weather, either. Bombarder-navigator Sgt. Tom Anderson had not said a word to the ground crew, while turret gunner Sgt. Joe McDonald had only shrugged when the *Mild and Bitter* crew chief wished him luck. Waist gunner Jim Bradford and tail gunner Floyd Sapp had merely brushed past the ground crew personnel, totally ignoring them.

But now, in the low skies over the English Channel, Lieutenant Ottley's B-26 looked no different than the other marauders of his squadron.

Behind the Nye's Annihilators' 449th and 450th Squadron, Lt. Col. Charles Olmstead stared from the cabin of *Pretty Baby,* the lead plane of the 332nd's other two squadrons. Olmstead would break off from the other Annihilator units when they crossed the French coast, because he would fly slightly north-northeast to attack the important railroad bridge at Letripad. This span was on the line that came from the low countries and into France. Without this bridge across the Seine River in northwest France, the Germans could not carry rail traffic to the Atlantic wall defenses on the Normandy coast.

Olmstead, a veteran with twenty-six combat missions, had flown with the 8th Air Force and the old 12th Air Force in the Mediterranean area. He had been among the experienced U.S. air officers who had returned to England to become part of the cardre to help newcomers who had come from the states in January of

1944 to expand the newly organized 9th Tactical Air Force. Olmstead had shown excellent leadership qualities in the several missions he had flown with the 322nd Bomb Group and had earned himself a DFC and two Air Medals.

The lieutenant colonel, the 322nd's deputy commander, had often led the group's 452nd Squadron. He preferred combat duty to administrative paper work. No doubt, Olmstead would be the 322nd's next commander, or he would be commanding some other medium bomber group.

Olmstead's *Pretty Baby* carried a quartet of thousand-pound delayed-fuse bombs in the bays and the Lieutenant colonel looked forward to attacking the Letripad Bridge, certain that he and his fellow B-26 pilots would knock out the spans. He squinted again at the dreariness ahead of him, then picked up his radio phone to call Maj. Hank Newcomer, CO of the 451st Squadron.

"Hank, keep the formation tight. We'll be over the French coast in about ten minutes."

"Where the hell is the escort?" Newcomer asked.

"They're a little late this morning, but you can be sure they'll catch up to us before we cross the Channel."

"Okay, Charlie," Newcomer said.

Co-pilot Lt. Mike Johnson listened to Newcomer's short conversation with Olmstead, but said nothing. The lieutenant looked at the instrument panel: a steady 190-knot speed, a thirty-eight hundred-feet altitude under the dense, low cloud cover, and all pressure normal. In the nose, navigator-bombardier Lt. Don Franklin peered from his blister and studied the water below. He looked at the diamond of planes ahead of him, and then the beading splashes of rain on the plexiglass nose blister of *Dolly*.

In the top turret, Sgt. Mike Whitehurst squinted at the dark, heavy clouds. He did not like the overcast. German fighters could dart suddenly out of these clouds and lace his B-26 before he got a chance to fire back. In the waist, Sgt. Al Aurelio looked first out of the starboard window and then out of the port window to stare at the other B-26s in his four-plane diamond. They hung above the Channel like levitating walruses. In the tail, Sgt. Ralph Wilson squinted through the drizzle at the Marauders behind him. Then, Wilson stared up at the clouds, wondering if he would be ready for any ME 109 or FW 190 fighters that might pop out of the dense overcast.

A few minutes later, a swarm of P-51s emerged from the mist to the northwest and closed swiftly on the droning B-26s. Col. George Bickel had arrived with his four squadrons of fighters, three from his own 354th Fighter Group and the P-38 392nd Squadron from the 367th Fighter Group. When Bickel came within a few miles of the Marauders, he called Colonel Nye.

"This is Spotlight Leader to Mayflower Leader."

"We read you, Spotlight."

"Spotlight I will accompany Mayflower 1 and 2 to Target 188, and Spotlight II will accompany Mayflower 2 and 3 to target 189."

"OK."

Colonel Bickel then called Col. Tom Seymoure of the 387th Bomb Group. "Spotlight Leader to Pallidin Leader."

"You're a little late," the Pathfinder group commander answered.

"Sorry about that," Bickel answered, "but we're with you now. Spotlight III will accompany Pallidin 1 and 2 to target 191 and Brightlight I will accompany Pallidin 3 and 4 to Target 192."

"Roger," Seymoure answered.

Then, Col. Ed Chickering of the 367th Group called Seymoure. "This is Brightlight I. We'll be hanging high over the Pallidin units while Spotlight 3 holds around you." Chickering was leading twenty P-38s of his 392nd Squadron.

Soon, the swarm of fighter planes, sixty from the 354th Group and twenty from the 392nd Squadron, assumed escort positions above and about the lengthy diamonds of B-26s.

In the first quartet of planes from the 387th Bomb Group, Capt. Sam Monk stared at the P-51s alongside of him. He felt more relaxed with the fighters next to him. They had done an excellent job keeping away German interceptors during the attacks on the Edex airfield two days ago. He was confident they would be just as capable today at keeping German fighters from interfering with the Pathfinder attacks on the Hasselt Bridge in Belgium.

On the right wing of the diamond, Capt. Ed James stared from the cabin of his B-26 at the P-51s on the starboard flank of the 556th Squadron. He too welcomed the arrival of the escort. He knew these 9th Air Force fighter pilots were good, and that the P-51 was superior to the 190 and 109.

In the B-26 *Flak Bait* of the 387th Group's 558th Squadron, Maj. Jim Keller craned his neck to look at the forked tailed P-58s of the 392nd Squadron that were above them. He saw only four of them so he rightly assumed that most of the Lightnings were above the clouds to make certain that no bandits dove through the overcast to surprise the droning B-26s.

Flak Bait's co-pilot, Lt. Ed Cook, also stared from the cabin at the other Marauders around him and the P-38s above him. He too felt more at ease with these fighter escorts. In the nose, bombardier-navigator Lt. Tom Clark looked out of his bubble at the P-38s. He fingered the trigger of his single .50-caliber machine gun and hoped that he would need to use it against German fighter planes.

In the top turret, Sgt. Tim Snyder swung his twin .50-caliber machine guns. They moved easily and smoothly. He then glanced at the other planes around him while trying to relax. In the waist, radio gunner Sgt. Tom Davis squinted through the starboard window, peering at the B-26s on the right point of the diamond and at the P-38s above. He looked at the long belts of .50-caliber bullets and knew he'd have plenty of ammunition if he needed to fight off German interceptors.

In the tail of *Flak Bait,* Sgt. George Morse eyed the B-26s behind him and the endless cloud cover above. He did not like this weather, for it necessitated flying and bombing at a relatively low altitude.

Far ahead of the long line of B-26s, Col. George Bickel sat calmly in his lead P-51 of the 354th Fighter Group. Bickel felt confident; he and his pilots had done well against German fighters two days ago. He called Maj. Bob Weldon, leading the 355th Squadron that would accompany the 322nd Group B-26s going to the Letripad railroad bridge. Weldon and seven more of his squadron pilots were flying high cover above the clouds.

"Captain," Bickel said, "any sign of bandits?"

"No, sir."

"We'll be reaching the French coast pretty soon; stay awake."

"We'll keep a sharp watch, sir," Bob Weldon said.

Weldon almost wished that German planes did loom from the east. He had thus far enjoyed excellent success against *Luftwaffe* pilots and he did nor fear any new donnybrooks high above the clouds. The 355th Sqadron CO knew that his Mustang was an awesome machine, a fighter plane that could outdive, outrun and outmaneuver the German 109 and 190. With a sharp pilot at the controls, the P-51 could do anything. Only an experienced, combat-honed German pilot had any chance to compete with the P-51 and, by mid-1944, the Germans had few such pilots left.

Above the clouds and to the rear, Col. Chickering droned his lead P-38 of the 367th Group's 392nd Squadron. He stared ahead for any sign of enemy fighters. His charges, the Marauders of the 387th Group, were below him, under the clouds. Like Weldon of the 354th Group, Chickering also flew above the overcast to make certain that no German planes dove through these clouds to surprise the B-26s. He called Capt. Joe Griffin, who led his squadron's 2nd Flight. "Any sign of bandits?"

"No, sir," Griffin answered.

Under the clouds, Maj. Jim Howard of the 354th Group's 356th Squadron stared from the cockpit of his P-51 at the hanging B-26s of the 387th Bomb Group. The Marauders were in tight formation so they'd have plenty of firepower against any Luftwaffe planes that broke through the gantlet of American fighters. He picked up his radio and called Lt. Glen Eggleston, whose P-51 hung on the starboard side of the B-26 diamond.

"Any bandits?"

"No, sir, Major, not a thing," Eggleston answered.

"Do you have a couple of scouts out?"

"One plane is up ahead and another is out about five miles at three o'clock," the lieutenant answered.

"Good," Howard said. "Stay alert."

"Yes, sir."

Still again, German radar teams on the west coast of France picked up a huge formation of American planes; more B-26s, P-51s and P-38s. Once more, reports went to Paris and once more Capt. Peter Heindorff and his aide, Cpl. Heidi Schroeder, drew lines on the huge table map. And, still again, Heindorff needed to wait before he could determine the probable course of this latest incursion into the continent.

As soon as the U.S. planes crossed the French coast, the B-26s broke off into four separate directions. The 449th and 450th Squadrons of the 322nd Group under Col. Glen Nye stayed on their current course to hit the Lille marshaling yards, only ten minutes ahead of them. The 322nd's 451st and 452nd Squadrons under Lt. Col. Charles Olmstead veered almost straight south by slightly southeast to attack the railroad bridge at Letripad. The destruction of this bridge would thwart German attempts to send trains northward along the west coast from the south of France.

Col. Tom Seymoure veered northeastward with the B-26s of his 387th Group's 556th and 557th Squadrons to hit the Hasselt Bridge in Belgium, while Maj. Jim Keller led the Marauders of the Pathfinders' 558th and 559th

Squadrons on a slightly eastward course toward the bridge at Louvain. This bridge was an important link on the Paris-to-Cherbourg rail line that ran off spur lines at Dijon and then toward the Normandy ports.

The four fighter squadrons also broke off. Col. Howard Nichols took his 354th Group's 353rd Squadron to accompany the B-26s heading for Lille, whle his 355th Squadron under Maj. Bob Weldon accompanied the B-26s heading for the Letripad Bridge. Maj. Jim Howard, leading the 356th Squadron of the 354th Fighter Group, droned northeast alongside the Marauders that were heading into Belgium to destroy the Hasselt railroad bridge, and the P-38s of the 367th Group under Col. Ed Chickering zoomed on toward Louvain with the B-26s of the 387th Group's 558th and 559th Squadrons under Maj. Jim Keller.

The Germans, of course, soon reacted to these American aerial formations. Most of the efforts against these American planes fell to Col. Joseph "Pips" Priller and the staffels of his JG 26 that were based in northwest France. At about 0915 hours, he got reports from Capt. Peter Heindorff in Paris.

"Herr Priller, it appears that these latest American air formations are after targets in your sector. One of the enemy formations is apparently flying toward a target in southwest Belgium. A second *gruppen* of enemy bombers is flying on a course southeast, perhaps to attack a bridge along the rail line from the south of France. The other two enemy bomber units are flying toward some potential targets in northwest France, perhaps around Lille."

"They have already destroyed our airfield at Lille-Nord," Priller answered somewhat bitterly.

"Then perhaps they have singled out other targets in your area," Heindorff answered, "possibly the Lille railroad bridge over the Seine River."

"We will do what we can," Priller answered.

However, when Pips Priller took inventory of his resources he counted only sixty combat-ready fighter planes in his Schlagetor *geschwader*. Thus, he could only mount staffels of ten to fifteen planes. Still, the JG 26 commander did what he could. He himself led twenty-four planes from his I Gruppen, two staffels of twelve planes each, to intercept the American bombers heading for Lille and Letripad. He sent Maj. Herman Graf with fifteen planes from the II Gruppen to intercept the bombers heading for the southwest Belgium, and he sent southward Capt. Emil Lang of the III Gruppen with fourteen planes to attack the fourth B-26 formation. But fifty-three FW 190s would not be enough to break through eighty American fighters to get to the American bombers.

The first dogfight came over Lille, when Priller clashed with the twenty P-51s of the 354th Group's 353rd Squadron under Col. George Bickel. The Germans met a solid wall, as the American pilots, in pairs, attacked the German 190s. Diving, whining planes screamed above the clouds while they unleashed chattering machine gunfire and thumping shells. The crews aboard the B-26s below the overcast heard the heavy dogfight and some of the U.S. airmen grew tense, waiting for German planes to come out of the clouds in blistering attacks.

But no FW 190s emerged from above. Bickel and his pilots quickly shot down six of the JG 26 planes to a loss of two P-51s. Bickel himself got a German fighter when he caught the FW with bursts of machine gunfire that sent the 190 spiralling to earth in flames. Priller, meanwhile, got a P-51 when he chopped off the tail with two accurate shell hits. Still, the Schlagetor staffel was shattered and Priller had no choice but to run off with his surviving planes.

Below the clouds, Col. Glen Nye soon reached the Lille marshalling yard. The diamonds of B-26s droned over the rail center and unleashed their thousand-pound HEs that struck the sidings, rolling stock, repair ships and locomotives with devastating effectiveness. The B-26s from Nye's Annihilators destroyed or damaged more than fifty box cars and gondolas, four locomotives and four buildings. The Marauders also tore up a square mile of siding. No trains would come out of this yard for some time.

However, the group suffered one loss from anti-aircraft fire when two eighty-eight-mm shells slammed into *Mild and Bitter* and exploded to ignite fires throughout the plane. The explosions killed all aboard: Lt. Alton Ottley, co-pilot Bob Grosskopf, navigator-bombardier Sgt. Tom Anderson, turret gunner Joe McDonald, waist gunner Jim Bradford, and tail gunner Floyd Sapp. The flaming B-26 crashed into a field and then disintegrated form a secondary explosion.

Only four miles to the northeast, Lieutenant Colonel Olmstead led the Annihilators' 452nd and 451st Squadrons toward the Letripad Bridge. "OK, in pairs; and stay at least thirty seconds apart."

"We understand, Colonel," Maj. Hank Newcomer said.

Soon, pair after pair of B-26 medium bombers zoomed at low level toward the bridge. Heavy AA fire downed two of the planes, but the Marauders continued on, lacing the three spans, the trestles, girders and piers with delayed-fuse thousand-pound bombs. *Dolly* nagivator-bombardier Lt. Don Franklin hit the second span squarely with three of his four bombs, breaking it loose from the pier.

"Good job, Lieutenant," Major Newcomer said.

"Yes, sir," Franklin answered with a grin.

As *Dolly* banked away, tail gunner Ralph Wilson and turret gunner Mike Whitehurst saw following B-26s blast the bridge until the second span plopped into the Seine.

Meanwhile, above the clouds, twenty P-51s under Maj. Bob Weldon successfully thwarted twelve FW 190s. Within a few minutes, Weldon and his pilots, from the 354th Group's 355th Squadron, knocked down four of the German fighter planes and damaged three more Folkwolfes, suffering not a single loss to themselves. Weldon himself got two planes. First he struck a 190 with a solid hit that ignited the fuel tank, then he literally chopped off an FW's left wing with machine gunfire. The 190 flipped over and plunged to earth.

In southwest Belgium, Maj. Herman Graf of JG 26/III had no more success than did the FW 190s of the Schlagetor's I Gruppen. When Graf and his fellow pilots roared into the P-51s of the 354th Squadron, Maj. Jim Howard and his fellow American airmen found themselves in a heavy dogfight. Graf displayed uncanny ability and the combat-wise German fighter pilot downed two P-51s, while Lt. Walter Schuck downed a pair of Mustangs. In fact, the Germans shot down six of the American Mustangs to a loss of four FW 190s.

"Those bastards are good, damn good," Howard cried into his radio. "Stay alert! Stick with your wingman."

Howard himself got his ninth and tenth kills. He blew apart one FW 190 with shattering shell fire and set aflame a second with chattering machine gunfire. Still, Graff and four more of his FW 190 pilots broke through the clouds and took after the B-26s heading for the Hasselt bridge. But by the time the JG 26 *gruppen* leader caught up to the B-26s, the Marauders had made the runs.

Col. Tom Seymoure and his 387th Group bomber crews from the 556th and 557th Squadrons made accurate hits on the Hasselt spans with delayed-fuse thousand-pound bombs. By the time the twenty-four Marauders left target, they had lost one medium bomber of AA fire, but they had dropped two spans of the Hasselt Bridge into the Muesse River. No trains would cross this bridge from the low countries. The Americans had enjoyed still another success in Operation Chattanooga Choo Choo.

But as the B-26s turned for home, the five German FW 190s caught up to them. While B-26 gunners downed two of the German planes, both Major Graf and Lieutenant Schuck downed Marauders to get their third kills each in this one engagement.

Meanwhile, Maj. Jim Keller droned towards Louvain and the bridge on the Paris-to-Cherbourg railroad line. Keller reached his target at 0950 hours. The B-26s ran into brutal AA fire that downed one Marauder and damaged two more. Still, Keller grimly led *Flak Bait* and a companion B-26 toward the bridge.

"Make the hits count," Keller cried to his bombardier-navigator Lt. Tom Clark.

"I'll make sure, sir," Clark answered.

And sure he was. The *Flak Bait* bombardier unleashed his delayed-fuse bombs accurately with all four thousand-pounders hitting the middle span, loosening it from the piling. More

B-26s followed to hit the bridge just as accurately. Sixty percent of the bombs from the two Pathfinder squadrons scored solidly. By the time the pairs of medium bombers left the area, they had dropped one span into the Muesse River and left a second span hanging over the river. No trains would cross this bridge from Nancy to reach the Normandy beaches.

High above the clouds, over Louvain, Col. Ed Chickering of the 367th Group's 392nd Squadron took on the last swarm of interceptors from JG 26. The American P-38 pilots macerated these final fourteen planes from the Schlagetor *geschwader,* knocking down seven of the FW 190s under Capt. Emil Lang. The Americans lost four P-38s. Surviving German pilots simply flew off to avoid a similar fate. None of the *Luftwaffers* got below the clouds to attack the B-26s.

By 1015 hours on this gloomy 4 June day, the Germans had suffered quite badly. These latest American air units from the Ninth Air Force had destroyed three vital railroad bridges and torn up an important railroad yard.

Before the day ended, other B-26 medium bomber, A-20 light bomber and P-47 fighter bomber groups ripped up six more marshalling yards in France and destroyed sixteen more bridges. The Americans had lost fifty-two planes by the end of the day, but they had shot down eighty-three German fighter planes, sixty-two by American fighter pilots and eighteen by A-20 and B-26 gunners. The Americans could afford these losses, however tragic, but for Luftflotte 3, eighty-three downed fighter planes was a devastating blow in view of the limited number of German aircraft in Western Europe.

CHAPTER TWELVE

By the time darkness had descended over the British Isles and Western Europe on this 4 June day, the rain had stopped, although dense clouds still covered the skies. In England, elation reigned among Ninth Air Force flyers, while in France, gloom again prevailed among the Luftflotte 3 airmen. In Paris, the Germans now understood the significance of the Ninth Air Force raids on 2 June against the airfields, and the attacks on the bridges, marshalling yards and road junctions on this 4 June. The air assaults were obvious preludes to an Allied invasion.

Adm. Wilhelm Canaris, chief of German intelligence, had finally learned the almost certain date of the Allied landings on the continent. Canaris had infiltrated agents into the French resistance groups and these spies had monitored coded messages between the Allies and the French underground. The agents had concluded that an Allied landing would come within forty-eight hours. The German infiltrators had verified the imminent invasion date when they learned that the lyrics to the French song "Chanson d'Atomne," the Song of Autumn, was the key for the invasion date—on 5, 6 or 7 June 1944.

The long song of the Violins of Autumn Wound my heart with a monotonous languor.

When the Allied radio played the song on the evening of 4 June with the coded number six, Admiral Canaris knew for sure that the invasion was coming on the morning of 6 June. However, none of his agents could learn for certain where the landings would come, for SHAEF headquarters command would not give this information to even their most trusted French partisans. Canaris only knew that the landings would come somewhere between Calais and Cherbourg, a 250-mile stretch of coastline in northwest France.

When Canaris reported this information to OKW headquarters in Berlin, the CinC of the German Armed Forces, Gen. Wilhelm Kietel, immediately told Hilter, who insisted on a meeting on the very night of 4 June. The Fuhrer ordered to the meeting Field Marshal von Rundstedt, CinC of the Armies of the West; Field Marshal Hugo Sperrle of Luftflotte 3;

production chief Albert Speer, *Luftwaffe* Deputy Chief-of-Staff, Field Marshal Erhard Milch; the *Luftwaffe* CinC, Reichmarshal Herman Goering; and Gen. Franz Halder, *Wehemacht* army chief-of-staff.

Most of these high-ranking officers were already in Berlin so they had only to drive to the chancellory. However, Field Marshal von Rundstedt and Field Marshal Sperrle needed to fly to the Reich capital from Paris in a fast transport. Gen. Franz Halder, who had been inspecting *Wehrmacht* troops in Holland, also flew to Berlin.

At 2100 hours, the meeting got underway.

Adolf Hitler wore his usual sober look and his dark eyes darted about the room, focusing first on one man and then on another. His face appeared pale and drawn and his small frame seemed bent and weak. His hands shook, as usual, from his palsy condition. Hitler was no longer the healthy man he had been only a short time ago. The series of harsh German defeats on all fronts during the past year and the numbing Allied bombing attacks throughout Germany had sapped his strength.

Now, although the Fuhrer had known for months that the Allies would attempt an invasion in northwest France, the report of an imminent landing had depressed him even further.

Hitler tapped his bent fingers on the desk impatiently, leaving the officers of the meeting quite nervous. They would have no easy answer for their Nazi leader because Germany had not the manpower, arms or planes to cope with the awesome Allied strength. And now, with the heavy coordinated air attacks by the RAF and Ninth Air Force on 2 June and 4 June, the Germans had also seen their air arm in western Europe badly depleted and their transportation system almost put out of commission.

"The reports are horrible, horrible," Hitler finally spoke as he gestured angrily, "and now we have irrefutable evidence that the enemy will attempt an invasion within two days. How could you allow this to happen?"

No one answered.

Hitler shuttled his glance among Goering, Milch and Sperrle. "I gave you special instructions on how you should deal with the aerial invaders, but as usual, you failed to carry out my orders. If you did as I suggested, one antiaircraft shell would have destroyed one enemy bomber and one fighter plane would have destroyed one enemy aircraft. But your airmen and gunners failed again. Now our airfields in France have been seriously damaged and many important rail and highway bridges have been destroyed. How are we to slay the enemy soldiers on the beaches without the *Luftwaffe?* Or how can we move troops to the front without highway and railroad bridges?"

"The airmen did their best," Field Marshal Sperrle said.

Hitler scowled at the Luftflotte 3 CinC. "The *Luftwaffe* failed," he said sharply. "But—" he gestured again—"we cannot dwell on these failures. We must determine how to deal with these enemy invaders."

"We have taken certain steps, Mein Fuhrer," von Runsstedt said. "We have reinforced the garrisons in the Calais area and we have sent the 709th Infantry Division to the Cotentin peninsula. It is almost certain that the enemy will attempt to make his landing in Calais or Cherbourg where he can use the Normandy port facilities."

"Field Marshal Rommel, who commands the Atlantic wall defenses, believes the enemy will land on the Normandy beaches somewhere between Le Havre and St. Mere," Hitler said. "Is it not his opinion that this stretch of flat beaches would be quite suitable for such landing?"

"I must disagree," von Rundstedt said. "This is the widest part of the English Channel and it is the area with the best coastal defenses. Every conceivable type of trap and mine has been laid along these beaches. I must tell you that the French partisans in the underground have been active in this area and they are well aware of these defenses. No doubt, the traitors have relayed this information to England. The Armies of the West staff doubt very much that the enemy would try his landings here."

"And I must tell you, Herr Field Marshal, that I have faith in Rommel," Hitler said. "He has exceptional ability and he has an uncanny foresight. However, I will not attempt to interfere with your plans to defend northwest France, but I would urge you to send at least one motorized infantry division and a Panzer division to reinforce the Normandy sector."

"Yes, Mein Fuhrer," von Rundstedt said.

Hitler now looked at Goering. "After these disastrous air strikes in France, what can the *Luftwaffe* do to stop this impending Allied invasion?"

Goering turned to Field Marshal Milch and to Field Marshal Sperrle. If there was more disheartening news for the Fuhrer, the *Luftwaffe* CinC preferred that his underlings take the blunt of Hitler's wrath. "Herr Milch?"

The deputy *Luftwaffe Kommando* referred to some papers in his hand and then spoke. "I regret to say, Mein Fuhrer, that the enemy air attacks on the French airfields have caused considerable damage and we will need time to make necessary repairs."

"Time!" Hitler barked. "With the expected invasion only two days away?"

"Some of the air bases are still in operating condition," Field Marshal Sperrle now spoke, "and we have sent aircraft to these bases. Unfortunately, we do not have many aircraft left in Luftflotte 3 because we lost so many during these massive attacks by the Allied tactical air units."

"How many aircraft do you have?" Hitler asked.

Sperrle looked at a sheet in his hand and then rubbed the jowls of his round face. "Between three hundred and four hundred."

"Between three hundred and four hundred?" Hitler scowled again. "You are the *Kommando* of Luftflotte 3 and you do not know the exact number of aircraft in your command?"

"All the reports are not yet in," Sperrle said.

"They should have been in your headquarters within an hour after the last enemy air attack in France and the low countries."

"Yes, Mein Fuhrer," Sperrle said. "I will make certain that we have an exact count of available combat-ready aircraft."

"In any event," Hitler said, "three hundred or four hundred aircraft is not enough to stop an invasion." He looked at Milch. "You will send another thousand bombers with fresh crews to the western front at once. Half of these bombers will destroy the debarkation ports on the English Channel coast and the other half will destroy the Allied ships that attempt to cross the Channel. Is that understood?"

Milch and Sperrle should have been absolutely stunned by this insane order, but they had come to realize the distorted thinking of their Fuhrer, who simply refused to believe facts. The two *Luftwaffe* leaders knew that even if they cleared out every airfield in Europe they could not find a thousand available bombers, much less the crews to fly them.

These German officers knew the exact locations of the Allied rallying ports on the English coast, but the enemy's air forces were so strong that no German air formation had been able to penetrate the solid wall of British and American aircraft that protected these sites. Any German bombers trying to attack these debarkation points on the British Isles would drop like flies in the English Channel from the thousands of Allied fighter planes that could rise to intercept them.

Indeed, by mid-1944, the Allies held no fear of exposed bases because they knew the German *Luftwaffe* could do little about it.

Now, here in the chancellory, the *Luftwaffe* commanders could only patronize their Nazi leader. "We will do what we can. Mein Fuhrer," Milch responded to Hitler's ridiculous suggestion.

Hitler nodded and then turned to General Kietel. "In view of the heavy damage to the transportation system in France, what steps can be taken to see that our armored and infantry units can still reach an invasion site and drive the enemy back into the sea?"

General Kietel looked at a sheet in his hand, glanced at von Rundstedt, and then looked at the Nazi dictator. "Unfortunately, the main railroad lines and principal highways through the low countries and into northwest France are out of commission because of the bridge losses at Hasselt, Gent and other areas along the routes. However, we still have the undamaged marshalling yard at Dijon along the Nancy-to-Brest railroad line and the Meziere marshalling yard on the Paris-to-Cherbourg line. We will have intact bridges at Juvisey and Elbeuf, and at several other trunk line points over which we can detour troops and supply trains along the Nancy-to-Brest line. We also have the Orival and Denain Bridges over which we can detour trains along the Paris-to-Cherbourg route."

Hitler looked at von Rundstedt. "You will move as many troops and supplies as you can to the Normandy areas as soon as possible. They must be in a mobile position to quickly reinforce Marshal Rommel's units wherever needed, whether at Calais, the Cotentin peninsula, the Normandy beaches or whatever."

"We will assemble such units tomorrow and move them during the dark hours to avoid enemy air attacks," von Rundstedt said.

"There must be no more failures," Hitler barked.

"No, Mein Fuhrer," the Armies of the West CinC answered.

Hitler now looked at Albert Speer. "You must amass all the ammunition, supplies and fuel that you can to bolster our combat forces in France. Such provisions will be sent to all units that face the enemy invasion forces."

"Yes, Mein Fuhrer."

Hitler looked next at General Kietel. "What arrangements have you made to rush new reinforcements into France."

"We have prepared four more armored divisions, ten infantry divisions and several artillery regiments," Kietel answered. "General Halder has assured us that several more divisions in Holland are also prepared to move promptly into France."

"And how will they get to the Normandy coast with the main railroad artery in the low countries out of commission?" the Nazi leader huffed.

The German Armed Forces CinC hesitated for a moment but then spoke. "We will move them south and then send them over the detour route between Paris and Cherbourg."

Hitler nodded.

"Be assured, Mein Fuhrer," Kietel continued, "we will do whatever is necessary to repel this Allied invasion. If we cannot destroy them in the Channel, we will destroy them on the shoreline. The defenses at the Atlantic wall are strong and Field Marshal Rommel is a capable commander. Even if some of the enemy troops break out from the beaches and come inland, our reserves will deal with them."

Hitler did not even react to Kietel's glowing promises. In fact, the Fuhrer's dark eyes reflected a slight hint of disgust and resignation. Perhaps a measure of sanity had returned to Adolf Hitler's mind and he did not really believe they could stop any Allied invasion. Perhaps he even realized that his suggestions, orders and demands were impossible to carry out, that his Anglo-Saxon enemies would soon begin a sweep across France. He calmed and spoke to his military leaders in a relatively quiet tone.

"I implore all of you to do whatever is necessary to repel these invaders. If they are thrown back into the sea, they will surely sue for peace."

"Yes, Mein Fuhrer," General Kietel said.

If the German reconnaissance plane observers had studied the Allied invasion preparation with the accumulation of massive arms and men, the Germans had probably underestimated the true strength of the Allies. Among the debarkation ports at Cornwall, Plymouth, Portland, Portsmouth, Shoreham and Kent were 14,500 tons of ammunition, food, medicine, clothing, tents, field telephones, signal corps equipment and a multitude of other items. Also in these ports were 14,000 motor vehicles that included 4,000 tanks of all types and more than 2,000 pieces of mobile artillery, And finally, stocked at the ports were more than 5,000 pieces of stationary artillery, from 37-mm to 205-mm cannons.

Among the Allied combat troops were three airborne divisions, two American and one British, two thousand planes would drop these paratroopers behind the enemy's Atlantic wall defenses to seize and hold key bridges, crossroads and railroad points. Of course, the Operation Chattanooga Choo Choo aerial assaults had made the job easier for these airborne troops.

Besides paratroopers, one hundred seven

thousand ground troops, including combat and service forces, would land on the Normandy beaches on D-day, D-day plus one, and D-day plus two. Fifty-three hundred ships, from huge twenty thousand-ton transports to small LCIs, would steam or chug across the Channel to deposit these one hundred seven thousand men and nearly fifteen thousand tons of supplies on the beaches. Also among this largest flotilla of vessels ever assembled in the history of warfare were auxiliary and service ships that would carry movable port structures, portable docks and flexible pipes that would be used to turn a flat beach area into a major port. The improvised harbor construction would make the artificial port as good or better than the port facilities at Cherbourg or Calais.

The Allied air force headquarters had sent out FO orders to almost every combat unit based in England. Some ten thousand fighters, light bombers, medium bombers and heavy bombers from the U.S. Air Force and Royal Air Force would ensure aerial support for the ground troop invaders. And, finally, more than two thousand warships—battleships, cruisers and destroyers—would begin a pre-invasion bombardment at about 0300 hours on 6 June and continue such assaults until dawn. The American and British naval units expected to lob more than ten thousand tons of shells into Germany's Normandy defenses. During the same wee morning hours, thirteen hundred

RAF heavy bombers would drop five thousand tons of bombs along the Atlantic wall from the Seine River delta to Cherbourg to soften German resistance even more.

On the evening of the 4 June, Gen. Dwight Eisenhower drew up last-minute instructions with his SHAEF staff at his headquarters in London. Operation Overlord would be the biggest amphibious operation in the history of warfare, an operation that might never be duplicated or surpassed in size and scope. The Allies needed a complete in-depth plan that did not neglect even the smallest combat unit. Otherwise, serious confusion could arise. Even the men of the lowest infantry squad, airmen of the smallest air flight, or a mere three man LCI crew needed to know their infinitesimal role in this huge operation.

"There is one problem, sir," chief-of-staff Gen. Walter Smith told General Eisenhower. "The meteorologists have made a dramatic change in their predictions. They now say the weather on 6 June is expected to be quite unfavorable, with high winds and churning swells in the Channel. That might be rough on the small landing craft and a little hard on the other ships."

"It's too late to postpone the operation," Eisenhower answered. "Every man is set to go, and I suspect the Germans also know we'll be coming across the Channel on 6 June. We can't give them a single hour to improve their

Atlantic wall defenses or to bring in reinforcements."

"The tactical air units have done a good job in disrupting communications," General Smith said.

"I know," the SHAEF commander said, "but they couldn't destroy everything. The Germans can still move at least some troops and supplies. We want to be well inland from the enemy's shoreline defenses before such reinforcements reach western France."

"General Spaatz intends to send out his tactical bombers again tomorrow to finish off anything they didn't knock out today."

Gen. Dwight Eisenhower nodded.

And, in fact, at USSTAF's Bushy Park headquarters, Gen. Carl Spaatz, Ninth Air Force CinC Gen. Lewis Brereton, and thirty-two group commanders were holding a conference of their own. Spaatz again referred to a huge map of France.

"You and your airmen did one hell of a job today," he told the Ninth Air Force officers. "The rail lines from the low countries are out; nothing can move over those pikes for quite a while, so the Germans can't bring any troops or materiel to Normandy from the northwest. You've also done a good job of cutting the Paris-to-Cherbourg line and the Nancy-to-Brest line with the destruction of bridges over the rivers in northern and central France. But—" Spaatz gestured—"we've studied the rail system quite carefully and we need to knock out a lot more bridges and several more marshalling yards."

"Take a look at these two lines," General Brereton said to his group commanders as he referred to the map. "The green line represents the Paris-to-Cherbourg railroad route and the yellow line represents the Nancy-to-Brest route. Please note these secondary spurs we've drawn on the map. The Germans could still run trains over these trunk lines if they use these detour routes."

Brereton tapped the map and then continued. "We've got to destroy quite a few more bridges, including the Orival Bridge here, the Denan Bridge here, the Juvisey Bridge in eastern France, and the Elbeuf Bridge, also in eastern France. We also need to hit several more marshalling yards, especially the Dijon and Meziere yards, here and here." He tapped the map again.

"Unfortunately, we can expect the same dreary weather tomorrow as you've had today," General Spaatz said, "but you'll need to fly out anyway. I'd like to see a full group of planes attack each target to make certain we knock them out."

Brereton looked at the stack of papers in his hand and then spoke again. "Let me start with the first sheet. I'm assigning the 365th Fighter Bomber Group to the Orival Bridge, the 366th Fighter Bomber Group to attack the Denan

Bridge, and the 368th Fighter Bomber Group to hit the Meziere marshalling yard. The fighter squadrons of the 370th Group will furnish escort. The 322nd Bomb Group will attack the Juvisey Bridge, the 387th Group will hit the Elbeuf Bridge with their B-26s, and the 391st Group will bomb the Dijon marshalling yard with their medium bombers. Fighter planes from the 354th Fighter Group will furnish escorts for these three medium bomber units."

Gen. Lewis Brereton then referred to more sheets on the table and explained the targets for the other B-26 medium bomber, A-20 light bomber, and P-47 fighter bomber groups of the Ninth Air Force. These other tactical air units would attack six more railroad bridges, five more marshalling yards, several more German air bases, and four highway bridges. When Brereton finished, he paused and then said, "My aides will pass out the FOs to the various group commanders so you'll all know your exact target."

The Ninth Air Force would again send out nearly fifteen hundred bombers, fighter bombers and fighters on mission tomorrow, 5 June. Besides all these communications targets, some Ninth Air Force units would even hit radar stations and suspected German encampments. The Second Tactical Air Force of the RAF would sent out swarms of planes to attack targets in Belgium and Holland, mostly road junctions and highway bridges, to make certain the Germans could not send tanks and motorized columns over the major highway arteries in the low countries.

By late evening, ground crews at more than sixty U.S. Ninth Air Force and RAF Second Air force bases in England were loading bombs in hundreds of American B-26s, A-20s, P-47s, British Mosquitos and British Typhoons. Other ground crews were loading ammo belts and cannon shells on hordes of fighter planes, U.S. P-38s and P-51s as well as hundreds of British Spitfires and Hurricanes.

Tomorrow, Allied planes would again blacken the skies over Western Europe.

The Luftflotte 3 fighter units had already been badly reduced by earlier air activities in the tactical attacks on airfields, bridges, road junctions and marshalling yards. They would be further depleted on this last phase of Operation Chattanooga Choo Choo. The Germans would have few planes to challenge the massive Allied invasion forces on D-day, 6 June 1944.

CHAPTER THIRTEEN

Dawn of 5 June emerged with the same gloominess as the day before: a drizzle and low-hanging clouds. A wind had also come up this morning. However, the airmen of the Ninth Air Force were not as nervous as they had been yesterday. Having already conducted their missions in this type of inclement weather, and suffered no particular problems, they felt more relaxed today. Further, the combat crews knew that fighter escorts had dealt effectively with interceptors, shooting down hordes of FW 190s and ME 109s during the assaults on 2 June and 4 June. The Ninth Air Force B-26 and A-20 crews suspected that German air units in France had been so badly decimated that they were not likely to mount too many fighters today.

At 0700 hours, Col. Lance Call and his wingman zoomed down the Beaulieu runway in England with his 365th Group P-47 *Magic Carpet*. He and his pilots carried pairs of five hundred-pound delayed-fuse bombs under their wings because the Hellhawks would be attacking another bridge today. Right behind these first two 365th Group Thunderbolts, Lt. Fred O'Connell and Lt. Bob Guillote roared down the same Beaulieu runway side by side. Behind them came forty-two more Thunderbolts. The P-47s then jelled into formations of four-plane diamonds, turned and headed south towards the Channel.

At 0700 hours in Thruxton, England, Col. Norman Holt roared down a runway with his wingman in the lead P-47 of the 366th Fighter Bomber Group. The 366th airmen also carried pairs of five hundred-pound delayed-fuse bombs under their wings for this group too would go after a railroad bridge. At thirty-second intervals the other P-47s of the 366th also zoomed down the runway and rose upwards. These Thunderbolts too jelled into four-plane diamond formations to turn south for the English Channel.

And at 0700 hours, Col. Gilbert Myers and his wingman rose from the Chilbolton runway into the low sky. These Thunderbolts from the 368th Fighter Bomber Group carried five hundred-pound HE bombs instead of delayed-fuse bombs because the Panzer Busters would be attacking the Meziere marshalling yards and not a bridge. Behind the first two 368th aircraft, other P-47s of this group, again in pairs, also zoomed down the runway: Lt. Col. Paul Douglas of the 396th Squadron, Capt. Bob Johnson in *Little Bill* of the 397th Squadron, Capt. Walt Mahorin in *Sally of Atlanta* of the 397th Squadron, and a host of other Thunderbolt pilots.

In total, forty-eight Thunderbolts from the 368th Fighter Bomber Group would attack the important marshalling yard on this gloomy morning.

In the medium bomber air group airdromes to the west of the P-47 airfields, three Marauder units prepared to take off. At Great Saling, Col. Glen Nye completed his briefing with thirty-eight bomber crews.

"All of us, the entire group, are going after the Juvisey Bridge in eastern France. It's a span on a spur line paralleling the main Nancy-to-Brest pike. The Nazis could use it to detour trains around the bridges we destroyed yesterday. So, we've got to knock it out."

"The entire group is going after a single bridge, sir?" Maj. Hank Newcomer asked.

"They want to make sure we finish it off," Nye said. Then he grinned. "But, maybe we're running out of pre-invasion targets for all Ninth Air Force groups."

"Yes, sir," Newcomer answered.

At 0730 hours, Col. Glen Nye sped down the Great Saling runway in his lead a/c, *Sandra Ann*. As soon as he hoisted his B-26 skyward, the next Nye's Annihilator roared down the runway to take off. Then came other bombers, including Lt. Col. Charles Olmstead in *Pretty Baby* and Maj. Hank Newcomer in *Dolly*. Soon, thirty-eight Marauders from the 322nd were airborne. They jelled into diamonds and then turned south. Nye's Annihilators carried four thousand-pound delayed-fuse bombs in their bays.

At Stoney Cross, less than ten miles away, Col. Tom Seymoure of the 387th Pathfinders Group completed his briefing. "Our target today is the Elbeuf Bridge. It's on a trunk line that runs a little south of the main Paris-to-Cherbourg railroad line. Intelligence thinks the Germans will use this spur to detour around the bridges the 9th Air Force knocked out yesterday. If so, the Nazis could still get troops and supply trains to the Normandy area."

"The entire group is going after one bridge, sir?" Maj. Jim Keller asked.

"That's our only target for today," Seymoure said. "I guess they want to make sure we put it down."

"Yes, sir," Keller answered.

At 0730 hours, the first 387th Group aircraft, Col. Tom Seymoure's lead B-26, zoomed down the runway. As soon as the Marauder rose from the end of the apron, Capt. Sam Monk roared down the runway, then Capt. Ed James, and then nine other planes of the Pathfinders' 556th Squadron. As these twelve planes were airborne, ten planes from the 557th Squadron took off. Then Major Keller swung his lead 558th Squadron *Flak Bait* to the head of the apron and, seconds later, he released the brakes. The B-26 jerked forward and shot down the runway.

By 0745 hours, forty-two Marauders from the 387th Pathfinders Group had risen into the low sky below the thick overcast and merged into formation. These Marauders also droned southwards toward the Channel.

A few miles southwest of Stoney Cross, at Matching, only a few civilians had come out to the field to brave the drizzle while they waited for the B-26s to take off. The crowd had been somewhat smaller than yesterday's because by today the novelty of watching planes take off in poor weather had worn off. Still, the Britishers stared apprehensively at the 391st Bridge Buster aircraft that were warming up before takeoff. They knew the Yank bomber crews would face the added danger of poor weather over France as well as German fighters and anti-aircraft guns.

Lt. Col. Bill Floak, who would lead the 391st Group today, had also given his medium bomber crews last-minute instructions. "Our target is the vital Dijon marshalling yard. It's a rail assembly point where the Nancy-to-Brest rail line joins the railroad pike coming up from the south of France. Even if our air units knock out the railroad pike bridges to the east, the Germans could still make a wide detour from the south to come north through Dijon."

Floak paused before he ran a finger over the map of France on the wall behind him. "One of the Ninth Air Force groups is hitting the bridges at Orival on the railroad line from the south. The destruction of this bridge and our destruction of the Dijon yard would just about put the Germans out of business insofar as moving anything by train to Normandy from Nancy or from the south of France. So let's do a good job."

"What about escorts, sir?" Capt. Jim Kahley asked.

"We'll have a squadron of P-51s from the 354th Fighter Group."

"Only one squadron?"

"Well," Floak said with a grin, "from all reports, the Germans only have a handful of fighters left in all of France. Ninth Air Force does not expect much opposition today. In fact, all the fighter units have instructions to strafe targets of opportunity if they meet no interceptors."

"Yes, sir."

By 0745 hours, the forty-two Marauders of the 391st Bomb Group were droning south toward the English Channel. They would join the B-26s of the 366th and 365th Groups before picking up their escorts for the flight to France.

Again at the Stoney Cross, England airfield, Col. Ed Chickering of the 367th Fighter Group gave instructions to his fighter pilots. "We'll be joining the three Thunderbolt fighter bomber groups over the Channel in about an hour. I'll take the 392nd Squadron to escort the 365th Group to the bridge at Orival. Captain Brown's 393rd Squadron will escort the 366th Group to the railroad bridge at Denain, and Major Gray's 394th Squadron will escort the fighter bombers of the 368th Group to the marshalling yard at Meziere."

"Can we expect much fighter opposition, sir?" Capt. Henry Brown asked. "We'd like to get a few more of those Kraut 109s and 190s."

"I'd be surprised if we meet many interceptors today." Chickering grinned.

"What do we do, sir?" Maj. Ron Gray asked.

"We'll make strafing runs on targets of opportunity," the 367th Group commander said. He scanned his fighter pilots. "Any more questions?"

None.

"OK, let's mount up," Chickering said. "We rendezvous over the Channel in an hour, as I said."

At the 354th Fighter Group base in Lasbenden, England, Col. George Bickel also gave last-minute instructions to his pilots. "As you've probably guessed, we're going back to France today to escort more B-26s on bridge busting and marshalling yard attacks. We'll be accompanying three medium bomber groups. I'll take the 353rd Squadron myself to escort the 322nd Bomb Group going after the Juvisey Bridge in eastern France. Major Weldon's squadron will escort the 387th Bomb Group to the railroad bridge at Elbeuf, and Major Howard's 356th Squadron will take the 391st Bomb Group to the marshalling yard at Dijon."

"Only one squadron for each bomb group, sir?" Major Weldon asked.

"I don't think we'll find many more German fighter planes in France after the pasting we gave them on the last two Chattanooga Choo Choo missions," Bickel said. He referred to a map behind him. "As usual, we'll pick up the bombers over the English Channel and then break off with our particular charges after we cross the French coast."

"Sir," Maj. Jim Howard asked, "if we don't meet any German interceptors over target areas, what do we do?"

"We strafe any kind of good targets in the area," the 354th Group commander said. "Anti-aircraft positions, trains, motorized columns, defense positions, anything like that. Those are the instructions from 9th Air Force. In fact, even some of the bomb groups have these kinds of targets."

"Yes, sir."

By 0830 hours, the sixty Mustangs of the 354th Group were droning swiftly toward the English Channel.

Throughout eastern England, more B-26 groups, A-20 groups and P-47 fighter bomber groups also took off to hit other communications targets in France. More P-51 and P-38 fighter groups roared down runways off an array of fighter bases to escort these other Ninth Air Force bombers and fighter bombers. By 0900 hours, under the low clouds, dozens of American Ninth Air Force combat groups were flying toward the English Channel.

At an array of Royal Air Force bases in England, scores of Second Tactical Air Force Mosquitos, Typhoons, Hurricanes, and Spitfires also took off at about 0900 hours to fly over the lower North Sea. These British planes would hit similar communications targets in Belgium and Holland.

In the U.S. 365th Fighter Group's lead P-47 *Magic Carpet,* Col. Lance Call frowned at the gloominess ahead of him. The clouds seemed lower today than yesterday and he hoped his bridge target at Orival was not closed in by the time he got there with his forty-six fighter bombers. Hanging next to the colonel in the same diamond of Thunderbolts, Lt. Fred O'Connell also frowned at the dreary weather. On the starboard point of the diamond, Lt. Bob Guillote squinted at the gray day and then tried to catch sight of the P-38 Lightning escorts that had not yet arrived.

In the Hellhawks' 387th Squadron, Capt. Vince Beaudrit in his lead P-47 could barely see the Thunderbolts in front of him because of the misty drizzle. He too feared that the target might be closed in.

In the lead P-47 of the trailing 366th Fighter Bomber Group, Col. Norman Holt stared down at the sea. The water was choppy today because of the brisk wind, and if these same rough seas prevailed tomorrow the invasion troops could have a difficult time. In the same group, Capt. Zell Smith of the 390th Squadron checked his instruments and, despite the weather, all gear was normal.

Col. Gilbert Myers of the 368th Fighter Bomber Group squinted at the other Thunderbolts in his lead diamond. The Panzer Buster commander could almost see the seriousness on the faces of his fellow fighter bomber pilots. they obviously felt the same fear as he did—a closed-in target at the Meziere marshalling yard. They might need to make their bomb drops at a very low altitude and thus face the peril of catching damage from exploding debris.

In the Panzer Buster's 397th Squadron, Capt. Bob Johnson in *Little Bill* and Capt. Walt Mahorin in *Sally of Atlanta* squinted through the wet windshields of their respective cockpits. They hoped the mist did not worsen and force them to abort the mission after they had come this far.

To the north, over the English Channel, Col. Glen Nye of the 322nd Medium Bomber Group stared at the hanging B-26s next to him. He hoped the weather did not worsen because he understood the vital need to knock out the Juvisey bridge. Inside the cabin of *Pretty Baby*, Lt. Col. Charles Olmstead checked the instrument panel and then called his crew to make certain all systems were normal.

Aboard the B-26 *Dolly,* Maj. Hank

Newcomer also checked with his crew. "Are you keeping an eye on the pressure, Lieutenant?" he asked his co-pilot.

"Yes, sir," Mike Johnson answered.

Newcomer then called his bombardier-navigator, Don Franklin. "Do you think you'll have any trouble on the bomb run?"

"The weather isn't that bad, sir," Franklin answered. "But if it gets worse, we'll need to bomb by radar from above the clouds."

"Hell, we'd never hit anything from upstairs." Newcomer scowled. Then he called his gunners.

"Turret guns okay, sir," Sgt. Mike Whitehurst said.

"Everything okay in the waist," Sgt. Al Aurelio said.

"No problems in the tail, sir," Sgt. Ralph Wilson said.

Newcomer sighed and then stared again through the beaded windshield of his B-26 pilot's cabin. He wished the mission was over.

In the 387th Bomb Group, Col. Tom Seymoure checked with his fellow pilots. "Are you having any trouble?"

"No, sir," Lt. Sam Monk said.

"We'll make it, sir," Capt. Ed James said, "unless the weather gets worse."

In the 558th Squadron, Maj. Jim Keller stared from the cabin of his Marauder and watched the heavy drizzle splashing rain drops on the left wing of *Flak Bait*. He hoped the weather did not get worse. When he turned, he saw Lt. Ed Cook, his co-pilot, squinting through the windshield.

"I hope this damn target isn't closed in," Cook said.

"It won't be if this rain doesn't get any worse and the clouds don't drop any lower," Major Keller answered. The 558th Squadron commander then called his other crew members. "Please report."

"I'm getting my H2X radar ready," bombardier-navigator Lt. Tom Clark said. "I want to make sure I'm ready in case we have to bomb blind."

"Good idea, Lieutenant," Keller said.

"Those clouds are almost on top of us now, sir," Sgt. Tom Snyder answered Keller from the top gun turret.

"I can't see much from the waist windows, Major," Sgt. Tom Davis said, "but I'll keep an eye out for any trouble."

"The weather looks real bad from back here, sir," tail gunner George Morse answered the *Flak Bait* aircraft commander. "I just hope we make it before we get closed in."

"Just stay alert."

"Yes, sir," Morse answered.

In the Bridge Buster group, Lt. Col. Bill Floak checked with his 391st Group pilots. They too gave him mixed answers. Some were highly optimistic and some were quite pessimistic. Floak told all of them the same thing: "Keep alert. We're going to get that goddamn marshalling yard even if we have to knock out rolling stock by running over them."

"Yes, sir," Capt. Larry Fogoneri said.

In the rear point of the 391st Group's lead diamond, Capt. Jim Kahley of the 574th Squadron was among those who answered Floak in the positive. "Everything looks good, sir," The *April Look* aircraft commander then checked with his own crew. "All stations report."

"Instrument panel okay," Lt. Frank Elder said.

"All systems operating properly," navigator-bombardier Lt. Ed Schweiter answered from the nose section.

"Guns swinging free," Sgt. Ed Bonham answered from the top gun position.

"Nothing wrong in the waist," gunner Al Mass said.

From the tail position, Sgt. Larry Carr was not so optimistic. "The weather seems to be getting worse. We could have trouble over target area."

"Keep me informed, Sergeant," Kahley said.

"Yes, sir," the tail gunner answered.

At 0915 hours, fighter escorts arrived with one squadron of either P-51s or P-38s closing around one group of B-26s or P-47s. By 0930 hours, with Ninth Air Force formation crossed the French coast.

Fortunately for the Americans, the weather would not worsen. The American airmen would be able to bomb easily from thirty-five hundred feet against the marshalling yards, and the weather would be clear enough for other planes to zoom in at deck level after the bridge targets.

At the Luftflotte 3 tracking station in Paris, Capt. Peter Heindorff soon got radar reports from stations along the Atlantic wall. "American aircraft crossing the west coast of France. They are again medium bombers and fighter-bombers under escort." Then came the monotonous follow ups: "We will let you know their destination as soon as we project their probable course. These enemy aircraft formations will no doubt break up and fly to different targets."

Captain Heindorff could only sigh. He would again need to call Luftflotte 3 fighter units to prepare for interception, but he knew the *geschwaders* had few planes left to send after these latest Allied aerial interlopers. The *Luftwaffe* had little chance of stopping these attackers, no matter what their targets.

Still, the Luftflotte 3 tracking captain sent out his coded radiograms to JG 2 outside of Paris, JG 54 with temporary headquarters at Epenon, JG 26, whose headquarters was now at St. Pierre, JG 27 at Vire, JG 1 at Argentan, and JG 22 at Metz. But now, all six fighter *geschwaders* combined would be lucky to mount 125 planes among them. Gen. Lewis Brereton, the Ninth Air Force CinC, had guessed right when he said the bombers would need few escorts on this morning's missions.

For more than an hour, continued radar reports from radar stations plagued Capt. Peter

Heindorff. More B-26 medium bomber formations, A-20 light bomber units, and still more P-47 fighter bomber units continued to pour into the continent. P-38 or P-51 escorts accompanied all of these bomber and fighter bomber units.

Col. Hans Hahn could mount only twenty-seven FW 190s from his JG 2 Richthofen unit. These few fighters could hardly stop the attacks on the Juvisey and Elbeuf bridges in eastern France. The 322nd and 387th Bomb Group Marauders laced the two bridges with minimum interference and dropped the spans from their piers and into the rivers. Thus, even this detour route on the Paris-to-Cherbourg and Nancy-to-Brest railroad routes was out of business.

To the west, in central France, Col. Erich Rudorffer of the JG 54 Green Hearts, with a mere twenty-three serviceable FW 190s, tried to stop the attacks on the Meziere and Dijon marshalling yards by the 368th and 391st Bomb Groups, but he had no chance against the forty accompanying American fighter planes. The American P-47s and B-26s left both yards in a mass of rubble, destroying seven locomotives, fifty-six box cars and passenger cars, two square miles of siding and eleven buildings.

In northwest France, Joseph "Pips" Priller could only mount thirty-one FW 190s from his JG 26 Schlagetor *geschwader,* and they were no match for the swarms of P-38s and P-51s that clashed with them. Priller lost half of his fighters in the lopsided donnybrook against three times his number. Thus, the 365th and 366th Groups easily demolished the bridges at Orival and Denain with little interference. No troop trains or supply trains would come up from the south through Dijon to reach the Normandy beaches tomorrow.

By early afternoon, some thirty more B-26, A-20, and P-47 groups had struck German targets in France to leave the rail transportation system almost totally crippled. All major bridges and marshalling yards had been destroyed or badly damaged. The American air attacks had utterly thwarted General Kietel's hopeful plans to send troops and supply trains into Normandy on the night of 5-6 June.

More American air units and droves of RAF units also made heavy attacks on the continent, destroying highway bridges, road junctions, and other targets in France and the low countries. The Germans would need to send any tank or motorized columns over poor secondary roads that could not carry heavy reinforcements swiftly to Normandy to bolster Field Marshal Rommel's Seventh Army along the Atlantic wall.

By the evening of 5 June, dismay prevailed throughout France. Field Marshal von Rundstedt knew he could not move combat units swiftly to any invasion site. Field Marshal Rommel realized that he would need to defend Normandy with his mere four divisions, and Field Marshal Hugo Sperrle recognized that he would have few planes in Luftflotte 3 to deal with massive Allied invasion forces and air units.

During the last hours of 5 June 1944, between 2300 and 2400 hours, thousands of Allied troops boarded transports for the sail across the Channel. Countless tons of supplies, hundreds of tanks, and innumerable motor vehicles had been loaded on ships. Shortly after midnight, this greatest invasion flotilla in history started across the choppy waters of the English Channel.

Between 0200 and 0400 hours, 6 June, 1333 RAF heavy bombers began lacing with five thousand tons of bombs the German defenses on the Atlantic wall between the Seine River delta and Cherbourg. During these same hours, 2,000 transport planes and gliders droned over the coast of France to drop behind enemy lines more than 40,000 paratroopers from two American airborne divisions and one British airborne divisions. The troops dropped on the Cotentin and Charles peninsulas to seize road junctions not already plastered by Allied planes during Operation Chattanooga Choo Choo. The airborne troops would hold these areas until the invasion forces on the beaches linked up with them.

At 0500 hours, Allied warships opened their pre-invasion bombardment of German defenses, blasting the Normandy beaches until heavy fires and dense smoke engulfed the area.

As dawn broke an endless stream of American B-24 heavy bombers, B-26 medium bombers, A-20 light bombers, P-47 fighter bombers, and P-51 and P-38 fighter planes droned over the French coast to hit anything that moved along the Atlantic wall. By noon of 6 June 1944, the huge American air armanda had dropped an astounding thirteen thousand tons of bombs and unleashed more than a half million rounds of strafing fire.

At 0558 hours, the first sixty landing barges puttered through the choppy water to Utah Beach. At 0630 hours, six hundred GIs from the Fourth U.S. Infantry Division spilled out of the LCIs and splashed onto the beach. In successive waves, more American infantrymen hit Utah Beach and then Omaha Beach, while thousands of British Tommies and Canadian infantrymen came ashore on the Gold, Juno and Sword beaches.

True, the Allied invasion troops met severe resistance, especially at Omaha Beach. The Americans alone would suffer 6,603 casualties during the morning hours of 6 June: 1465 killed, 3184 wounded, 1928 missing and 26 captured. The British and Canadians would suffer about 4,000 casualties. However, by noon, Allied troops had broken out of the beaches. The British had come four miles inland and the Americans two miles inland. Allied infantry and armor units moved swiftly eastward, with the British and Canadians racing towards Caen, while the Americans sped towards Carantan.

Within a month, the Americans would land 903,061 troops, 176,620 vehicles, and 853,436 tons of materiel in France. The British would land 660,000 troops, 156,000 vehicles, and 750,000 tons of materiel. The Germans lacked the resources to stop this huge Allied army driving across Western Europe, especially with 15,000 Allied planes supporting the drive through France.

Operation Chattanooga Choo Choo had enabled Allied troops to make its breakthrough in Normandy before the Germans could move reinforcements swiftly to coastal areas to aid Field Marshal Rommel's Seventh Army.

"The Allied tactical bombers successfully destroyed our communications systems in France," said Gen. Hans Spiedel, Rommel's chief-of-staff. "Our forces at Normandy were doing a good job against the initial Allied invaders. If we could have swiftly brought in more infantry, artillery and Panzer units, we might have delayed or even stopped the Allied invasion. But the Allied air forces had carefully and wisely destroyed major highway and railroad bridges, marshalling yards and road junctions. These coordinated air attacks cut our communication routes from the low countries, from eastern France and from the south of France."

"We had no chance to muster our full strength at Normandy before thousands of Allied troops expanded a bridgehead," said Lt.

Col. Erik Hoffman of the German 709th Division in the Contentin peninsula defenses. "We had ample troops to face the Americans, but arms and equipment never arrived in time because of the destruction of the vital railroad bridges at Orival and Letripad."

"We had no more air force," Col. Pips Priller said. "What the American tactical air force did not destroy on the ground, they shot out of the air. We did not even have two hundred serviceable aircraft in all of Luftflotte 3 to attack the invasion sites. Thousands of Allied planes over northwest France on the morning of 6 June easily shot down what few aircraft we had."

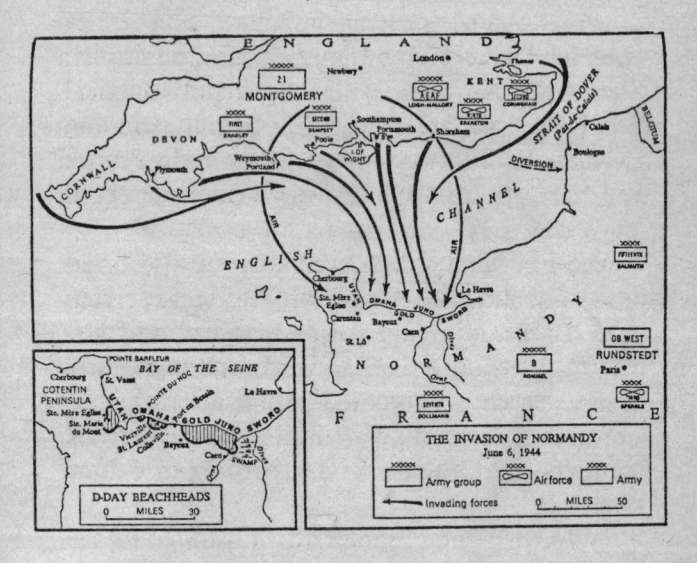

In fact, Colonel Priller himself led the only successful attack on the Normandy beaches during the morning of 6 June, when he and one pilot, Lt. Walter Schuck, attacked British troops at Juno Beach and caused about thirty casualties and the destruction of a ton of stacked supplies. Priller and Schuck miraculously got away from a skyful of British fighter planes. But this attack was like throwing pebbles at a foot-thick concrete wall.

Gen. Dwight Eisenhower, CinC of SHAEF in the ETO, said: "We took heavy losses during the first day of the invasion because of stiff German resistance on the Omaha and Utah Beaches. But our losses could have been much worse and our delay much longer had it not been for the critical pre-invasion air operations. The Ninth Air Force and the Second Tactical Air Force did an excellent job in destroying German airfields and communications in France and the low countries. These airmen deserved much credit."

And in fact, the American airmen alone had destroyed twenty-six airfields, thirty-four railroad bridges, eleven highway bridges and fourteen marshalling yards, while destroying nearly ninety percent of the Luftflotte 3 aircraft. The Germans had less than a hundred planes totally, bombers and fighters, on the morning of 6 June 1944.

Said Gen. Omar Bradley, commander of the U.S. First Army. "If the Germans had air power, and if they had been able to move reinforcements quickly into Normandy, we may never have reached the Cotentin peninsula as soon as we did. We no doubt would have suffered many more casualties."

Thus the tactical air operation in France and the low countries had paid off. The series of Chattanooga Choo Choo air strikes had enhanced the success of Operation Overlord, the D-day invasion. Allied troops were able to establish beachheads quickly and with fewer losses than expected.

Participants

AMERICAN

SHAEF CinC (ETO)—Gen. Dwight Eisenhower
U.S. Strategic Air Force (USSTAF)—Gen. Carl Spaatz
Eighth Air Force—Gen. James Doolittle
Ninth Air Force—Gen. Lewis Brereton
  332nd Bomb Group (Nye's Annihilators)—Col. Glen Nye, commander
    Lt. Col. Charles Olmstead, deputy commander
  387th Bomb Group (Pathfinders)—Col. Tom Seymoure, commander
    Maj. Jim Keller, CO, 558th Squadron
  391st Bomb Group (Bridge Busters)—Col. Jerry Williams, commander
    Lt. Col. Bill Floak, deputy commander
  416th Bomb Group—Col. Harold Mace commander
    Maj. Don Willits, CO, 669th Squadron
  365th Fighter Bomber Group (Hellhawks)—Col. Lance Call, commander
    Capt. Vincent Beaudrit, CO, 387th Squadron
  366th Fighter Bomber Group—Col. Norman Holt, commander
    Capt. Zell Smith, CO, 390th Squadron
  368th Fighter Bomber Group (Panzer Busters)—Col. Gilbert Myers, commander

Lt. Col. Paul Douglas, deputy commander

354th Fighter Group—Col. George Bickel, commander
    Maj. Jim Howard, CO, 356th Squadron

367th Fighter Group—Col. Ed Chickering, commander
    Maj. Ron Gray, CO, 394th Squadron

370th Fighter Squadron—Col. Howard Nichols, commander
    Maj. Seth McKee, CO, 402nd Squadron

474th Fighter Group—Col. Clinton Wesem, commander
    Capt. Bob Milliken, CO, 492nd Squadron

Twenty-First Army Group—Field Marshal Sir Bernard Montgomery, OTC, Operation Overlord
    First Army—Gen. Omar Bradley
    Second Army—Gen. Miles Dempsey

Second Tactical Air Force (RAF)—Air Marshal Sir Leigh Mallory

Participants

GERMAN

Armies of the West CinC (AOW)—Field Marshal Gerd von Rundstedt
- Seventh Army (Normandy)—Field Marshal Erwin Rommel
- Army Group G, (Western Europe)—Gen. Johannes Blaskowitz
- Army Group H, (Western Europe)—Gen. Gunther Blumentritt

Luftwaffe CinC (OKL)—Reichsmarshal Hermann Goering
- Luftlotte 3 (Western Europe)—Field Marshal Hugo Sperrle, CinC
  - Jagdkorps IX (bombers)—Gen. Dietrich Peltz
  - Jagdkorps II (fighters)—Gen. Werner Junck
  - Luftflotte 3 tracking officer—Capt. Peter Heindorff
- JG 2 (Richthofen)—Col. Hans Assi Hahn, commander
  - Maj. Heinrich Ehler, II Gruppen
- JG 54 (Green Hearts)—Col. Erich Rudorffer, commander
  - Maj. Horst Adameit, II Gruppen
  - Maj. Franz Eisenach, III Gruppen
- JG 26 (Schlagetors)—Col. Joseph "Pips" Priller, commander
  - Maj. Herman Graf, II Gruppen
  - Capt. Emil Lang, III Gruppen

JG 27—Maj. Gustan Roedel, commander
JG 1—Maj. Hartman Grasser, commander
JG 22—Lt. Col. Erick Hartman, commander

BIBLIOGRAPHY

Books:

Asher, Lee. *The German Air Force*. Duckworth Pub., London, 1946.

Baldwin, Hanson. *Battles Lost and Won,* Chapter 8, "Normandy, the Beginning of the End." Harper & Row, New York City, 1966.

Bambauch, Werner. *The Life and Death of the Luftwaffe*. Coward McCann, New York City, 1960.

Bekker, Cajus. *Luftwaffe War Diaries*. Doubleday, Garden City, L.I., 1968.

Brereton, Lewis. *The Brereton Diaries*. Wm Morrow & Company, New York City, 1946.

Craven, W.F. and Cates, J.L. *The Army Air Forces in World War II, Vol. II, Europe: Argument to VE Day*. Univ. of Chicago Press, Chicago, 1952.

Fitzimmons, Bernard. *Warplanes and Air Battles of World War II*. Beekman House, New York City, 1973.

Freeman, Roger. *Mustang at War*. Doubleday & Co., Garden City, L.I., 1974.

Galland, Adolph. *The First and the Last*. Henry Holt & Co., New York City, 1954.

Gurney, Gene. *The War in the Air*. Crown Publishers, New York City, 1962.

Irving, David. *The Rise and Fall of the Luftwaffe*. Little, Brown & Company, Boston, 1973.

Jablonski, Edward. *Flying Fortress*. Doubleday & Co., Garden City, L.I., 1965.

Johnson, Robert S. and Caiden, Martin. *Thunderbolt*. Rinehart & Co., New York City, 1958.

Killen, John. *The Luftwaffe*. Muller Pub., London, 1967.

Maurer, Maurer. *Air Force Combat Units of World War II*. Franklin Watts Pub., New York City, 1963.

Nowarra, Heinz. *The Folke Wulf 190: A Famous German Fighter*. Harley Ford Pub., London, 1965.

Rumpf, Hans. *The Bombing of Germany*. Holt, Rinehart & Winston, New York City, 1963.

Rust, Kenn. *The 9th Air Force in World War II*. Aero Publishers, Fallbrook, Calif., 1967.

Saundby, Robert. *Air Bombardment*. Harper & Bros., New York City, 1961.

Tantum, William and Hoffschmidt, E.J. *The Rise and Fall of the German Air Force*. WE Publishers, Old Greenwich, Conn., 1969.

Toliver, Raymond and Constable, Traver. *Fighter Aces of the U.S.A.* Aero Publishers, Fallbrook, Calif., 1979.

Toliver, Raymond and Constable, Traver. *Horrido: Fighter Aces of the Luftwaffe*. MacMillan Publishers, New York City, 1968.

Van Ishoven. *Messerschmidt BF109 at War*. Charles Scribner & Sons, New York City, 1977.

Wolff, Leon. *Low Level Mission*. Doubleday & Co., Garden City, L.I., 1951.

Wood, Tony and Gunston, William. *Hitler's Luftwaffe*. Crescent Books, New York City, 1977.

Archive Sources:
All archive records from the Albert F. Simpson Air Force Historical Research Center, Maxwell Field, Alabama

AMERICAN

AAF Evaluation Report #46, summary on "The effectiveness of Air Attacks Against German Rail System in France"

322nd Bomb Group Combat Narrative History, May-June 1944
    Mission #968, 2 June 1944
    Mission #971, 4 June 1944
    Mission #973, 5 June 1944

387th Bomb Group
    Mission #100B, 2 June 1944
    Mission #172B, 4 June 1944
    Mission #176B, 5 June 1944

391st Bomb Group
    Narrative "Mission to Abbeville," 2 June 1944
    Narrative "Mission to Lille," 2 June 1944
    Mission #140, 4 June 1944

368th Fighter Bomber Group, Narrative History, May-June 1944

416th Bomb Group Narrative history, May-June 1944

365th Fighter Bomber Group, combat history, May-June 1944

368th Fighter Group, Missions #303, 316, 2 June, 4 June 1944

366th Fighter Bomber Group, combat history, May-June 1944

354th Fighter Group, Combat Narrative Summary, June 1944

367th Fighter Group, Combat Narrative Summary, June 1944

370th Fighter Group, Combat Narrative Summary, June 1944

Ninth Air Force
    Doc. #43, Missions summary, 2 June 1944
    Doc. #45, Missions summary, 4 June 1944
    Doc. #48, Missions summary, 5 June 1944

GERMAN

ATIS Reports: Interviews of German officers
    Gen. Werner Junck, II Fighter Corps Headquarters
    Field Marshal Hugo Sperrle, Third Air Fleet Command
    Gen. Hans Wimmer, General der Flieger, Belgium/N. France
    Albert Speer, Minister of Production
    Field Marshal Gerd von Rundstedt interrogation
    Ninth Air Force interrogation of Hermann Goering, 1 June 1945

Summaries of German Air Force Operations
    F23, Operations in France, June 1944
    F22, Operations in France, May 1944
    Report #158, Fuhrer Conference, 4 June 1944
    OKW Report #74, Jagdkorps II—"Aspects of German Fighter Efforts," May-June 1944

PHOTOS: All photos from the Albert F. Simpson Research Center and National Archives (including Boehm collection, German Archives, Bonn)

MAPS: All maps from the Albert F. Simpson Research Center

ACKNOWLEDGMENT

The author would like to thank the staff at the Albert F. Simpson Research Center for their time and efforts in digging out research material for this book. I am grateful to director Cargill Hall and his aides: Mr. Pressley Bickerstaff, Mrs. Margaret Claiborn and Mrs. Judy Endicott.

I would also like to thank Mr. Elias Mallouk for his help in searching through volumes of the archive records to find significant army air force mission reports pertinent to Operation Chattanooga Choo Choo.

DYNAMIC NEW LEADERS IN MEN'S ADVENTURE!

THE MAGIC MAN (1158, $3.50)
by David Bannerman
His name is Donald Briggs O'Meara, and since childhood he's been trained in the ways of espionage—from gathering information to murder. Now, the CIA has him and is going to use him—or see to it that he dies . . .

THE MAGIC MAN #2: THE GAMOV FACTOR (1252, $2.50)
by David Bannerman
THE MAGIC MAN is back and heading for the Kremlin! With Brezhnev terminally ill, the West needs an agent in place to control the outcome of the race to replace him. And there's no one better suited for the job than Briggs—the skilled and deadly agent of a thousand faces!

THE WARLORD (1189, $3.50)
by Jason Frost
The world's gone mad with disruption. Isolated from help, the survivors face a state in which law is a memory and violence is the rule. Only one man is fit to lead the people, a man raised among the Indians and trained by the Marines. He is Erik Ravensmith, THE WARLORD—a deadly adversary and a hero of our times.

THE WARLORD #2: THE CUTTHROAT (1308, $2.50)
by Jason Frost
Though death sails the Sea of Los Angeles, there is only one man who will fight to save what is left of California's ravaged paradise, who is willing to risk his life to rescue a woman from the bloody hands of "The Cutthroat." His name is THE WARLORD—and he won't stop until the job is done!

Available wherever paperbacks are sold, or order direct from the Publisher. Send cover price plus 50¢ per copy for mailing and handling to Zebra Books, 475 Park Avenue South, New York, N.Y. 10016. DO NOT SEND CASH.

THE SURVIVALIST SERIES
by Jerry Ahern

#1: TOTAL WAR (960, $2.50)
The first in the shocking series that follows the unrelenting search for ex-CIA covert operations officer John Thomas Rourke to locate his missing famly—after the button is pressed, the missiles launched and the multimegaton bombs unleashed . . .

#2: THE NIGHTMARE BEGINS (810, $2.50)
After WW III, the United States is just a memory. But ex-CIA covert operations officer Rourke hasn't forgotten his family. While hiding from the Soviet forces, he adheres to his search!

#3: THE QUEST (851, $2.50)
Not even a deadly game of intrigue within the Soviet High Command, and a highly placed traitor in the U.S. government can deter Rourke from continuing his desperate search for his family.

#4: THE DOOMSAYER (893, $2.50)
The most massive earthquake in history is only hours away, and Communist-Cuban troops, Soviet-Cuban rivalry, and a traitor in the inner circle of U.S. II block Rourke's path.

#5: THE WEB (1145, $2.50)
Blizzards rage around Rourke as he picks up the trail of his family and is forced to take shelter in a strangely quiet Tennessee valley town. But the quiet isn't going to last for long!

#6: THE SAVAGE HORDE (1243, $2.50)
Rourke's search for his wife and family gets sidetracked when he's forced to help a military unit locate a cache of eighty megaton warhead missiles. But the weapons are hidden on the New West Coast—and the only way of getting to them is by submarine!

Available wherever paperbacks are sold, or order direct from the Publisher. Send cover price plus 50¢ per copy for mailing and handling to Zebra Books, 475 Park Avenue South, New York, N.Y. 10016. DO NOT SEND CASH.

NEW ADVENTURES FROM ZEBRA!

SAIGON COMMANDOS #1 (1283, $3.25)
by Jonathan Cain
Here are the mysterious streets of a capital at war—filled with American men, adrift with deserters and orphans of war... and always the enemy, invisible and waiting to kill!

SAIGON COMMANDOS #2 (1329, $2.50)
CODE ZERO: SHOTS FIRED
by Jonathan Cain
When a phantom chopper pounces on Sergeant Mark Stryker and his men of the 716th, bloody havoc follows. And the sight of the carnage nearly breaks Stryker's control. He will make the enemy pay; they will face his SAIGON COMMANDOS!

THE BLACK EAGLES: (1249, $2.95)
HANOI HELLGROUND
by John Lansing
They're the best jungle fighters the United States has to offer, and no matter where Charlie is hiding, they'll find him. They're the greatest unsung heroes of the dirtiest, most challenging war of all time. They're THE BLACK EAGLES.

THE BLACK EAGLES #2: (1294, $2.50)
MEKONG MASSACRE
by John Lansing
Falconi and his Black Eagle combat team are about to stake a claim on Colonel Nguyen Chi Roi—and give the Commie his due. But American intelligence wants the colonel alive, making this the Black Eagles' toughest assignment ever!

Available wherever paperbacks are sold, or order direct from the Publisher. Send cover price plus 50¢ per copy for mailing and handling to Zebra Books, 475 Park Avenue South, New York, N.Y. 10016. DO NOT SEND CASH.